LOST SOUL SEARCHING

LOST SOUL SEARCHING

Revised Edition

Jean Solbert

ISBN:	Hardcover	978-1-4363-3379-5
	Softcover	978-1-4363-3378-8

This book was printed in the United States of America.

To order additional copies of this book, contact:
Xlibris Corporation
1-888-795-4274
www.Xlibris.com
Orders@Xlibris.com

49070

CONTENTS

SOUL

By Webster Definition

"An entity, which is regarded as being
The immortal or Spiritual part of the person and, though having no physic-
Cal or material reality, is credited with the functions of thinking and willing, and hence determining
All behavior

That means that the soul is the controlling factor, the hand so to speak at the controls of the brain, or the master computer in our bodies. It pulls all the strings and pushes all the buttons that keep the muscles working as they should, and we have a lot of muscles to control.

The fact that it has the functions of thinking and willing means that it must have a very large memory bank to draw from in making decisions.

The brain, in which it resides, has a certain amount of memory, but stores only what it is given in the lifetime of the body in which it resides. The Soul also has access to this memory bank and adds it to it's own memory bank to use when needed.

It appears that the soul can leave or enter the body when that body is near death or near birth.

How many times have you heard about a person who was in an accident and near death, say that they had an "Out of body experience" where they found themselves looking down at the scene of the accident and seeing themselves on the ground.

Evidently when the body functions slow down to a near death condition, the "Soul" can no longer have any control and leaves the body. In some of the cases somehow the Soul decides it might still have control and returns to the body and brings it back to life with the right muscle control where it is needed.

This fictional story is written on that premise and should be considered as strictly fiction in all respects and instances.

Solbert

ATTACK

The three young women, all in black robes came down the narrow path walking quietly they came into the park and walked directly to a small court yard and sat on one of the rock benches that were there. It was quickly apparent that one of them was a person of high esteem. As the bench was approached, one of the other girls moved ahead and spread a silken cloth in a position for the taller of them to sit. As the taller one sat down, the others positioned themselves on each side of her.

With their robes opened and their faces visible their Tanganese heritage was visible. All three were very beautiful to look at and appeared to be in their late teens or early twenties. The tallest one was the daughter of the emperor and had been trained in all the required mannerisms and actions that befit a princess. The other two were the bodyguards for the Princess. They were trained and ordered to protect her with their lives, to kill if the action was called for to see that nothing happened to the princess. The daily routines of the Princess were different than this night mission. During the daylight hours there would be no real danger to the princess so the guards were merely close by and watching. Only the many handmaidens were close to the Princess. The handmaidens were also trained in all types of self defense and would protect her as best they could, but the guards were the best in the country for her protection and two or three were always around her. They were taught the deadly art of Machedo, "the killing art". All were young and strong and experts in the art of self defense.

PRINCESS LI CHAN

The training of a princess begins very early in life. She begins learning how to walk, talk, how to move evenly and quietly, and many other things. From the time she can stand up the learning begins and it never ends. She is a princess and she must never forget that. All young men were taught different fighting techniques along with their education. In the case of a princess, Her mother and father, the Emperor picked most of her instructors. She was taught all the fighting techniques the boys were and in addition she was taught secretly the little known art of Machedo, a last resort type of fighting meant to kill with a single blow. She had mastered everything and the use of the little Ninja short sword and the Samuri.

When she reached the age that young boys and men would look at her like a woman instead of a young girl, her father had a metal worker make her a beautiful Ninja short sword with a secret compartment in and a handle that glittered with fine gemstones from around the world and a sheath of beautifully tanned leather in which to keep it. He knew that there may come a time when she might have need of it.

At the age of eighteen Li Chan met a young officer in the royal Guard that immediately caught her attention. He was two years her senior but was about the same height. Li Chan's hair was black and his was a very dark brown. His name was Chen Li. There was instant pleasure for both of them, when they were together they seemed as one. They loved the same things and their minds were usually in the same vein with their likes and dislikes. Their love grew as time went by and now, after two years of being together they were deeply in love and had no other thoughts but for each other.

Due to the places in their society that each held and had to uphold, their time together was not as they would like, but it was their tradition and they were forced to follow.

Li Chan's father approved of the meetings and expected his daughter to follow the protocols and demands of her position. He had no other children so she was in his thoughts always. He knew of this meeting this night, for the two handmaidens were loyal to him also, but he trusted his daughter.

They were very good friends and when alone, formalities were forgotten. Su Lin spoke; "Li Chan, your father would not approve of this, you must be careful".

"I know, but I so want to see Chen", Li Chan replied. "It has been nearly a week since I last saw him and I love him so. Everything is so wonderful when he is around and with me. Sometimes we talk without saying anything, and we both understand. It is such a deep love I have for him and he has for me. I do not know what I would do if he ever left me. I would grieve myself to death".

Yoko Dhe spoke up," It is danger here, darkness comes."

The evening shadows were growing as the darkness came. Chen Li was late in his coming or they were early with Li Chan's anxiety to see him. There was a light rustling of cloth.

Suddenly they found themselves surrounded by half a dozen black clad figures. They stood up wrapping their robes around themselves the handmaidens on either side of the princess. The figure in front of them spoke, We came for the princess. We do not wish to hurt anyone. Do not resist." Two of the other black robed figures came forward to take hold of the princess. They were met by the two guards and were soon in trouble, for the handmaidens were now fully trained fighting machines and had produced deadly curved swords and short daggers.

As the other black robed figures entered the fray the two hand maidens switched to the ancient, art of Machedo, killing blows, and soon, two of the attackers were down to stay and the others were being more careful.

In the darkness, all of them dressed in black, there was no telling each other apart. Suddenly three more figures came into the fight as Chen Li and two of his friends were in the middle of the battle. Their clothing was lighter in color and military.

Li Chan, in the middle of the fray was resisting the leader of the thieves. She had drawn her little ninja short sword and just as she felt it go deep into the leader she felt a sharp pain in her side from behind her. Su Lin's sword plunged into the side of her attacker, but was not quick enough to stop the short sword from killing Li Chan.

As she began to fall, she felt the gentle hands of Chen Li catch her and lower her to the grass. The two thieves that were still alive were quickly dispatched.

Chen Li slowly lowered Li Chan to the soft grass and knelt beside her, holding her head. When he removed his arm to lower her to the grass, he saw that his hand was covered with blood and he was filled with fear. "Li Chan, are you hurt?" He asked, "I should have come earlier! Go get some help" he shouted to his two men. They quickly left.

Tears were rolling down the cheeks of Chen Li as he cradled his love in his arms. He knew she was bleeding, but did not know what else to do but hold pressure on the spot where the blood kept coming, and she was getting weaker and weaker.

Li Chan opened her eyes and looked up at her lover and whispered," Do not grieve, I have loved you and we will meet again, my Darling." Her eyes closed and her body suddenly went limp.

Chen Li held her until the soldiers came and carried her away. Su Lin saw the glittering handle of the dagger and reached down and picked it up, then slowly followed.

The soul of Li Chan looked down at the scene below her and watched as Chen Li held her in-life body in his arms and shed tears. She remembered what had happened, but there was no emotion now. She knew she had left the body. The liquid that had kept the real life alive in the body had slowly disappeared until she had no means of controlling the life that was there. So she had left. With the life giving fluid gone there was no way to keep anything going. She saw the glitter of the little jewels in the handle of the ninja dagger as it lay on the ground where she had dropped it after killing the leader of the bandits. She saw Su Lin pick it up and follow Chen Li.

Li Chan was thinking of the wonderful times she had spent with Chen Li. The love they shared and wonderful feeling that they shared just being together. Her father, the Emperor knew of the romance and had agreed to his daughter seeing the young soldier, but he had put restrictions on the times and places. He wanted proper protocol and did not want Royal embarressment over the actions of his daughter. If there were to be any marriage, it would come after the soldier became more important to the army and had become an officer with some rank of distinction. That would be a few years in the future, but they were young and could wait.

The memories, she still had. Now what? She thought as she slowly drifted off, maybe she could find a body with some of the life fluid still in it. There was no hurry now. The memory of Chen Li was still with her. Somehow she must find a way to go to him again for there was a deep love between them and she would like to find it again. She had not known many boys her own age. Her father, the Emperor had kept her pretty much confined and she had often wondered about the other young people she had seen, both girls and boys.

Oh, well, she thought as she drifted off slowly, there is no hurry, but she knew that she would be watching for the soul of Chen Li.

ROBERT

The soul of Li Chan drifted aimlessly around the Universe for unmeasured time. There seemed no interaction between souls and so there was nothing but the memories. With the memories there was no feeling and no activation of the pleasant memories. There had to be a physical being to make the memories real.

As she was drifting past a huge planet, she noticed a greenish hue and instantly remembered the one she had drifted away from and the young man Chen Li. They had met several times over the past nearly two years. Both of them were conscious of the protocol they must follow and there had never been any sexual action except for the kissing and caressing. The tutors and her older attendants who were much wiser in the ways of love would have noticed anything else.

Li Chan had never experienced love as other lovers do. Her tutors had told her things that she would encounter, but the encounter had never happened. She was curious.

She let herself drift lower and soon she was drifting along over the green fields and woods of the planet she had left so long ago. She suddenly came across a field with a large building at one end. A group of young people were playing a game of some kind and were shouting and running around. She stopped to look. At the far end of the field she noticed a person on the ground that seemed to be in trouble. She looked down on the young man and saw he was hurt in some way so she drifted lower to get a closer look at the body and face of the young man. She looked at him closer and saw that there was some of the life giving fluid on his face and on some of his clothing.

She saw no sign of movement so she went to the body and as she felt no resistance, slowly slipped inside. She sensed another soul, but there was no power or will to do anything. Nothing was being controlled, but the large muscle that pumped the fluid around and the large sacs that were drawing in the required air. There was still life in the body but no effort to stay alive was being made by the soul, what little of it there was. The boy or young man had very little will power and no inner strength. The soul of Li Chan immediately absorbed the memories and power of the soul that had been in the body. It willed the large sacs to work harder and the pump to pump harder.

Soon the strength came back to the muscles and the arms moved. Then the eyes opened and the head was raised up a little as the young man looked around.

Absorbing the memories had given the soul of Li Chan the knowledge she needed to take control of the body. She now knew all about the young man and she willed him to get up and walk quietly away from the field and go to his home. As she directed him back to his home she mused over what she had found out. He was also male which was new for Li Chan. She had not been looking for a lover. She had just seen a physical being and without thought had entered the body to see if she could bring it to life and save it. He was a good student with very good grades and seemed to like to learn new things. The language he spoke was English. She had heard it spoken a few times but had not been able to understand it. Now, after absorbing the contents of this body's memory banks she could speak the language if she needed to. When he was in the third grade he said he wanted to learn to play the piano. His parents located a good piano instructor and he took piano lessons through the third, fourth and fifth years of grade school. As a result he became quite good. His self esteem, as a result of all the teasing and being made fun of all those years was very low and if he saw anyone listening to his playing, he would stop playing and leave. As a result of that not too many of the students knew that he could play the piano. His parents had found a good used piano and bought it for him to play and practice on at home. There was one at the school in a room off of the auditorium that he would play once in a while if there was no one around. His full name was Robert Richardson, Bob for short. It seems he was born with a speech impediment and the doctors could not do anything about it, so he had to endure the pain inflicted by his classmates and people around him. Now, at the age of seventeen he was tired and about to give up. Some of the other boys in the school had recently started to pick on him and make fun of the way he talked. Two of the bullies had started hitting him to see him cringe, laughing all the time. They had destroyed his will to live or fight back in any way. He had about given up on life.

She knew now that he loved football and that he was on the football team but very seldom played because of the attitude of the other players. Some of them liked him and gave him no problems. He was a good athlete and could run and handle the ball well. The years of being made fun of and treated like there was something wrong with him had made him so non-confrontational that he now had no aggression at all. Football, being an offensive game more or less, called for confrontation. If someone would throw him the football and he saw the other team heading toward him to tackle him, he would instantly drop the ball and run. Not good for a football player. Therefore he was usually on the bench during any games with opposing teams. The team captain kept hoping that he would somehow work up some courage and become a good player.

On this day he had been playing on the team in a practice game with the opposing team being from the same school and he knew them all. Two of the opposing teams' blockers were Jeffrey and Leonard. They were two of the bullies that had been teasing and playing tricks on him during the past years of high school and even back through the grade school years. When one of his teammates had thrown him the football and he had seen Jeffrey coming at him for a tackle, he had dropped the ball and turned to run. Jeffrey tackled him and threw him to the ground. As Bob went down his foot came up and hit Jeffrey in the face hard. When Jeffrey got up, he started hitting Bob and the other boys pulled him off. Bob left the field and stayed to watch at the end of the field. After the game Jeffrey and Leonard caught him as he was leaving to go home and the beating ensued.

There did not seem to be anything wrong with the physical parts of his body. The problem had to do only with his throat and voice box. There was something wrong there. Li Chan's soul had plenty of will power to give and as much controlling power as she would need. Li Chan was having a little trouble assuming the role of a male. The basic soul memory was of a female and now she had to stay in the memory banks of the male to keep control and think like a male.

As he was walking back to his home, the soul was willing him to think about fighting back. He was as big as most of them and it was not his fault that his voice box had been formed that way. His muscles were a little soft he knew, but that could be remedied. He began to walk a little straighter and think about ways to fight back. He knew that he would stay away from them until he was ready to fight back.

When he walked into the house, his mother immediately saw there had been trouble. She had seen it all before many times and did not know exactly what to do about it. Her son had become quieter and reserved over the last few weeks and months. He was so passive and had no will to go on living, it seemed. The doctors that she had taken him to said there was nothing they could do. He was not an aggressive person and very non confrontational.

She immediately treated his cuts and was completely surprised to hear him say," Mom, I am going to fight back. It is not my fault that I have to speak this way, and it is not fair to blame me for it."

"What are you going to do?" She asked him.

"Starting tonight I am going to exercise and toughen my muscles. I am as big as they are and I can be as strong, if I exercise." he answered.

"Are you sure?" She asked.

"Yes mom, I'm sure." He said. "I am tired of being beat up all the time and for some reason, today. I decided to fight back. Things will be different from now on."

His mother watched as he left the house and walked into the large garage in the back yard. She noticed the air of confidence he seemed to have as he walked, it seemed he even stood straighter. She wondered what had happened.

As Bob walked into the garage, he looked around for something that he could use to exercise his different muscles. Against the back wall of the garage was a neatly stacked pile of cut logs that his father kept for the fireplace in the family room of the house. The pile of cut wood contained cut pieces of the trunks of dead trees, all about the same length but varied in size from two and three inches to eight inches in diameter. Walking back to them, he picked up two of the smaller chunks one in each hand and hefted them to see what size he would need to start the strengthening process. He cleared a large enough area in front of the pile that he could perform the exercises he wanted to do. He found an old rolled up rug that his mother had not needed, but had not thrown out, and unrolled it in the space he had made for himself. Now he could start.

As he stood there, it occurred to him that something was different. Something had changed. He had never even thought about doing such a thing. Now it was being done. Something had happened. He was now thinking things that would never have occurred to him a day or two ago. His memory was now full of things that he did not fully recall and yet he remembered them. He was really looking forward to the exercise and was even thinking about what would happen when he encountered the two bullies who had beaten him and knocked him down. He walked back to the house and to the piano. It always quieted his nerves and made him feel better when he played the piano for a half hour or so.

During the day at school he avoided the other boys as much as possible and then went straight home when he left the school. He had avoided friendships with the girls his age because of his speech problem, but now he thought he would try speaking and see what would happen. As he had told his mother, he was just as good as they were except for the speech problem. If they did not like him as he was, then he would leave them alone. The girls did not laugh as much as the boys did when he answered the teacher's questions. He would wait till he had his strength built up before he would tackle that problem. He knew that the boys would resent his speaking to any of the girls and would probably start something. He wanted to be ready when that time came.

The next evening when he got home, he went right out to the garage and decided what he was going to do. There was over one half hour before his mother would have the evening meal ready so he started exercising. He lay down on the rug and started doing push-ups. He discovered he was weaker than he thought. He could only do ten pushups before he had to stop, which surprised him. He really was in bad shape physically. He continued exercising till his mother called to him.

When he was in school, he continued to act as he had before as best he could. He knew he was not succeeding because of the new glances he was getting from some of the students that were normally around him. They seemed to be trying to be friendlier, but were waiting for him to start the encounter. He held off, knowing that there probably would be some kind of trouble and he did not think he was ready for it yet.

One evening while bob was out in the garage exercising, his mother and father were talking in the family room.

"What has come over Bobbie this last week or so?, he seems different somehow?" his father asked his mother.

"I know," his mother answered, "It started one day last week, he came home with blood on his face and bruises all over, and while I was cleaning him up and fixing his cuts he told me he was going to fight back. He wasn't going to take it any more. That it was not his fault that he could not talk right, it was a physical thing and he could not help it. He was really angry. Now he has started to build up his muscles so he will be ready for them if they try to do it again. Whatever happened on the playground that day really had an effect on him. He seems more confident and ready to fight whatever battle comes his way. He reminds me of you when we were first married."

"I think he is putting on some weight," his father said, "and he looks like he is about ready for anything. I am glad. There for a while I thought he had lost all the backbone and will power in him. I have been giving some thought to getting some exercise equipment, but he seems to be doing alright with the logs and the mat on the floor. I will wait till he mentions it before I do anything. They are pretty expensive and we are pretty tight for money."

The soul of Li Chan was quite content with the results of her willing and controlling. When she had first entered the body of Bob, it had been hard to start any kind of control She had used a lot of her will power to get him to raise his head and then pull himself up and start home. Now, with all the memory that was already in his brain and the added memory from Li Chan he knew a lot and could use his brain to figure out things and come to a good conclusion without the help of his new soul. If he could not come to a logical conclusion, his new soul was there to will or control with a push or thought, in the right direction.

The soul of Li Chan gave little or no thought to the fact that she had entered the body of a male and the body that she had left had been a female. To a soul these were minute things that would be worked out in the process of willing and controlling. Of course the memories she had were of a female body, and now she knew about the male body, so she was vastly prepared for whatever came up to will or control. The pleasure the body would get from that would be reflected in the brain of the body she was in at the time. As she remembered, there had been much pleasure in the touching that had occurred in the many times that she and Chen Li had been alone. That had been all, but she remembered it was pleasure. As Bob's brain was working quite well with the knowledge in its memory banks the soul was quite content to just supervise the whole situation. Now that he was on the right track, so to speak, the soul only needed to keep him there with a little pushing and willing along the way.

The exercise was working. Bob was feeling much better and he was becoming much stronger. He was different in a lot of ways and the other students noticed.

His grades even improved. When he talked, the sound of his voice was now more definite and sure, but still uneven and some stuttering.

By the end of March, he had been exercising nearly a month and his body was now in nearly perfect shape. He began to think a little of talking to some of the girls that he liked and that had been glancing at him in the halls and the classrooms.

Bob was seventeen years old, about five foot ten and one half inches tall and weighed close to one hundred sixty five pounds. Most girls would say he was handsome with his dark brown hair and gray eyes, evenly tanned face and arms. He usually wore blue jeans and short-sleeved shirt of one color or another, none of them bright or gaudy

An encounter came the next day during a classroom change. Bob was walking along the right hand wall and turned a sharp corner. Approaching the same corner was one of the two bullies that he was trying to avoid. Both stopped.

"Well, looky here," The bully said. "if it isn't the dummy himself, get out of the way."

As he spoke he raised his hand and put it against Bob's chest to push him out of the way.

Bob had seen it coming and as the bully's hand reached Bob's chest it was caught in a tight grip that stopped it, then slowly forced it back and down causing the bully to drop to his knees.

"I do not want to hurt you so leave me alone." Bob said and it was clear enough to be understood.

Then Bob shoved out and down. The bully went over sideways and down. Bob walked on past him along the wall to his classroom.

Some of the students had been watching, but being careful not to laugh for they feared reprisals from the bully. The bully, whose name was Jeffrey Haliday, had dropped his books when he fell and was now picking them up off the floor. The other students now were walking away snickering and whispering to each other.

Bob knew that it wasn't over. He would have to face Jeffrey later and probably with his buddy Leonard. Well, he would meet that when it came. He went to his assigned desk and sat down putting his books on the desk. He felt a tap on his shoulder and glanced around. The girl who sat there was looking at him and smiling. It caught him by surprise.

"Hi, I'm Pamela," she said, "You know that he will come after you later so you had better be careful. He had that coming for a long time."

"Hi, my name is B-B-Bob, y-yes I know he will, b-but I am not afraid of him any m-more. Now we will f-f-fight," Bob replied. "And thank you Pamela"

Bob was blushing at the meeting with a girl his own age, he was flustered.

Word of the incident soon spread and it was the talk of the school. That was no help to Bob. It just made the bullies more determined to get even with him. Bob lived a little over three blocks from the school and as he left the school property and was walking along the sidewalk. Pamela was suddenly beside him walking with him. It caught him unawares and he stammered as he looked at her and said,

"What are you doing here?"

"I thought you might like some company for awhile on your way home." She answered. "Do you mind?"

"A-a-a-of course not." He answered, "But no girl ever a-a asked before."

"You were not the same then. You have changed, you were, well, sort of wimpy and we were afraid to approach. Now you look different and you look nice and even friendly, and the girls think you are handsome." She told him.

"Don't you think I talk funny, like the other boys think I talk?" Bob asked.

"Of course we think you talk funny, but that is not your fault, you were borne with a defect and it cannot be corrected. There is nothing to do about it but to accept it and go on with your life. The way you look and are acting now. It seems you have accepted it and are already going on with your life and fighting back those who will not accept you as you are." She answered him. She continued, "I noticed the difference a few weeks ago and it is a nice difference. I liked you before, but you seemed so unapproachable. Now you do not seem that way."

"That makes me happy." Bob said, "I was sure you all hated me and wanted me to stay away from you. I was afraid of the big boys and afraid to fight back for fear that they would hurt me more The last time they beat on me something happened, I don't know what, but while I was lying on the ground I suddenly decided I was not going to take it anymore. I decided to fight back. That is just what I am going to do even if they kill me."

"A lot of the boys don't like the way Jeffrey and Leonard are treating you, but they do not want to make the bullies angry." Pamela said.

They stopped in front of Bob's house and he said, "Th-Th-Thanks Pamela, you have made me happier than I have been for a long time. Will I see you tomorrow in school?"

"Yes, "She said, "Any time you want and please call me Pam."

The next day as Bob approached the school, he saw Pamela waiting outside on the steps. His heart beat a little faster and he felt a surge of anxiety. Did she really like him like she had said? He had been feeling so sorry for himself that he had not given girls a thought. Now he was feeling the full normal attraction for a girl of his own age. It was a new feeling and he liked it. He was beginning to have the feelings he had missed for so long.

He was so engrossed in his thoughts of Pam that he had dropped his alertness where the bullies were concerned. As he was climbing the steps and looking at Pam as she talked. He did not see the foot that was put in his way as he stepped up. Too late, he saw the foot, but could not stop the fall. As his hands softened the fall on the steps, he immediately pushed himself back up. As he came back up he twisted to see who the tripper was and at the same time started his left fist in that direction. Bob's fist caught the bully on the side of the head and sent him sprawling sideways on the steps.

Bob and Pam walked on up the steps and into the building. They did not look back.

Things went smoothly. Bob saw the bully team several times, but he ignored them and they stayed away from him. His reaction to their last attempts to bully him had been surprising to say the least. They now had to figure a way to get even with him

The football coach noticed the change in Bob and started to find out just what the difference was. At practice one after school session he watched as Bob was hitting the dummies and throwing blocks. The new aggressiveness was very apparent and he was pleased. He decided to see how good Bob would be at passing the football. He had two of Bob's friends take Bob to one side of the field and pass the ball back and forth. He watched as they started short passes, then gradually opened the distance between them until they were nearly the length of the field apart. Bob was still throwing the ball the full distance and with very good accuracy.

The coach decided to put Bob in as quarterback in the next after school game to see what would happen.

The next afternoon when the game was about to start and the teams were being made up. The coach announced that Bob would be first quarterback. Most of the team members had been seeing Bob at practice and they went along without comment, but Jeffrey complained. The coach said "I want to see if he is as good in a game as he is at practice, so give him a chance, and you leave him alone" he added.

The game went along well and Bob completed seven out of eight pass attempts. He was watching Jeffrey and noticed that Jeffrey's blocks were not always successful and that he let some of the other team members get through to tackle Bob. The Coach was pleasantly surprised at the way Bob was playing. Every one of the completed passes had been as accurate as they could be, right on the money and at a moving target. Bob had been tackled a few times but after the ball had been thrown. There had been no problems with Jeffrey.

One morning in April as Pam and Bob were walking to school, Pam said, "Bob, don't you forget about Jeffrey and Leonard, they will try to get back at you sooner or later, you promise you will be careful."

"I will Pam, I know that they will try something and I will be watching." He said "It has got to end sometime, the sooner the better.".

"You know Bob, you're grades are almost perfect now. They were above average before, but you have even made them better, and I have been watching you at football practice and you are getting very good." Pam said as they were nearing the school.

"You may be in line for student of the year if you keep it up. As a graduating senior you may win a scholarship."

"I am not that good." Bob said. "And what college would accept me, the way I talk? Bob answered. He still stuttered and stammered when he talked, but he was a lot more confident in the way he did other things. He did not pay attention to what the other kids were doing when he talked, because he did not care what they thought. He was doing the best he could. Lately his throat had been feeling funny and he had a little trouble swallowing his food

They entered the school and parted, she squeezed his hand as she left him, he smiled happily and thought how much he liked her. That was as far as he ever thought about her. He was fully convinced that no girl would ever get serious about him that they were all sorry for him. It would take a lot of talking and convincing to change his mind about that matter. He had felt sorry for himself for so long it was hard to think otherwise

He left school quickly that day and walked fast to keep from seeing Pamela. He wanted to be alone to think a little about the situation. As he entered the house and walked to the kitchen his mother noticed the different expression on his face and motioned him to a chair by the table. He sat down and looked at his mother.

"Mom" he said, "Pam told me that I may be awarded a scholarship for my grade average and improvement. I don't want it. I don't want to go up on the stage to get it in front of all the other kids. I would not be able to say a word for fear of stammering and stuttering. Why don't they just leave me alone?"

"We can get around that Bobbie, I'll just tell them you don't feel good on that day and keep you home. Your grades are good enough that they won't say anything."

"I didn't see Pamela when you came home, didn't she come with you?" she asked him.

"No." he said. "I left fast, I don't want her to think she has to walk home with me every night because she feels sorry for me." He thought he should not have said that, but sometimes he thought that was the way she felt. He was so sure that everyone felt that way for so long that it was hard for him to think otherwise. In his heart he was hoping that she really liked him and enjoyed walking with him

"Bobbie, I want to ask you a question and I want you to tell me the truth, OK?" his mother said.

"OK mom" he said, "Ask away".

"That day back in March when you were beaten up and came home all bloodied and dejected. Tell me everything that happened and how you felt. That is the day you changed and became a new son of mine that I am very proud of I loved you before and love you now, but now I am also very proud of you and the way you are. You have nothing to be ashamed of. There are many people with speech impediments and they are all loved for who they are, not the way they speak. Now tell me what happened that day.

"Well, I was watching the football game and did not see Jeffrey and Leonard coming up behind me until one of them grabbed me and threw me to the other one, then he threw me back, then one of them tripped me and I fell to the ground. When I got up Jeffrey hit me in the face and knocked me back down. When I got back up Leonard hit me in the face and knocked me back down. Then I started covering my face with my arms to keep from being hit in the face. Then they started kicking me in the stomach and when I bent over they kicked me in the legs. They finally stopped kicking me and left."

"What happened then?" his mother asked

"I remember feeling like I must be dying, I was so weak and could hardly breathe. I was just lying there and thinking, no more beatings, no more beatings and stammering with people looking at me like I was some kind of freak. Suddenly I felt like there was a breeze blowing and I wondered how it could be blowing through my body too. I thought they must have beat me pretty good for that to happen. Then I started to feel stronger and a few minutes later I even thought about fighting back the next time those bullies started something. That was a new thought for me. I don't think I ever thought that way before. As my strength came back I finally got up and came home, all the time trying to think how I was going to fight back."

Bob was quiet for a minute or so then started to talk again.

"the strangest part of all is that I now know a lot more things than I remember learning. I seem to know how to say and do things that I don't remember doing before. I must have read and remembered them, like hitting Leonard when he tripped me on the steps at school. I immediately twisted and came up with a fist and hit him on the side of the head. I guess I hit him pretty hard for he went down on the steps and I left. He has stayed away from me ever since. But I know they will try again to hurt me. Now I know I can fight them and I know that the way I talk is not my fault and that I will always be this way. My grades show that I am as smart as any one else and maybe even smarter than some, so now I know that I am right and will fight for those rights. I don't feel like the person I was before the beating, but I do not understand what happened."

His mother looked at him and saw the confidence and the lack of fear in his eyes. There was no doubt in her mind that he was a changed person. As he was talking there was stuttering and stammering in the sentences with some words, but the flow of his voice was even and steady and he could be understood very well in spite of the hesitations and breaks. How well she remembered the cringing, scared almost helpless little boy she had raised. How helpless she had felt because she did not know how to help him. How the doctors had tried to do something to change the way he felt about himself. Nothing had helped in any way. His lack of will power and ambition was apparent from the time he was born. The defect in his voice box and control could not be corrected it seemed, and that only added to the problem.

"Well," his mother said, "whatever happened made a great change in you and I am very glad it happened. You understand yourself a lot better now and your attitude toward other people has changed for the better. I am very happy for you and if you do get a scholarship and want to try college. Your father and I will try to see it happen. Now what about Pamela? I do not think she just feels sorry for you. I think she really likes you for what you are. The way you talk does not bother her either. You ought to think about that. You should be able to see in her actions if she just feels sorry for you or not. Give her the benefit of the doubt until you are sure."

"Ok mom, I do like her a lot and she is a smart girl." Bob replied. "Pretty too" He added.

Then he went to the piano and played till he was called to dinner, much to his parents delight.

As they were talking at the dinner table that evening, his mother detected a slight change in the way he talked, so she watched him covertly. He seemed to be having a little trouble swallowing his food. She said nothing, but she was worried.

Pamela met him at the corner up the street the next morning and they went to school as usual. Bob did not talk much and Pam asked him why.

"There is something wrong with my throat" Bob told her. Talking rather soft and low, "I don't want my mother to know, she will worry."

"She probably already knows something is wrong", Pam said. "I noticed the way you swallow and I could tell it was in your throat. You better tell her so she can make an appointment with your doctor, and have him check it out."

They were a bit early this morning and they walked into the auditorium to sit and talk. There was no one else in the auditorium so they sat in the front row to talk. Someone had moved the piano down in front of the stage for some reason.

Bob kept looking at the piano and he did not seem to want to talk. Maybe his throat hurt. Finally he got up and went over to the piano, sat down and started playing some of his favorite tunes. Pam stared and listened with disbelief as his fingers moved over the keys so softly and at the music that came out of it. She sat there entranced as he played several of his favorite pieces. He played by ear now and did not need the sheet music. She saw him glance at the large clock. He got up and walked to her and they each went to their respective rooms. Before she released his hand she said, "Bob, that was beautiful, and I really mean that,"

Bob had been playing well in the past weeks of football practice and the coach was planning in using him in the playoff series at the end of the school year. He was a very good quarterback and could throw the ball as good as any of the regulars. Jeffrey and Leonard had stayed away from him. They both knew that one on one they were not good enough and they were waiting for a chance to gang up on him and beat him up. They knew that on weekends he and Pam usually went to the local park and talked.

The final game of the season was nearing and they wanted to beat Bob bad enough to keep him out of the game.

The last weekend before the game, Jeffrey, Leonard and another friend of Jeffrey's, Edward Bailey were waiting in the park when Bob and Pam came walking in to the usual bench area to sit and talk. The three came out of the brushy area behind the bench the two used to sit on when they were talking Bob and Pam stood up as they came from behind and confronted them.

"Ok dummy, we're gonna fix you this time. You won't be able to play in the big game. You'll be in the hospital." Jeffrey said as he swung a fist at Bob.

The memories of Li Chan came into use as Bob spun on his heels and caught Jeffrey in the stomach with his foot, then Leonard on the side of the head with his elbow as he slowed his spin. Ed bailey was standing ready to hit Bob. His feet planted apart and facing him. Bob was still in motion as he came around and he continued the motion and brought his foot up between the legs of Ed Bailey. As the foot met solid body, Ed screamed and fell to the ground holding his private parts and screaming at the top of his lungs. Leonard was now coming back in to take a swing at Bob, so Bob moved toward him instead of backing away and grabbed his head and pulled it down as he brought up his knee. The result was a bloody nose for Leonard as he fell back to the ground stunned. Jeffrey was still trying to get his breath back to normal.

This all happened so fast that Pam had hardly moved, except to step a little to get further out of the way. Bob had not said anything and now he just looked at each of the bullies and then said to Pam, "Come on Pam, let's get away from here.".

Pam said nothing, just took Bob's hand and held on to it. As they walked away Pam spoke. "Bob, when did you ever learn to fight like that?" I've never seen anyone move that fast before and I have seen a lot of fights."

"I don't know," Bob said. "When I first saw them moving around us I suddenly remembered fighting like that before and I just did what came to me as they moved toward me". It is an oriental form of fighting that is rather deadly I remember reading about it as I was growing up. Maybe that is where I learned it, although I do not remember practicing it any time."

"Poor Ed," Pam said. "He did not really want to be mixed up in this but the other two talked him into it I believe. I hope he is not hurt too bad."

"How is your throat now Bob?' Pam asked as they walked out of the park toward a little restaurant up the street a ways.

Bob hesitated for a while then spoke. "It is getting worse, and I am going to a doctor for a check." he said softly. "It is getting very hard for me to swallow, even water, I am scarred Pam, but I do not want Mom to worry so much. The Doctor's appointment is right after the game and I would like you along if you will come."

Pam was nearly in tears as she said, "Of course I'll come if it is ok by your mother."

The game was just two days away.

When they were in the restaurant and the waitress took the order. Pam noticed that Bob ordered soft food and hot chocolate. She watched carefully and noticed that he ate slowly and swallowed very often, but she said nothing.

As his house was on her way home she walked with him they stopped in front of the house to talk. Then Bob said, "Would you m-m-mind if I kissed you Pamela?"

Pam moved closer to him, took his face in her hands, said "Of course not, silly." Then she put her lips to his in what was their first kiss. Bob put his arms around her waist and pulled her close to him and held her there while they kissed. It was his first kiss ever with any girl and he was shaking with delight as he held her then released her a little and said," I-I H-Have wanted to do that for a long time Pamela, but I was afraid you would not want me to."

"I have wanted you to do that for a long time too Bob, but I wanted you to want to do it first. I think I have fallen for you I like you an awful lot Bobbie."

They stood there holding each other, kissed again, but both felt awkward there in the street so Bob said, "I better go in now, will I see you tomorrow?"

Pam said, "You bet you will. It is Monday and I'll be here to walk to school with you, bye now."

When Bob entered the house his mother was waiting. "How do you feel son?" She asked.

"I feel about the same," Bob replied. "It hasn't gotten any worse. I kissed Pamela. Do you think Pam will get a sore throat too?" He added.

"No son, I don't think whatever is wrong is contagious so do not worry yourself, Pam will be Ok." His mother reassured him. While she was talking to him she noticed that his breathing had changed a little, perhaps a little faster, she was not sure.

"Mom" Bob spoke. "I had a fight with Jeffrey and his friends today. I think I may have hurt them a little. I knocked them all down and gave Jeffrey a bloody nose, and I kicked Ed Bailey where it hurt bad, and knocked the wind out of Leonard too. We left them there. I don't think they were hurt bad. I think they will leave me alone now."

"Did they hurt you at all?" she asked.

"No" Bob told her, and walked into the living room to lie down.

His mother looked after him, wondering what had happened to her son these last few months. She was happy, yet unhappy, and very worried about his throat. She was anxious to get him to the doctor so she would know just what was wrong with his throat. Three full grown strong boys his own age and he said he knocked all three of them down, and he did not think he had hurt them. Pam must have been there with him, I will call her when I get a chance and find out just what had happened.

Bob ate a good breakfast the next morning and did not act like anything was wrong, but he did not talk very much. He left the house when he saw Pam coming up the street. They hugged and kissed when they met and then walked on to school. It was nearly the last day of school and they only sat around talking and turning in the things that belonged to the school. Bob would be at football practice all afternoon. The big game with the Bristol school team was tomorrow and they all wanted to be in good shape for it. The Bristol Team was just an average team, but the team that won tomorrow would be the best in the local league and would win the pennant for their school.

The three boys that had accosted him on the weekend were there, but they did not look at him except when he wasn't looking their way. He caught them looking at him when they thought he wasn't looking. He did not expect any trouble from them with all the other young people around. He knew he was not going to start anything. He was ready to forget it all.

During practice, he threw passes to Jeffrey and each one was accurate and Jeffrey was at the right place at the right time to receive them. It was the same with the other receivers. He only had one interception and that was when he was throwing to the regular receiver. He was good and therefore he was watched closely.

The coach was happy and satisfied that they could beat the other team. They stopped practice early and he told them to all get a good nights rest and be ready for the big day tomorrow.

Pam had been watching the afternoon practice and when Bob came out of the dressing room and walked toward her, she ran to him and said, "Bob, you played real well. How do you feel after such a workout?"

"I feel Ok now, but a bit tired and my breathing was a little tight when I was playing but now it is not so bad. Let's go to the park where we can sit and talk and be alone. Can we Pam?" he asked.

"Yes we can Bob, come on." She told him and took his hand. They started toward the Park. Not talking. Pam was full of questions, but she did not want to make him talk with his throat hurting the way she knew it was. She just talked about things that she knew he would not have to answer but that would break the silence between them.

The soul that had came from Li Chan was doing all she could do to will Bob's physical being, and to control his physical being in the best way she could. She was doing quite well she thought. The problem with his throat was beyond her control and there was nothing she could will him to do that would help the situation in his throat. She was willing him very strongly to be sure to go to the doctor. She had made strong suggestions to go to a doctor much earlier, but he had practically ignored her wishes. The Soul could only do so much where the will power was concerned. There had to be a little help from the brain she worked through for her wishes to come true. The years he had lived with the very weak soul, before she entered his physical being, left his brain in a stubborn and weak condition that she had to overcome. She had overcome a lot and the change was very noticeable in the behavior of his physical being and his way of thinking and acting.

In the park they sat on a bench that was away from the other benches far enough that they could not be heard talking and only a few other benches could be seen. Bob let her sit down, then sat down beside her and pulled her close and just sat there holding her. Pam turned her face up to look at him and he leaned down a little and kissed her on the lips. Then he held her close, not saying anything. Pam glanced up and saw a tear rolling down his cheek. She snuggled closer. She noticed his breathing was a little faster than it had been. She was worried. She knew that if his throat was not hurting he would be telling her what he felt and what was wrong; or rather what he thought was wrong. Therefore his throat must be hurting pretty bad or his breathing was getting harder and harder. She thought he should not play in the game tomorrow, but she did not want to be the one to tell him. She knew that he really wanted to play and was looking forward to it. He could not get enough oxygen to supply his physical requirements for a hard played football game breathing the way he was now. He must be able to see that, she thought. Maybe he knew it and would pace himself so that he could still play, but not so vigorously. That must be it she thought. He is a very smart boy.

The next day Bob did not arrive at the school until lunchtime. His mother had called the coach and told him ahead of time that Bob would not show up till noon, but that he would be there.

Pam was sitting in the stands with some friends and was watching the doors that the players would come out of as they came onto the field. She was eagerly waiting for the sight of Bob.

The game started and Bob had not shown up. She began to worry and all kinds of thoughts were going through her mind as she waited. The regular quarterback was now playing and the regular receiver was on the field as well as Jeffrey, who was also used as a receiver.

Bob came out and took a seat on one of the benches during the second quarter. Pam watched and tried to see if everything was as it should be. She could not detect any sign of problems. She saw him looking toward the stands, but she could not be sure if he saw her or not.

The teams played back and forth across the centerline during the third quarter with the score tied at thirteen. Coach had still not put Bob into the game.

At the start of the fourth Quarter the coach put Bob in as quarterback. Pam could not see any difference in his movements to show problems. The game continued back and forth in the center of the field for a few plays. Then she noticed that the lineup had changed and it appeared that there was to be some long passing coming up. Bob's blockers were doing a good job of giving him time enough for a good pass. He was tackled once and pretty hard too, by one of Bristol's men. It did not seem to bother him.

On the next play, his receiver ran out to his left and down the sideline to go into the end zone for the pass. Bristol's men followed him and boxed him all the way. Bob went back for the pass and watched as his receiver entered the end zone. He was covered so tight that Bob could not see any way he could complete a good pass. Bob quickly scanned the field for an alternate receiver and saw Jeffrey twenty yards from the end zone and open, watching him.

The bullet pass that he threw went straight to Jeffrey's hands and Jeffrey turned and crossed into the end zone about three seconds later for a touchdown.

It had happened so fast that the spectators were caught off guard and there was silence for a moment. Then the home stands burst into applause and shouting.

The field goal was made and the game ended that way.

The home team gathered around Bob and was shouting and clapping him on the back. That much excitement was too much for his heart and the amount of oxygen it was getting. His body suddenly went limp and he fell. The team was trying to hold him up and they did not realize what had happened at first.

When Pam saw him go limp in the hands of the team she immediately knew what was wrong and ran to the ambulance at the side of the field and told them. They raced onto the field. The nurse in the ambulance checked and found that his heart had stopped.

Minutes later they were at the hospital and in the intensive care unit, They had somehow started his heart beating again

Pam called Bob's mother on the local pay phone and told her what had happened, and asked her if she would pick her up at the school and take her with her to the hospital. She said she would be glad to.

When they arrived at the hospital, Bob was still in the intensive care room. They had to wait nearly an hour. Then the doctor came to them.

"How is he?" Bob's Mother asked. Pam was beside her and listening.

"Not good," The doctor answered. "I an afraid I have bad news for you all. The checks we have made on your son have given us reason to believe your son is dying and there is nothing we can do to prevent it. I am truly sorry, If what we have discovered is true and I believe it is. Your son has had cancer since he was very young and it has grown along with him until his chest cavity is nearly full of the cancer. I have to tell you that he has very little time left. It is a wonder that he is still alive. You may see him now."

The doctor led them to the door of a room down the hall, then left them. They walked in. Pam stayed behind his mother as they approached his bed.

Bob was awake when they approached and smiled weakly.

"Did we win the game/" he asked weakly.

"Yes we did, thanks to you." His mother told him. "That pass of yours took them all by surprise."

His mother was about to say something else when she noticed he was looking past her. She turned and looked back. Jeffrey had come into the room and was waiting to talk to Bob. When Bob's mother motioned him forward, he stepped over to the bed and looked down at Bob.

"Why did you do that?" he asked Bob.

"Y-You were open and I K—knew you could make it to the zone." Bob replied.

Jeffrey mumbled, "Thanks." And as he turned to go, Pam saw what looked like a tear and moisture in his eyes.

Pam and his mother were beside the bed again and there were tears in his mother's eyes. "Mom, don't cry; I'm ok. The doctors did not tell me anything yet, but they will".

"Pam, lean down, I want to tell you something." Bob said.

Pam leaned down and kissed him. Pam was looking into his eyes and the look of love she saw was more than she could stand. The tears were coming and she could hardly keep from crying out. It seemed that all the love he had been holding back for years was showing at once.

Then she turned her head and put her ear to his mouth

"Pam," he whispered. "I-I-I Love you." His eyes closed and his body went limp.

Pam burst into tears and turned away as the nurses rushed in

One of the nurses that had been standing by at the door rushed over to Bob and took over. Pam and Bob's mother stood back, crying silently and let the nurse do what had to be done. They rushed Bob out to the emergency room. Everyone knew that it was useless, but they had to try.

What had been the soul of Li Chan and was now the soul of Robert Richardson drifted slowly out of the physical being of Robert Richardson and rose slowly upward.

Looking down, she saw Bob's mother and Pam, still sitting on the chairs in the empty room and both were crying silently as they watched the body of the son and boyfriend for the last time. Li Chan had felt the deep love that Bob had for Pam and she knew the feeling, for it was the kind of love she had had for Chen Li. She thought about all the memories she had now and wondered where she would go now that she was not occupied by willing and controlling a living being. She still wondered about the loving part of the male and female beings. That should be interesting.

LEAH

For years the soul of Li Chan drifted endlessly through the universe. Time meant nothing to it as it gave no thought to anything, there seemed to be no interaction between lost souls.

Years later it became aware of a surface below and noted the difference of where it had last been, and what was appearing now as it floated above. The surface was the same, yet different somehow. The land was not so green and looked dry and desolate.

It drifted slowly, not really concerned about what it was looking at, but memories began to come to it and the real life it had been involved with.

Green grass and trees began to go by beneath and then a small lake appeared. At one end of the lake a group of creatures similar to the ones it had left when the life had stopped were gathered around one of their number that lay on the grass.

Dropping lower the lost Soul could sense life still in the body, but there seemed to be no controlling action going on. Water was in the body's mouth, but none of the figures standing around were doing anything to help the figure on the grass. Two girls about the same age were trying to roll her over, but were not succeeding. There seemed to be no life in the body.

Dropping beside the body, the lost soul slipped inside of it.

One of the young women was shouting, "Leah, wake up, Can you hear me?" "Leah, say something!" There was no answer.

As it entered the body it knew that the body should be rolled over first to get the water out of the breathing passage. It tried to get the hand to move first and the fingers did move. One of the bystanders saw the movement and knelt down and said, "She's alive, roll her over and get the water out of her mouth, quickly".

One of the bigger figures, a huge man reached down and, grabbing her around the waist lifted her up, turning her over as he did so. The weight of the girl, hanging over his arm pushed the water out of her and as he lowered her to a sitting position on the ground. The lost soul now willed her to try to breath in some air. She gasp, then tried again, until she drew in more and more, She coughed and spit out some more water until she began to breath a little more evenly.

The girl was young, in her late teens and very beautiful with long golden hair that looked very cared for. Two other young women were very concerned about the girl and hovered like mother hens around their chicks. The other figures were other young girls and a couple of young boys, who stood next to the huge man watching with big eyes and scared faces.

One of the two young women that had been hovering around the blonde spoke "Leah, are you alright, how do you feel?"

"I am feeling better now, but my body still hurts" the blonde girl replied a little weakly. "Just let me rest a little here in the sun and I will be alright." The two girls put down a small pillow and a blanket and moved her to it. Then stayed there to serve her if need arose. The Lost Soul had a new life and name again. The new Soul did not sense any feeling or strength that would be coming from the other soul if it were still in the controlling area of the Brain of the young girl, so it moved in and immediately took control. It first absorbed the memory area and learned all about the young girls past. It assumed her identity, and was ready to become the Soul of Leah

The memories she had absorbed told her that Leah was eighteen years of age and was the daughter of a very strict rancher who controlled with an iron hand. Leah was his favorite daughter and had been given nearly everything she asked for. She Loved music and could dance for hours, loving every minute of it.

Leah now knew she was in a group of people at a lake. They had come to the lake on a picnic and had a table and chairs at one end of the lake near the spring that fed it. The water was cool and she had taken off her shoes and walked out into the lake to walk around in the shallow area. It was a sandy bottom and she was enjoying the feel of the sandy bottom when she slipped over a drop off into deeper water. She went under and when she came up tried to reach the shallow part again. Her foot slipped off again and the water filled her mouth as she went under again. She tried to breath and only made things worse as she swallowed more water.

Both of her sisters had seen her slip and immediately ran out and each one grabbed an arm and pulled her back to shore and out on the grass. She seemed unconscious.

Now, on the bank after the scare she was feeling much better. The hot sun had warmed her body and she felt all right again. Her clothes were soaked and she had to stay in the sun for a while and let them dry out a little. The little group relaxed a while and let her lie there and dry out. Later she started to get up and her two sisters were instantly at her side helping. It was a relatively large lake and she wanted to walk around it and see who else was using the area for a picnic. She had seen a small group of people on the opposite side from where her father had stopped, and she was curious.

She started walking that way and the little group followed. As they came closer, Leah's eyes caught the eyes of one of the young men in the group, and it seemed she could not stop looking at him. Her legs felt weak and she did not know what to do. Her face felt hot as she began to blush. She was beginning to lose control of everything. She had never felt this way before, what was the matter. She knew, somehow that the young man was still looking at her.

Her sisters could see what was happening and being a little older and wiser, took her hands and led her towards the lake. With her back toward the young man they helped her compose herself and tried to build her confidence.

They were trying to keep from giggling and were not doing too good a job of it. The young man was very good looking and was beautifully dressed. The sisters were interested themselves. Their sister had always been so self-confident that they were surprised to see that something had caused such confusion.

Leah spoke, "Be quiet you two, I do not know what came over me. I have seen boys before and I did not feel like this. I am so attracted to him it is embarrassing. He is so very handsome I cannot keep my eyes away from looking at him. Come, let us go on around the lake, I must get farther away from him."

Diana, the elder sister spoke, "Leah, I have never seen you blush before, what happened?"

Leah replied, "I do not know, I have never felt this way before. It felt like I was being drawn toward him, I could feel the strong attraction. He is very handsome and he is so very well dressed. I wonder who he is. He must be a stranger to this area."

Melanie the second sister spoke, "He looks like he may be a soldier, he has the bearing, and he looks about the right age and there are no women with them, they may all be soldiers".

As they were walking away, Leah spoke again, "He must still be looking at me, I can still feel the attraction, it is like he is pulling me towards him, I must meet him, not now though, I must have time to prepare for a meeting like that."

The little group that had been with her had walked on, laughing as they went. Leah ignored them and let them go. She hoped they would not say anything to her father about what they had seen. She had not been paying attention to anything but the handsome boy so she did not know what they had seen She wanted to look back, but she knew that she should not, at least not till she could compose herself and be prepared for the meeting. She just had to see him again and this time she would be calmer and ready for the meeting.

The young man that was the cause of Leah's blush and looking away was aware of what had happened and knew that he was the cause. Their eyes had met for just an instant, but that had been enough. He had felt the same attraction. It was a new experience for him as well and he was stunned that the instant had caused him such emotions. He had encountered other young ladies and had felt no such feelings before. He watched as Leah and the two other girls walked away. He seemed to understand why they had not came on over as a group to talk to them. He was oblivious to the other young men around him. His mind was completely on the young lady he had just seen. The attraction he was feeling was new to him also. It was so very strong it was all he could think of.

He watched as they disappeared into the wooded area at the other side of the lake. He felt they were destined to meet again. This had been a special meeting.

A very confused and shook up Leah walked back to the picnic area and sat in one of the lawn chairs there to collect her thoughts and compose herself. She could not get her thoughts off of the young man she had seen by the lake. She could not even remember what he was wearing. It was an all encompassing feeling that she felt and she still felt in it's grasp.

Her father had seen her and her sisters return and knew that something had happened that had made a deep impression on his daughter. His other daughters, he noticed were talking and giggling about something, but he had no clue. He caught his eldest daughters' eye and signaled her to come over.

"What happened to Leah" he asked her.

"Oh, nothing, she just saw a new boy on the other side of the lake, and it threw her for a loop, she just fell apart, "She answered, "and he is handsome" she added.

"What do you mean, a new boy?" he asked.

"He was with a small group of people and I have not seen any of them before, and I know most of the young people who live around here". She told him.

Leah sat in the chair for a while. She was refreshed after the swim, but the scare of nearly drowning left her tense and seeing the boy had not helped. She let herself completely relax and tried to get the thought of the new boy out of her mind, but could not. Who was he? Where had he come from? Why was she feeling this way? She caught herself looking in the direction of the group of young men on the other side of the lake but she could not see past a few trees that were in the way. They were several hundred yards away and she did not feel the young mans eyes on her any more. She felt more in control of her feelings now and had regained her composure.

Her mother had set out the lunch on the portable table and Leah saw that it was ready for eating. And she was hungry. As she put a sandwich together she was trying to figure out how she was going to arrange a meeting with the young man she had locked eyes with earlier. The feeling that had came over her was at first scary, but she thought it was also very pleasant and somehow safe. She had felt as if he was trying to draw her to him she had barely been able to take her eyes off of him and look somewhere else.

After a few minutes of thinking and enjoying her lunch, she decided to ask her elder sister to come along and go with her and they could walk that direction and "by accident," "walk past the young men as they walked around the lake.

Having reached that conclusion, she relaxed and went back to the lunch table and finished her meal. Her mother was a great cook and had prepared a really good meal. She picked a lawn chair that faced the lake and was positioned so that most of the lake could be seen. As she sat there looking toward the other side of the lake, the group of young men came into view and were walking along the opposite shore.

Her heart started beating faster and she began to feel the attraction again.

Leah's father had been watching Leah as she walked around getting her food and walking to her chair. He was not sure of what it was but there was something different about her, the way she walked or the way she stood. He had not been told of how she had come close to dying as she lay on the ground with her lungs and throat full of water. It had all happened so fast that the other people around her had not grasp the full situation and the grave danger she was in. If the big man, who was her uncle, had not grabbed her around the waist, rolled her over and lifted her up, thereby forcing the water out of her lungs and mouth, she surely would have died. He could not define any particular difference, but he knew there was a change.

Charles Madison was a strong man with practical ways and beliefs. Honest and hard working, he had bought an ageing ranch with several thousand acres and built it into a prosperous and popular ranch.

There were five children from his marriage to Elizabeth, a quiet woman, the same age as her husband. Two boys, John and Jeremy, Jeremy being the eldest, age Twenty-five, John age twenty-three and then there were the three girls, Diana age twenty, Leah, age eighteen and the youngest, Melanie, age sixteen. All were very dependable and helped run the large ranch.

Leah's father watched as Leah and Diana left the table and walked toward the lake. With Diana along he put aside his worries and relaxed to enjoy the company of his wife. The older boys, actually young men had left after they had enjoyed the luncheon their mother had spread out on the table. They had returned to the ranch, located only a few miles down the highway south of the lake.

Leah and Diana walked slowly toward the lake and looked ahead to see where the group of men was. They had moved to a spot near the drinking fountain that had been put in near the spring. They were all sitting on the grass and talking.

Leah and Diana walked to the fountain to get a drink of the fresh water. Leah had been glancing covertly in their direction and had noticed the young man she was looking for was sitting not far from the fountain. While she was drinking she felt the presence of the young man drawing closer. She knew it and could hardly keep her composure. Diana noticed the flush of a blush in Leah's cheeks and looked up to see the young man coming in their direction.

When Leah straightened up from the drinking fountain, she looked into the Bluish-gray eyes of the handsomest young man she had ever seen. He was smiling as he said,

"I was hoping you would come this way. My name is Kenneth Altman, and I would like to ask a favor."

Leah had kept her composure and said, I am Leah Madison and just what kind of favor do you have in mind Mr. Altman? This is my sister Diana." She nodded toward Diana

It was his turn to blush and he turned away for a few seconds then looked at Diana as he said, "Hello Diana" Then he turned to Leah and said "I am here with some of my friends. We have a band and we are on our way to Baker Springs. We are playing there tomorrow night. We are new to the area and we don't know where the Arena is and how to get to it. We also need the location of the motel nearest to the arena."

"Oh, Good, finally some excitement in this town. I've seen the signs around town." Diana said.

"The Arena is right on the main drag the other side of town on the right. And there is a motel almost across the street. You can't miss it if you stay on the main road." Leah told him.

"Will you two come, It is a dance you know and we do play pretty good music." Kenneth said quietly. "And bring some friends, we like big crowds."

Leah had been watching Kenneth closely and she saw his eyes looking at her hair, face, then down to her mouth, then her full breasts. When they reached her breasts, they quickly returned to her eyes and he blushed a little before he said. "Was that some of your family you were with before?"

"Some are family and some are just friends. We came here for a picnic today. We come here quite often. It is quite beautiful here most of the time during the summer and fall. How did you happen to be here today?" Leah asked him.

"We drove up from downstate and stopped for a rest when we saw the Park sign." He replied.

Leah turned and slowly walked toward the edge of the grass along the shore of the lake and he fell into step along with her, matching step for step. Diana stood for a minute. She was undecided as to what to do so she trailed along behind at a respectable distance, just out of hearing range. They were walking slowly, glancing at each other every once in a while. They came to a spot where a small stream entered the lake and Kenneth stepped across it first then reached out his hand for Leah to hold as she stepped across.

Diana noticed that when they continued walking they were still holding hands. Boy, that was fast, she thought. They were so engrossed in each other that they were oblivious to anything around them. She studied the young man a little closer and noticed how neat and trim he appeared in his sport clothes. He was as tall as Leah with light brown hair and his face was lightly tanned. Very nice looking she thought.

Leah heard him talking, but she seemed to know what he was saying before he said it

She felt like she was part of him, an extended part, but she felt like they, together were one. The attraction she had felt when she was away from him had came together and they were one. It was a new feeling for Leah and she was not sure how to handle it. She only knew the feeling was beautiful and she did not want to leave it. She felt so completely safe and comfortable just being close to him.

She heard him talking but she had already known what he was going to say and she answered him practically before he was finished. They both smiled at that. They stopped at the side of the water and were talking when they heard someone calling him. He was one of the group of men he had come with and when he looked up the man motioned him back toward the group. They headed that way.

As they approached the group of men, Leah noticed that they were all about the same age and height. Except for one man who looked foreign, who was about five feet six inches in height. She could see most of the men, as they looked her up and down. All of their eyes lingered on her breasts as they passed. She was used to that. It had happened a lot in her senior year at school.

They stopped in front of the group and ken spoke, "Guys, I would like to introduce you to my new friend, Leah Madison. She lives south of here She is picnicking here today with her family. I have invited her to the dance tomorrow night to hear us play."

He pointed to each one as he said their names,

"Leah, this is Ted Butler, our Drummer, This is Harry Dillon, our Bass player, This is Michael Bowers, our Lead Guitarist, and this is William Bagley "and he pointed to the short man." Our violinist."

Leah noticed that Michael Bowers paid the most attention to the introduction. She did not know just what it was about him, but she instantly felt a dislike. Maybe it was the way that he looked at her so openly and kept his eyes on her body so long. Even Kenneth noticed it and said," Mike is the band leader and runs the scheduling etc for the rest of us."

Mike Bowers spoke up, "Ken, if you can tear yourself away from the young lady, we have to get going, it's getting late and I have a lot to do."

Ken and Leah walked way from the men a little ways and stopped to talk. Ken said, "Leah, can I see you tomorrow night after the show for a cup of coffee or something? I truly want to see you again."

"Ok Ken" Leah said. "I'll see you tomorrow night after the show."

She wiggled her fingers at him as she turned and walked toward Diana who was not far away and had been watching the whole affair.

Diana and Leah walked slowly back toward the picnic area and the family. Neither spoke for a while then Diana said,

"Boy," Leah you sure can pick them, he sure is good looking and he seems so nice."

"I know Diana," Leah answered, "but looks are only skin deep. I know by the feeling I have when I am around him. It is a feeling of complete safety and assurance and a very pleasant feeling of love and contentedness. I really don't know how to explain it."

"I don't like that Michael Bowers though," she continued. "He looks like trouble. The way he looked at me gives me the creeps, and he is the boss of the group."

"Are you going to the show and dance tomorrow night?" Diana asked.

"Yes, "Leah answered, "I told Ken I would see him after the concert and go for coffee or something. I would like to dance with him, but I don't know whether he can get away or not. He is one of the Guitarists. That Bowers guy is the Lead guitarist so maybe Ken will be able to get away for a dance or two."

"I kind of like the first one you were introduced to." Diana said. "He is not bad looking and he looks about my age too."

"That was Ted Butler, I suppose his name is Theodore, he is the drummer for the band."

The band members walked away from the lake area and disappeared.

Leah and Diana walked back around the lake to the picnic area and the family. Their mother was cleaning up and repacking the leftovers and the dishes. They helped their mother pack the boxes in the station wagon and they all returned to the ranch.

Leah's younger sister "Melanie" was curious about the band and the dance and that is about all they could talk about on the way home. Melanie assured everyone that she was going to the concert alone and was going to have fun.

The coming concert and dance was the talk at the evening dinner at the Madison house. When the meal ended it was common knowledge that the whole family was going to be there. There were not many concerts and chances to dance and listen to music. When one did come along, nearly everyone went.

The concert had been advertised and a large crowd was expected. The arena could only seat two thousand and they were expecting a full house. The basketball court was used as a dance floor. The stage was at one end of the court and was elevated above the court level by three feet. The dressing rooms were behind the stage.

The entrance from the parking lot was at the other end of the building and came in under the seating section.

The Madison family came a little early in order to get seats down near the dance floor. Everyone in that family liked to dance. The two older sons were married and they brought their wives with them.

When they arrived and entered the arena they found that there were already people in the first two rows, mostly teenagers that wanted to be there to watch the setup and then be free to quickly get on the dance floor to dance when the music started. The speakers and musical instruments were already in their places on the stage and the microphones were in place. Leah did not know if there was a singer with the band. She had heard no mention of a singer so she wondered if one of the band members could be a singer too.

By eight o'clock the seats were nearly filled and the place was noisy with everybody talking at the same time. There were quite a few Mexicans living in the area and worked for the ranchers. They had picked a section of the seats and were making quite a bit of noise with their Spanish language and natural love of music.

Leah had taken Spanish in high school for that reason. Her father had several Mexicans working for him on the ranch and she had learned well.

The band members then came out and took their positions by their instruments and the noise quieted to a low hum.

When the music started, it appeared that Mr. Bowers, the bandleader had done a little research. The first song was one that was a favorite of the area. As soon as it was recognized, the first three rows moved nearly as one onto the dance floor and the night began.

The music, as it turned out was very good and all had a good time. The crowd was appreciative and showed their enthusiasm with thunderous applause. The crowd was clapping for more and more until Bowers finally had to hold up his hand until the noise subsided low enough that he could talk.

"I and my friends wish to thank you for your generous applause and promise that we will return as soon as arrangements can be made. It is late and we have a long journey tomorrow. Again, we thank you and Goodnight."

Leah stopped outside the front entrance and waited for Ken to come around. When he came she went to him and he put his arms around her and held her tight and whispered quietly, "Oh Leah I don't want to leave you, but I must. We all rode up here in vans with the instruments and we have to go back together."

"I know," Leah whispered back. "I came with the family in the station wagon too, will I see you again, I must, you know."

"Yes" Ken replied. "We don't live very far from here and I'll drive up in my car the first chance I can get. We have a long drive tomorrow because we have another gig downstate a ways for tomorrow night. Will you give me your phone number so I can talk to you and tell you when I can come up?'

"Of course." Leah said and then reached in her purse for pencil and paper to write the number on. He put it in his shirt pocket and said. "I'd better get back to help pack the instruments."

Then he turned her head to kiss her on the cheek. Leah saw it coming and turned back so their lips met. She knew that was what he wanted to do in the first place. After the long first kiss, she said,

"You be sure and call", but she knew inside her heart that he would. She had such an inner feeling. She was not scared or afraid he would not come back. She knew that he wanted to come back and that he had to leave for now. Those were facts. He disappeared in the crowd and she went to the waiting station wagon.

The Madison family talked about the concert and the music. They all really had a good time and were wishing the band would make another appearance in the near future. As it turned out Michael Bowers done what singing had been performed. His voice was not the best but it did sound pretty good.

Diana had not had a chance to meet Ted Butler, but she knew she would eventually because Ted and Ken were good friends and she knew that Ken would be coming around soon. He and Leah were so wrapped up together that she knew it would be soon.

The next day Leah was in a dream world of her own and wasn't much good at helping out around the house. She could not talk about anything but the band and Ken.

Late in the afternoon, Mrs. Madison was working in the kitchen when she heard piano music coming from the recreation room at the back of the house. She walked quietly back the hallway that led to the recreation room and stopped at the door and looked in. Leah was sitting at the piano and softly playing one of her favorite songs.

She almost cried out in surprise at what she saw. To her knowledge, Leah had never learned to play any kind of musical instrument, let alone a Piano. She was so surprised she quickly left before Leah saw or heard her, afraid she would say something and she wanted some time to think about what she had seen and heard.

She stood at the sink and listened as the music continued. Leah was playing some of her favorite songs on the piano, and she had never had a lesson in the world. What had happened to her that now she was playing music, and doing it very well. She finally went back to her preparation for the evening meal. The music was soft and beautiful with a melancholy sound to it. She could hardly contain herself, but she had to wait till she could tell Leah's father.

Charles Madison came in a little later and hung his jacket on a peg beside the back door. Then he walked into the kitchen and sat down on one of the empty chairs. The soft music was still coming from the recreation room. He listened for a while then looked up at his wife.

"Good music." He said, "Who's responsible?"

"Leah." His wife replied, looking smug.

"Leah is playing the piano like that?" He practically shouted.

He listened some more then asked his wife, "How long has she been playing like that?"

"All afternoon." His wife told him.

Just then the front door opened and Diana came in. She saw them sitting at the table and seemed to be listening to something. She stopped and listened. Soft piano music was coming from the recreation room. She looked at her parents and asked,

"Who is playing the piano?"

Diana did not wait for the answer. She just walked down the hall to the rec room and walked in. Leah looked up and stopped playing. Diana asked,

"When did you learn to play a piano like that?"

Leah looked a little stunned for a while then looked up at her big sister and said.

"I don't know Diana; I walked in here today and saw the piano. I walked over to it and it seemed familiar to me. I sat down and put my hands on the keyboard and it slowly came to me.

My fingers started to search the keys and suddenly I was making music. It is a wonderful feeling and I truly enjoy it. Since I fell in the lake, I have felt different somehow. I don't know why, but I seem different to myself, if that is possible. Do I seem different to you?"

"Well, now that you asked." Diana replied. "Playing the piano so sudden like that is a little different, but yes Leah you do seem a little different, but it is a good difference so don't knock it. Go with the flow. If it feels right accept it and enjoy it. Life is too short to miss any of the good stuff. That piano was there for a long time and you hardly looked at it. Like you say, that fall in the lake must have changed you somehow."

"Thanks Diana." Leah said. "I like the way I feel now. I seem to know a lot more things than I can remember learning and it makes me wonder how I learned those things."

About that time Leah's mother and father came into the room. Her father said.

"Leah, where in the world did you ever learn to play a piano like that?"

Leah replied, "I don't really know dad, since I fell in the lake and nearly drowned I seemed to have changed somewhat. I seem to know a lot more things than I knew before."

"Stop right there, what is this about nearly drowning?" Her father asked then continued, "Diana, you tell us, What happened?"

"Well, you remember the other day at the picnic when Uncle Bob and us went for a walk around the lake. Leah went wading in the shallow end of the lake and stepped off of the shallow part into deep water and went under. She got a mouthful of water and then choked. We thought she had fainted, but she was unconscious. Her mouth was full of water and she had stopped breathing. We didn't know what to do. Then we saw her fingers moving and uncle Bob picked her up and put her over his knee upside down. That knocked the water out of her and then she started to breath again. She rested for a while then we walked on around the lake where she saw Ken, the new boyfriend." Diana explained.

Leah's mother went to Leah and put her arms around her daughter and hugged her close as she said.

"Oh daughter, we nearly lost you, My God.' I could not stand that. How are you feeling now, are you alright?"

"Oh yes, I feel great now." Leah said.

A few days later, Leah was out in the back yard working with the flowerbeds. She suddenly felt as she had when she first met Ken. It was weak but she knew that Ken was coming so she ran around the house to watch the road. A minute or two later a small car appeared, slowed down and finally turned into the Madison driveway. Kenneth Altman was at the wheel.

Ken jumped out of the car and Leah ran to him. He put his arms around her and held her close for a quick kiss. "Hi Peaches." He said to her.

"Why Peaches?" Leah asked

"Your lovely cheeks look like two beautiful ripe peaches." He told her.

They turned and she led him into the house to meet her father and mother.

Ken's attitude and courteous manner impressed both Leah's father and mother. They felt comfortable talking and being around him. As the afternoon progressed, they learned many things about him. They liked what they heard.

They learned that the band was not only going to play this coming Saturday night, but that they were contracted to play every Saturday night for the next six weeks which pleased them. They had really enjoyed the one dance they had been to and were now looking forward to more nights of dancing.

They learned also that the band's leader, Michael Bowers was looking for a house to rent and intended to open a small retail craft store in the town of Baker Springs. All the band members liked the little town and were pleased at the prospect of living in it for a while. Ken was also looking for a rooming house or for a motel that would let him rent a room by the week.

The band had already been giving permission to use the arena for their practice. They had found out that there were some songs that the local people liked that they needed to practice. As the afternoon was ending, Ken turned to Leah's parents and asked,

"I would like to take your daughter into town for a snack at the local restaurant and check the rooming houses, if it is alright with you. She probably knows just where they might be and I would have to search for them?"

"Just be careful and bring her back safely." Mr. Madison said.

After Ken and Leah had left, he turned to his wife and said,

"I wonder what made Bowers decide to sell crafts in this town. This is not a craft-loving town. There are a few crafters here but they are older people looking for something to do. I wonder what kind of craft he is going to sell and who does the crafting."

"Oh well, we will find out sooner or later." He turned to his wife and said. "I am looking forward to another night of dancing with you, I enjoy that very much."

Saturday came and the Madison family was all looking forward to the evening concert. Diana was counting on she sister to introduce her to the drummer Ted Butler. Melanie was looking forward to being the queen of the ball and all suitors asking to dance with her.

Diana and Leah wanted to arrive earlier so that Leah could talk to Ken, so Diana asked her parents if they minded if she and Leah went on ahead in her car. Her father said,

"No, we don't mind, just be careful and let us know what's up after the dance so we won't worry about you both."

Diana and Leah arrived early and went into the arena. The band was already there and all the instruments were on the stage in their proper places and some of the members were on the stage. Diana looked around and could not see Ken or Ted. She looked at Leah and Leah said,

"Ken is not here yet."

"How do you know?" Diana asked.

"I would feel it if he was and I don't feel anything. So he isn't here yet." Leah replied. Diana Just looked at her and nodded.

They were standing close to the stage and talking when a group of their peers came in and walked to the stage. They were laughing and talking with the two musicians on the stage. One of the group, a young man of Leah's age who had evidently been drinking, came up behind Leah and put his arm around her from behind. Placing his right hand on her breast he moved his head around to kiss her. It was a kid named Jerry. He had been a classmate of Leah in her senior year in school and seemed to have a running crush on her.

Leah turned to face him, rammed her right fist into his stomach. Then she brought her left knee up into his face. The result was he went over backwards to the floor where he lie trying to get his breath back and groaning all the time.

About that time Leah felt the presence of Ken and she turned to Diana and said,

"Kens coming," They turned and walked toward the entrance. Ken and Ted came walking in and saw Leah immediately and went to her. Ken spoke,

"I am sorry Leah, I am a little late, I am glad you came. I think I will be able to dance a little with you tonight"

"That's ok," Leah said, "Ken, I want you to meet my sister Diana. Diana this is Ken Altman and this" she pointed to Ted Butler, "is the band's drummer, Ted Butler."

"My pleasure, I can assure you both." Ted said.

"We'll see you later." Ken said and he and Ted ran on behind stage to get ready for the concert.

Diana looked at Leah, "Little sister, where in the world did you learn to do what you did to Jerry back there?"

"I don't know Di." Leah said. "I just reacted that way; I seemed to know just what and when to do it and did it. I have wanted to do that to him for a long time. He is a pest."

The rest of the Madison family came in a little later and they all sat together in the second row and waited for the concert to start.

After the fourth song Leah saw Ken get up and leave the stage and she knew he was coming to dance with her to the fifth song. She immediately got up and walked over to the door from the back stage area. He came out as she got there then the music started and they went out on the dance floor.

Neither spoke as they moved around the floor. It was enough to just be holding each other so close and the feeling was beautiful. The song ended far too soon for them. Leah's father and mother had been dancing also and had passed them on the floor. It brought back memories for them.

As the dance ended Ken asked,

"Will I see you after the concert?"

"Of course, we'll wait at the car." Leah said.

Leah went to talk to her parents and tell them that she and Diana were going with Ken and Ted for a bite to eat at the fast food place after the dance, then they would be right home.

They were waiting at the side of Diana's car talking when the ex-classmate of Leah and two of his friends showed up. Jerry said,

"Leah, you shouldn't have treated me that way, I thought we were friends."

"We were friends, only friends; you should not have done what you did. You asked for what you got." Leah replied.

"Now you will see how it feels, hold her guys." Jerry said as he reached for Leah's arms.

Leah reacted quickly, grabbing his arm she pulled him close then brought her knee up to his groin. Turning to the other two she grabbed an arm of one and pulled, throwing him over her shoulder then turned and kicked the other one in the stomach. All three were on the ground when Ken and Ted came up.

"What happened?" Ken asked.

"They were fighting over us girls." Leah answered. "Come on, let's get something to eat at the Diner. You drive Di."

Leah climbed into the back seat as Diana got into the drivers seat and Ted got in the front seat beside her. Ken entered and sat beside Leah.

Diana was still in a daze. Everything had happened so fast she had not had a chance to say or do anything. She just started the car and headed for the restaurant. She tried to turn and look at Leah, but decided to keep driving. Something had happened to her sister. She sure had changed.

When they had ordered and found a table. Diana started again to say something, but a look from her sister stopped her and they proceeded to eat and chitchat about the band and the music.

Chitchat ended and they left the restaurant. As they sat in the car talking Ken told them that he and Ted were sharing a motel room by the week and it was just across the street and down a ways from the arena.

Diana started the car and headed it toward the arena. Ted pointed out the motel room that he and Ted shared. She parked in front of it and shut off the motor.

Diana and Ted got out of the car and went to the porch of the motel and sat on the edge of it.

Ken and Leah stayed in the back seat of the car. A kiss or two later they got out and Leah called to Diana,

Come on Di, time to go."

They left and stated for the ranch. Diana started to say something, then hesitated, then started again.

"I think that Ted is a pretty nice guy Leah. He seems honest enough and he is rather nice looking. He and Ken seem to get along real good too." And she added, "You and ken sure are getting along very good. When are you going to see each other again?

"I don't know, "Leah said, "He said he would call. I know it will be soon though, we really love being together"

"Leah, "Diana said. "You were pretty rough on Jerry and his friends. And they deserved it, but where in the world did you learn to fight like that? I have seen fights before, but not like that. It only took you a few seconds to put all three of them down. I did not have time to help you at all. I barely had time to think what was going on. Maybe now they will leave you alone."

"I hope so," Leah said. "The boys taught me how to kick in the stomach and groin, even the knee in the face, but I came close to using the ancient battle type of Machedo. I have memories of fighting using killing blows. I have been holding back, but if they try again and I fight from my memories too hard I may accidentally hurt them bad. It is an ancient Tanganese battle form of fighting. I do not know where I learned it. It scares me a little when I think of what could happen. I hope they do leave me alone. Please don't tell mom and dad Di. If it happens again, then I'll tell them."

Their parents and Melanie were in bed when they got home and they said goodnight and both of them went to their rooms for the night.

Ken knew that the Madisons were church going people and so he waited till afternoon before he called Leah. They talked for a while then decided to meet at the park where they first met for a picnic. Leah made up some sandwiches and lemonade and they spent the afternoon as lovers do. Both were amazed at how each one almost always knew what the other was thinking or wanted. They just fell deeper in love with each other.

Ken told Leah that Michael Bowers had found an empty store and was trying to rent it for a craft shop. There were small living quarters in back and he would live there

While Ken and Leah was talking, Ken told her that they were having band practice the next day in the afternoon and asked her if she would like to come and sit in.

"Oh yes," Leah said. "I would love to sit in, I love your music."

They learned much about each other as the afternoon passed. They learned that they had very many things in common and their likes and dislikes were similar. Leah was in his arms much of the time and they kissed often when the other people in the park were not watching. Lying there in Ken's arms Leah felt so safe and comfortable. She felt that they were part of each other and it was such a good feeling.

The next afternoon Leah walked into the arena and to the stage. Mike, Ted and Ken, along with Bill Bagley were on the stage setting up the equipment. Harry Dillon came in and joined them on the stage. Leah noticed that there was a piano on one side of the stage in the curtain area. The boys had never used the piano so she had not seen it before,

She needed a place to sit so she walked over to the piano and sat down on the bench. The lid was down on the keyboard. She lifted the lid and looked at the keys, then lifted the lid up to the upright position.

She could not resist. She let her finger slide over the keys, then started playing one of her favorite songs. The band members worked on, then slowly stopped, stood up and listened. Slowly they started walking toward the piano. They gathered behind her. She felt their presence and glanced up to see Ken smiling and he looked a bit surprised.

She ended the song and Ken said.

"I had no idea you could play a piano, you did not tell me, that was beautiful Leah."

"Why thank you Mr. Altman." Leah replied smiling her thanks.

"Can you play any of the songs we do on stage? Mike asked her.

"I think so." Leah said. "I would have to practice with you a while to get used to the rhythm of the band. It should not be too hard to pick it up."

"Good." Mike said. "Let's practice.

A few hours later, after Leah had played with them on the songs requiring piano, she had picked up the bands singular style and they felt good about the new addition. Leah had enjoyed the afternoon.

Diana had quietly slipped in while they were playing and took a seat in the corner inside the front door. No one had seen her and she had heard most of the show. Now she came forward and approached the stage.

"I don't mean to flatter you guys, but that was beautiful, the piano added a final touch and made it darn near an orchestra." She said.

Ken and Ted came down off the stage with Leah and the four of them decided to go out for a snack, before they went home.

Days went by, then it became weeks. The band played each Saturday night and the arena was crowded all the time now. Many of the people in the town knew The Madisons and knew Leah personally.

Mike Bowers had rented a shop and living quarters near the arena and had opened a woodcraft shop. He carried all kinds of wooden articles, from birdhouses to little wooden chairs. One of his main sellers was cut wood for fireplaces and campfires and wood burning stoves. No one seemed to know where he bought his firewood. A truck would bring in a load of logs and unload them beside his shop and he would then cut it into the desired length.

If anyone asked any of the band members, they would just shake their head and say it was none of their business and they did not asked. They left Mike alone except where the band was concerned.

Leah and ken were together constantly. They could be seen in the restaurant or around town at different places, but always together.

Leah was a little apprehensive the first time the band left Baker Springs to play in a neighboring village or town but she got over it after a few new places. The people liked the music and one night in a neighboring town. Leah sang one of her favorite songs for the audience.

She had been practicing and Mike thought she was really good enough. She did not want to sing the first time in public in her home town, so he waited till they had a gig in a neighboring town and let her sing for the first time.

She was very flattered and surprised at the audience reaction. After a few times at the microphone she began to relax and really enjoy the event.

The next Saturday night in Baker Springs Mike announced that the hometown girl would sing her favorite song for the opening number and Leah sang before her friends and family for the first time. The reaction was terrifying for Leah. The audience stood up, clapped, shouted and whistled till Leah thought the roof would fall in. They seemed to love her and she could not be happier.

Mike Bowers approached and took the microphone from Leah. He turned back and motioned Ken to come up to the microphone. When Ken came up beside of Leah he called for silence and waited till the arena was quiet, then said.

"Friends, we have enjoyed playing in your town and will continue to enjoy it we hope. This announcement will not surprise some of you, but will some others. Leah has asked me to tell you that today, Ken Altman, our guitarist has asked her to marry him and she has answered "yes".

The uproar started when he said yes and lasted for what seemed to Leah to be hours.

Leah kissed Ken and they both went back to their instruments.

Mike still had the microphone and after the noise stopped he said.

"Maybe I'll be able to talk them into having the ceremony here on Saturday night on this stage and we'll have a party afterward, by starting the show an hour or two early."

The reaction of the crowd signaled their approval and the louder hum of the crowd the rest of the evening signaled their interest.

The wedding of course was to take place in the church they had been members of for practically all their lives. It was what Leah wanted and everybody agreed. By virtue of the fact that she came from a large family it would be a large wedding.

The reception was a different thing and was to be held in the arena with the band playing for the dance that followed.

Needless to say, the church was packed. The church organist was to handle the musical end of the program and Leah's older sister took care of the whole affair. Diana made all the arrangements and Protocols.

Leah and Ken had shopped together for the ring and wedding dress. It was what Leah wanted. Ken did not see Leah when she tried the dress on. Diana with Melanie's help handled everything else. Leah's mother monitored everything and was enjoying it all.

It was a bright sunny day in early June that the church began filling up with people. Both church members and lay people filled the church pews to capacity as the town showed up for the wedding. Saturday morning in Bakers Springs was going to be remembered for a long time.

The organist started the music at about nine-thirty and played softly until exactly ten O'clock. She hesitated a few seconds while the minister walked out and took his position. Then she played "here comes the Bride,"

Leah's father started down the center aisle with Leah on his arm, looking proud as a proud father could look. Leah was a sight to see. Dressed in pure white and trailed by a long beautiful white tail, her beautiful blonde hair and lovely face were glowing.

The happiness and love were overflowing as Ken slipped the plain gold ring on her finger. When he kissed her, the undying love they both had for each other was too much. There were tears of happiness in their eyes as Ken held her and kissed her gently, then kissed her again before they turned and walked back up the aisle.

Leah did not want to the dance in her wedding dress so she asked Ken to drive her home so she could change into something for dancing and for the reception. Ken tried to follow her into the bedroom while she changed dresses, but she stopped him at the door and kissed him and told him he would have to wait till tonight. They then went to the arena to be there when the guests arrived. They were also hungry so they wanted time to eat a snack before the crowd arrived.

The reception was to start at two O'clock at the arena. Diana with the help of her mother had made arrangements with the local caterer for food and refreshments along with tables and all the required condiments etc. to be ready at two o'clock. The reception would last till four thirty. The floor would be cleared and the dance would start at six o'clock with the band playing till ten o'clock.

At about eight o'clock that night the sheriff called an ambulance for one of the young men. The young man had feinted or passed out and they could not revive him. The sheriff suspected an overdose of narcotic and ordered a test when they got him to the hospital.

There had been two other occasions of narcotics overdose. The sheriff was trying to find where the young people were getting the stuff.

The band played live music, without Ken until eight o'clock when the rest of the band wanted to dance, so Mike put on some records for the rest of the night's dancing and joined the crowd of dancers.

The band members all wanted a dance with the new bride and ken reluctantly gave in. Even William Bagley, the short violinist tapped her shoulder and danced with Leah. Leah thought that the short man's eyes looked a little funny, but she shrugged it off as not important.

Ken finally got control again and then held on to her for the rest of the evening. The floor was so crowded that they could barely move around at all. People were continually congratulating them and wishing them well. Finally at a little after nine o'clock, they worked their way to the edge of the dance floor and then quietly slipped off into the crowd and disappeared. They hopped into Ken's car and drove to the new living quarters for a chance to be alone.

Leah and Ken had been looking for a house to live in after the marriage and they found one about a mile from Leah's parents' house on the other side of the road. They had rented it and had fun buying the furniture for it. They had never lived in it but it was ready for them after the wedding.

As they pulled into the driveway, Ken pulled the car up to the garage door. He got out first and opened the door for Leah to get out. Then as Leah walked to the house he opened the garage door and pulled the car into the garage then shut the doors so the car would not be visible then he also entered the house.

Leah was waiting just inside the door. She had not turned any of the lights on. As he closed the door and turned, she slipped into his arms and kissed him. His arms closed around her and he picked her up and walked back the hall to the bedroom. He lowered her feet to the floor and continued kissing her on the neck and throat as he unbuttoned her blouse and unsnapped her bra. Leah closed her eyes and let him remove her top covering. He continued kissing her mouth, neck, throat then down to her now exposed breasts. She began to moan as his lips caressed the nipples and firmness of them. As he lowered her to the bed she loosened the ties that held her skirt. She had waited a long time for this night and she was anxious.

The Soul of Li Chan, Robert and Now Leah is finally finding out what the emotions between the male and females of the living bodies are like. Li Chan's soul had learned that touching between the male and females produced pleasant feelings. Now she was to learn what the complete interaction was to produce. The Soul had never been in a living body when it experienced the complete act of lovemaking and the brain had felt the true feelings of love and desire along with the physical pleasure of the act. Tonight it would be in the body of Leah and would feel the overflow of love and desire from her experience. The brain would know and it would reach her very soul. It would be that intense. The willing and controlling would be used very little as Mother Nature and built in desires and natural instincts would take control. She would know the heights and depth of the feelings and would have them in her memory banks for eternity.

When the sheriff was called to the first overdose patient, he began to keep a sharper lookout for signs of narcotics use. Narcotics in his town were the last things he wanted. Then came a third, and then a fourth case and he started to watch a lot closer. When Mike Bowers opened his craft shop the sheriff began to wonder where the man expected to sell all the wooden artifacts he brought in. The wooden logs that were delivered did not come from a local source and that puzzled him. There were plenty of places locally he could buy lumber.

Mike himself cut the logs into the proper size for a fireplace or wood furnace and stacked it beside and behind the building he had rented. Some of the birdhouses and other craft items were also purchased locally from the town's crafters.

The one thing that bothered the Sheriff was that there were a lot more cars coming into town with out of state license plates and nearly all of them stopped at the craft store. They stopped at the restaurants and sometimes at the local grocery.

The sheriff had asked two of his deputies to stop one of the out of state cars after it left town and search for narcotics. He told them to tell the people in the car it was a random check of out of state cars and had not been selected. Nothing had been found but the sticks of firewood in the trunk.

Ken and Leah were now living in their new residence and were set to settle down to raise a family. Ken had been looking at finding a good job now that he was to be head of the household and would need more of an income. He had been looking at a service station that was and had been operated by an elderly man. The man was ready to retire and had put a for sale sign in the window.

Ken and Leah stopped in one day to talk to him about the property. After some negotiating with the owner Ken and Leah decided to see if they could get the proper financing to buy the property, lock, stock and barrel so to speak. Leah's father and mother agreed to help and three weeks later Ken took over the operation of the station. He and Leah still played in the band when it played locally.

Two months after the wedding Leah was with Ken on the porch swing after he had closed the station for the night. She was snuggled close to him with her head on his shoulder when she looked up and said,

"Ken, I am pretty sure I am pregnant, I waited a while to tell you."

Ken hesitated for a few minutes before saying,

"Are you happy about that? You are pretty young to be starting a family you know."

"Ken, I am the happiest girl in the world right now, I love things the way they are and a little boy or girl with you will just make things better and happier, if that is possible" She said.

"Well." Ken said, "The station and the band will let us live comfortable and we will both be busy.

Leah kept herself busy around the house and she loved to spend time at the piano. She loved to play soft and low and just enjoy the music. Ken spent his days running the service station and after keeping his accounts and finding out that the station was in reality making a good profit. He asked the sheriff if he knew a good man to take over for him in the evenings for four or five hours. That way he could spend his evenings with Leah.

After a few months Leah began to feel uncomfortable sitting at the piano and mike found a replacement. To keep her physically fit. Leah found a health club and spent her afternoons there.

Time passed and the winter came and went. During the winter holiday season there were a couple of narcotic overdoses, but no one would say where the stuff was coming from and the sheriff was baffled.

March came and Ken was called one day by his mother-in-law and told he better come home and be ready to take his wife to the hospital. The child was about due.

A few hours later, he was the proud father of a beautiful baby girl, they named Leanna.

Leah remained in the hospital overnight and Ken brought her and the baby home the next day. The joy felt by the parents was boundless. She was so filled with joy tears were rolling down her cheeks.

She did not really want to go back to the band so she told Mike she was going to stay home and take care of her child. Ken was still playing with them, and sometimes Leah would go and listen, but she was not interested in playing.

It had been an experience for the Soul of Leah. The Soul had not lived through the birth of a new living body before and it did not really know what to do, It did not remember how it had been developed so it did not know if it was to do anything or not. It had its own living body to care for and was kept busy. The new baby girl had probably developed a young Soul of it's own

Leah's Soul had felt no contact or need to enter the young body when it was being carried and formed, so it must have developed its own Soul.

One week after Leanna reached her first Birthday; Leah left her with her grandmother and went into town to do a little shopping. Mike had sent Leanna a birthday present and as Leah approached the craft shop she decided to stop and thank Mike for the present.

She parked the car and ran into the shop. When she entered there was no one in sight and she walked on into the shop and toward the back. No one seemed to be around. Then she heard voices from the room marked "tools. Keep out" she opened the door and looked in.

Mike was standing in front of a workbench talking to Bill and another man Leah had not seen before. Leah glanced at the bench and saw little packets of white powder stacked at the back of the bench. Bill was standing beside some round pieces of firewood that were fastened to the bench somehow. There were round holes in the top of the pieces of firewood. It appeared that Bill was putting the little packets of white powder into each hole.

Bill and Mike jumped to get between Leah and the packets and firewood. The stranger grabbed for Leah's left arm. Leah saw immediately what was going on and her right hand swung hard to the side of his neck in a chopping blow that sent him to the floor.

Mike and Bill followed her as she backed out of the room into the open store. As Bill rushed her, she spun and her heel caught him in the neck. She had kicked as hard as she could and Bill flopped over backward to the floor. Leah turned then to Mike who was standing behind her waiting for her to turn around so he could hit her with his fist. She turned swiftly and her right foot smashed him in the stomach, knocking the wind out of him and sending him into a pile of firewood hat lay on the floor.

She glanced at all three of them then rushed to the telephone on the counter and shouted to the operator.

"Send the sheriff to the craft shop quick, there is a fight, send an ambulance too, someone is hurt."

Then she dialed the number of the station. When Ken answered she said.

"Ken come here quick, I am at the craft store and mike attacked me, I had to hurt him."

Leah did not know just what to do now. I had better just wait for the sheriff I suppose. She suddenly heard the siren of the police car and ran to the front of the store.

The sheriff and one of his deputies came rushing into the store. Leah led them to the back of the store and showed them the tool room. They turned back to the men on the floor and the Sheriff ask Leah,

"Leah, what happened here?"

Leah explained,

I came into town to do some shopping and I wanted to stop and thank Mike for the birthday gift he sent Leanna. There was no one in the store when I came in so when I heard voices in the tool room, I opened the door. When I saw the white powder I knew I was in trouble and I tried to back out, but they grabbed me, and the fight started. I am sorry, I did not want to hurt anyone but it happened so fast I could not hold back my punches,"

The sheriff spoke. "You did this to three men, it looks like one is dead and the other might be, what did you hit them with?"

The sheriff was standing facing Leah and the deputy was standing over the stranger and looking at Leah.

Suddenly Mike hollered, "Leah, You Bitch, you ruined everything." And the gun in his hand fired twice at Leah.

Both the sheriff and the deputy drew their weapons and fired at the same time at Mike, both shots were true and Mike fell back to the floor.

The sheriff turned to Leah. She had fallen to the floor and was moaning.

The ambulance crew came through the door and the sheriff motioned them to Leah. As they loaded her on the canvas, her eyes opened and she looked at the sheriff, but no words came. Just then Ken came running in and he followed the nurse into the van for the run to the hospital.

The sheriff went from body to body and checked each one. All were dead. The tool room spoke for itself and cleared up the situation as far as Baker Springs was concerned. They found the two-inch holes drilled in the ends of the firewood were filled with packets of cocaine. Different amounts were put in according to their destination. A two-inch plug was covered with glue then pounded into the hole in the firewood. The grain of the wood was cut to match and looked natural. The sheriff expected to find records somewhere in the tool room with names, dates etc. that would put a lot of people in trouble.

In the Ambulance, the nurse found two bullet holes in Leah's side. At least one of the bullets had hit her heart and she died on the way to the hospital.

The Soul of Leah Madison could tell that the life giving fluid was going somewhere and that she was fast losing control. The pump was slowing down and she could not keep it pumping. She was using all her willing power to keep parts of the body moving. There was no response, the air sacs would not respond.

The Soul was slow to leave the body of Leah. Her time there had been filled with memories and they were all enjoyable. The Soul feels the stronger emotional happenings more than the everyday events. The stronger emotions and disturbances seem to make a deeper impression and are memories that are never forgotten. The love between Ken and Leah was of an intensity that is seldom felt by most humans. A deep understanding of each others feelings and love for each other.

As the Soul drifted out of Leah's physical body she thought," maybe I can find another body with a love like that of Leah" or maybe I can find another "ken". I would like another encounter like that and hope that it would last longer. Perhaps I can find another Chen Li.

The Soul lingered above Leah and Ken for a while. Leah's face was serene and beautiful, but a shade too white. Ken was looking down at her, crying into an already wet handkerchief. It had all happened so fast he had not fully comprehended what had happened.

He would find a duplicate of Leah in his daughter as she grew into a beautiful young woman. He would not ever marry again.

The Soul which had been Li Chan, Then Robert, Then Leah, now slowly drifted off into who knows where, with her memories, mostly of love which now, thanks to Ken and Leah she knew just how deep the love could be and how much pleasure could be shared. Oh well she thought I will find another somewhere. Hopefully, like Ken or Leah. Then the memory of Chen Li and their love came to her and she drifted off thinking how nice it would be if she could find Chen Li's Soul in a physical body like Ken only a Tanganese. She thought she might just drift over toward the little Island of Tanga. She had learned much Geography from her contacts with the physical beings she had entered to save. I will get to see my homeland again she thought as she drifted off.

JESSICA

The young Italian girl had just turned thirteen years of age and was thinking, "Now I am a teenager". She looked down at her breasts. They were not large they looked like she had cut an orange in half and put the two halves on her body. To her way of thinking they were big enough for her to hold them out so the boys could see the bulge they made in her blouse. She had just come from school and was on her way home.

As she turned on the shortcut through the orchard and grape vineyard she was thinking of what the boys were thinking when they looked at her and saw the two bulges in her blouse.

Suddenly she was grabbed from behind and thrown to the ground. Two people had grabbed her arms and forced her to the ground on her back. She started to fight back, but her arms were now held together above her head and one of them sat on her legs. A third boy now appeared and pulled her blouse up over her head so she could not see who they were. She had already seen the two and recognized them as schoolmates.

When Jessica began to holler and scream, one of them pushed the blouse into her mouth till she shut up and stopped kicking. When they pulled her little Bra up and exposed her breasts, she began to shout and cry again. The third boy was older and he hit her hard with his fist on the side of the head, she went limp and quiet.

When the boys left, she lay on the ground, bruised and bloody. They had pulled her blouse and skirt back down and left quickly. She was no longer a Virgin.

Li Chan, after leaving the physical being of Leah, drifted aimlessly until she found herself drifting over southern Europe. She drifted down closer to the surface and then down out of the high mountain area into the lowlands of Italy. With the knowledge she had acquired while in the other bodies, she knew the geography of the earth now and could use her memory to go wherever she wanted.

As she drifted slowly over the lowlands she saw the vineyard at the outskirts of a small village and noticed the body lying on the ground between the rows of grapevines. Lowering herself, she hovered over the body and looked for signs of life. She saw the chest rising and lowering and sensed the body was still alive. Slowly she drifted into the body and then entered the brain area. She felt no opposition from an internal soul so she absorbed the memories and took control of the body. Now she was fully aware of all that had happened. The lungs were operating correctly, but the head had received a damaging blow and needed faster flow of the life giving fluid and more help from the lungs.

In a few minutes the eyes opened and the girl began to move her arms and was breathing easier. As she became more alert she looked down at herself then reached her hand to her head and felt the lump that was forming. Tears were starting to flow from her eyes and she started to get up. As she sat up she reached her hand under her skirt and felt the wet bloody area. When she saw the blood on her hand as she pulled it out from under her skirt, she started crying more.

Jessica got slowly to her feet and still crying walked slowly toward her parent's house at the other side of the vineyard. She knew that her mother was there and that her father was still at work. She was thankful for that. Her mother was in the kitchen at the back of the house when Jessica entered and her mother, sensing something was wrong came out of the kitchen and saw her, she burst into tears again and ran to her mother.

"Oh mother,' Jessica cried. "I think I've been raped."

"You don't know?, her mother asked.

"They hit me hard and I don't remember anything after that." Jessica said. "I am bleeding and it hurts a lot."

"Come with me into the bathroom and we will clean you up." Her mother said and then led her daughter into the bathroom beside the kitchen.

Jessica was in a mixed up state of mind. She was trying to be scared and angry about what had happened but her new state of mind with the added knowledge that had been entered into her memory banks when Li Chan had entered her body and taken over was telling her new things to do and think about. She was trying to be angry about what had happened but her new soul was telling her to be angry at the boys that had committed the assault. What was done was done and it could not be changed. Just get on with life and learn from it. She was wondering where all the thoughts were coming from and when did she learn all the things that popped into her thoughts as she was just thinking.

As she sat in the warm water she helped her mother clean the blood and necessary places that needed cleaning on her body she relaxed and her mother noticed the change in her daughter and wondered at the change. The teen aged girl that left the house this morning would still be crying and scared and would be saying how she would never leave the house again. It was not like her daughter to be so calm and thoughtful after a violent rape. What had changed her? It was like she had aged a few years, but she still looked the same.

As Jessica got up and stepped out of the tub, she felt a lot better. Her mother found a robe in the closet and put around her. The hurting had nearly stopped, but her head still ached and her mother fixed a compress to hold over the swelled area where she had been hit. She walked to the living room and stretched out on the divan to rest and relax. Her mind was still searching her memory for things that she was wondering about. She was very perplexed about the whole afternoon. She was soon asleep and her mother kept a close watch over her daughter and wondered.

Jessica opened her eyes a little later and thought about her father. What would he say or do? She got up and went into the kitchen, as she approached her mother she said,

"Mother, lets not say anything to father about what happened. He would probably get very angry and if I told him I knew the boys that did it. He would go after them and start a fight or call the police. I do not want all that publicity and I am really not hurt that bad. I will get even with the boys that did it on my own time. They will regret it."

"Alright Jessica, if that is the way you want it. You are right about your father. He would probably make a lot of problems. What will you tell him about the bruise on your head?" Her mother answered.

"I'll tell him I bumped it at school on the corner of a wall," Jessica said.

The rape had happened on Friday on her way home from school so Jessica had plenty of time to recover and plan for Monday. She was planning on acting like nothing had happened and see what the boys would do. Her new frame of mind puzzled her but she felt good about it. She knew so much more about things now than she had before and it gave her a new outlook and gave her new courage to face whatever came up. She felt like she was ready for anything. It was a nice feeling.

During the day at the school with so many other students around the boys did nothing but occasionally glance at her. The two that had grabbed her and threw her on the ground looked a little ashamed, but the one that had hit her on the side of the head just leered at her and smiled. She instinctively knew that he had been the instigator and he was the one that she wanted to get even with.

She lingered a while outside of the school talking with her girl friends before starting for home As she entered the vineyard and walked out between the rows of vines. the boy that had hit her suddenly appeared standing in the aisle between the two rows of vines. He was standing in the center of the aisle with his two legs spread out to prevent her from running past. Beautiful, she thought, just the way I want him.

"You want some more of what I gave you the other day?" He said as he leered at her.

"You think so." She asked as she kept walking toward him.

As she got closer to him he put out his arms as if to grab her. She stepped out with her left foot to get closer to him and then brought her right foot forward and hard up between his legs at just the right place. He screamed and grabbed his privates with both hands and fell to the ground, still screaming.

Jessica ducked under the vines and disappeared. Good, she thought now he knows how it feels to be hurt. He was still screaming as she left the vineyard and entered the house.

"Was everything alright today?" her mother asked

"Yes, Mother." Jessica replied. "No one said or did anything. So I guess it is all forgotten. I will stay away from those boys and hope they leave me alone."

The boy Leonardo, was not in school the next day. The other two boys just glanced at her a few times, but stayed away from her altogether.

Leonardo was out of school a full week and no one knew why.

Weeks went by and Jessica heard nothing. Leonardo had returned to school and completely ignored Jessica. Jessica had not forgotten him. She figured that he would try to get back at her so she kept on the alert for anything that might happen. She was finding new things that she could occupy herself with. She kept thinking about playing a piano and she could not remember having a piano in the house. She knew that her mother and father could not afford to buy one. She thought she knew how to play one and she was anxious to try. The upperclassmen were taking piano and other music lessons and there was a Piano Recital coming up in the spring. She began thinking about going to the recital and listening to the music.

She had a girl friend that was in a higher grade level and one day she asked her friend if there was a piano at the high school.

"Yes Jess, there is a piano there in the auditorium, would you like to see it?" her friend Terry answered. "We can go over tomorrow after school if you would like."

"Great". Jessica told her." I think I can play one and I would like to try."

"What makes you think you can play a piano, you haven't been taking lessons have you?"

"No, but I remember Playing the piano and way back I remember taking lessons, only it was so long ago" Jessica said. "It is a puzzle I know, so I want to go and see if I can really play."

The next day after school Jessica started walking toward the High school, which was only two blocks away on the same street. Terry came out of the big building and met her on the steps and they went back into the High School and Terry led the way to the Auditorium.

As they walked down the aisle toward the stage Jessica spotted the piano and they walked toward it. Terry sat on a little chair that was next to the stage and watched as Jessica walked over to the piano and sat down on the bench that was in front of it.

She watched as Jessica put her hands on the keys and studied them, then slowly pressed the different keys and listened to the soft sounds.

As Jessica's fingers began to search out certain keys and press them down, Terry sat stunned at the soft sounds that came out of the piano. Then watched in amazement as Jessica's fingers began drifting back and forth over the keys producing a beautiful melody of the past, but was still beautiful as ever.

Jessica was lost in her music, enjoying herself as she played through the musical passages she had been given by the new Soul from the memories of Robert Richardson. Of course Terry knew nothing of all that, but it was coming to Jessica as she played.

The Auditorium was small, but the acoustics were great and soon the music began to draw a crowd of admiring listeners. Jessica played on until she happened to look up and see the crowd. She stopped instantly and looked embarrassed.

"Don't stop now", someone in the crowd said "You are doing very well."

"Jess, where in the world did you ever learn to play like that?" Terry asked. "That was beautiful".

One of the people in the crowd was a music instructor and she immediately approached Jessica and asked her if she would be interested in playing in the coming Piano Recital.

"I don't know." Jessica answered "I will ask my mother if I can and tell Terry, she can tell you tomorrow.

Now that was going to be a problem, Jessica thought. My mother does not know that I can play a piano. Maybe I won't have to tell her about the Recital.

As Terry led Jessica out of the auditorium she could hardly contain herself.

"Jessica, I have known you for a long time and you never once wanted to play a note on a piano. What happened and how did you learn to play like that so quick?" Terry asked.

Jessica led Terry out away from the people standing around and said,

"Terry, do you remember the week end that you wanted me to come out and go with you somewhere, I don't remember where, and I said I couldn't come out? Jessica continued. "Well, that Friday as I was going home from school. I cut through the grape vineyard like I always do. I was grabbed from behind, thrown to the ground and raped by three boys from school. One of them, Leonardo Giano hit me so hard on the side of my head that I nearly passed out. Maybe I did for a little while. Anyway, when I felt better it seems as if I remember a lot of things that I did not know before, like the Piano playing."

"Jess, did you have anything to do with his being in the hospital and out of school for a while?" Terry asked.

"Well," Jessica said, "I did kinda have a fight with him. I was angry at what he had done and I wanted to get even. I'll get the other two too if I get the chance."

"Will you put them in the hospital too?" Terry asked.

"Probably not, if I can help it. I think Leonardo put them up to it and they really did not hurt me much." Jessica answered.

Terry looked at her friend Jessica and now noticed the subtle change that had happened in her. There was no fear and lack of confidence. She had not been that strong looking and sure of herself before. She asked herself what could have happened that could change her little friend so much, and what had she done to Leonardo to put him in the hospital and keep him out of school.

Jessica did not say anything to her mother about the piano playing for a couple of days. Then one day at dinner with her father present she looked at her mother and asked,

"Mom, can we get a good used Piano, I would like to have one to play on. I seem to remember playing one years ago, but I am not sure. Did I ever take piano lessons when I was younger?'

A very surprised Mom looked at her daughter and then said,

"No, you have never had any lessons and you have never expressed an interest in learning to play a piano. Wherever did you get that idea?"

"You remember the other day when I bumped my head." Jessica said and looked sharply at her mother.

"Well since then I have thought a lot about playing a piano."

"Well, "her mother answered. "Your Aunt Isabel has one and no one there even thinks about playing it so I think we can get it over here and you can see if you like to play."

The next weekend Jessica's father and Uncle used a friend's truck and spent the day moving the old upright piano to the house where Jessica lived. The living room had a small alcove off on one side and the piano was put in there along the wall. There was a small bench that had a lift top and when Jessica lifted the lid she saw old sheet music and a lot of old papers.

Jessica ran her fingers over the keys and the notes seemed to be pretty much in tune. As it was near dinnertime Jessica thought she would wait till after the dinner to go in and see how the piano sounded. Her father would be in a better mood after a good dinner.

After dinner Jessica helped her mother clean the table and then the dishes. She then went to her room and did the homework assignments. Her father and mother were sitting in the living room as Jessica came out of her bedroom and walked to the alcove and sat down at the piano. They were listening to the radio and at first did not here the soft notes of the piano, for Jessica liked to play softly and enjoy the sounds of the music as she played.

Her mother was the first to hear the soft sounds as they came from the piano, for she had watched as Jessica went into the alcove. She reached over and turned down the volume on the radio and let the sounds of the piano become prominent.

Jessica's father had not said anything during the other conversations about the piano. Now he just sat there and listened. He opened his mouth to say something but his wife held her finger across her lips and turned the radio volume on down. They sat there and listened as the soft sounds came out to them. As it happened the song Jessica was playing was a favorite of her fathers. He sat there and listened intently as the soft music came to him. He relaxed and sat back and seemed enthralled in what he was hearing.

Neither her father nor her mother could fathom what had happened to their daughter. It was nothing short of a Miracle, for as far as they knew Jessica had never even been in contact with a piano, let alone learn how to play music on one. More importantly, it was not the music of an amateur.

In one end of the alcove that the piano was placed, there was a stand on which stood a statue of the Virgin Mary in a blue robe. Jessica's mother now walked softly into the alcove and Knelt in front of the statue. Tears were evident below her eyes as she spoke silently to the statue

Jessica finished the song she was playing and switched to a song she had heard in their church many times. Softly the music came from the piano and drifted through out the house. When the song ended she stood up and walked out into the living room. She knew she had to explain something she herself did not really understand

She sat down in one of the lounge chairs and faced her parents, who did not know just what to say first. Jessica spoke first so she could answer most of the questions before they were asked.

"Mother, you remember when I got the bump on the head. Well since then I keep remembering things that somehow I learned a long time ago and they are coming back to me. I cannot explain the piano playing. Since the bump I have had a desire to play the piano and once I put my hands on it and felt the notes as I pressed the keys I seem to remember the tunes and then my fingers do the rest, It seems to come naturally for me, as if I was born with the knowledge. I can not explain it any more than that, I love to play it and The teacher heard me play in the auditorium the other day and she wants me to play at the piano Recital next week and I told her I would ask you. Can I Mother?"

Of course her mother said yes and Jessica was a big hit at the Recital. Mostly due to her young age and the way she played. There were more Recitals and invitations to play at Concerts around the country.

Whenever Jessica's friend Terry could accompany her, Terry was along on the concert trips. On one of these trips to an Amphitheater on the outskirts of Rome, Terry received another surprise from her young friend. Jessica had just finished a lengthy period of playing before an intermission. As usual, a crowd of her admirers formed around her and Terry.

A man and woman, obviously American by their dress approached Jessica from the crowd and addressed her, speaking English.

"Miss Levanti, have you a moment," The man asked.

"Of course, thank you", Jessica replied in perfect English.

Terry turned and looked at Jessica with an amazed look on her face.

"We wish to tell you how much we loved your music, and we are surprised how young you are to be playing music like that." The man said, and the woman nodded in agreement.

"I am sixteen years old now and I have been playing since I was thirteen. I love playing the piano and I thank you for your kind words." Jessica replied.

The man handed her a program and ask,

"Will you please autograph this for us, other wise no one will believe we actually were here and met you?"

"Gladly."

Jessica answered and with the man's pen, signed the program sheet.

Terry finally was able to speak and as the couple walked away she looked at Jessica and said, "There you go again, doing something completely unexpected, when in your sixteen years did you go to America and learn to speak English like that?"

Jessica looked flustered and then returned to Italian.

"Oh, I was speaking English wasn't I?' She seemed a little surprised. I do not remember learning it. When I heard my name and then the English words, my memory brought up the language and I replied to it automatically. Now I remember it well. It is like it was in the back of my mind all the time and it took the sound of it to bring it to my mind".

Terry looked at Jess and wondered what her friend would say or do next to surprise her.

Terry did not have long to wait. That evening as dusk settled over the city, they were walking through a mall near the Amphitheater; Jessica was looking in the storefront windows as they walked. She suddenly saw the reflection of a man coming towards them at a fast run. She started turning and as the man grabbed Terry's handbag and turned to leave with it Jessica's foot caught him in the stomach and stopped him. As he fell to the sidewalk gasping for breath, Jessica grabbed Terry's handbag and backed away, still watching the man on the cement.

Jessica handed the handbag to terry and stood watching the man. He was still holding his stomach as they walked away.

Terry had a lot she wanted to say, but all she could come up with was,

"Thanks Jess."

The next two years passed quickly. Jessica was now in demand for professional playing and by her eighteenth birthday was a very well paid Pianist. It was at this time that her father sat them all down at the dinner table and said;

"I think we should move to America. As you know, my brother Angelo moved there a few years ago and is living very well now. He has a good job and he has bought a house and he says there is much work there. Think about it. Jessica could play her piano all over the United States and make a lot of money and maybe become a star."

Jessica had a smile on her face and she could not stop smiling. She had been dreaming of just that same thing for weeks now and hearing her father suggest the same thing was beyond her best wishes.

Her mother looked at her and said.

"What are you smiling like that for? We have not made a decision yet. We have a lot of friends and relatives here, you were born here, you have friends here. Why would you want to leave this place?'

"Mother" Jessica said. "For the last six months I have thought of nothing else. I can keep playing here, but America has so much more to offer, so many new places, more money, and I could play a year and not play in the same place twice. I will go in a minute and love it."

The smile was still on her face she was so happy.

"We will see." Her mother said.

The next spring Jessica graduated with high honors and the family began preparations for a move to the United States of America, It was a big move, going to a new country, leaving most of your life experiences and favorite places and things behind.

The War had been very bad for them. Italy was a very poor place after the War and they had heard a lot about America.

Her uncle had found a house and rented it for them and he even had a Job located for her father to apply for. Everything was working out fine so far. He even had an Italian grocery store that said they needed another girl to help around the store.

It took them nearly three weeks to make the journey from southern Italy to Philadelphia, Pennsylvania. Jessica's use of the English language came in very handy as they traveled. Her mother and father looked at her in amazement as she conversed with the different people. They used busses, trains and ships. They were finally getting off the train at the Philadelphia train station and being greeted by Jessica's Uncle Angelo. They had only lost one small valise, which held mostly dainty underclothes for the women. These could all be replaced. The trip had been a real experience for the two elderly Italians. Jessica took it all in stride, but with a lot of wonder and awe at the things she was seeing.

Jessica missed her friend Terry more than she had thought she would. A young lady of nineteen needed another lady of near her own age to keep her company. As luck would have it she had a cousin two years her senior who was still living at home with her parents. Her uncle Angelo had only one daughter and she met them at the station.

The trunks with a lot of their personal stuff in them were a problem. Uncle Angelo had to make a few phone calls before he could hire some one with a light truck to come and get the trunks and haul them to the rented house. The house that Angelo had rented was only three city blocks from his own house and they were in a good section of the city near the outskirts. Not out of town, but not deep in town either.

When they reached the house, they were surprised at the nice condition of the house and the lawns. They had been kept in livable condition and even the lawn had been mowed recently. The owner came by after they had moved what little stuff they had into the building. He lived only a few houses away and was a good friend of Angelos.

Angelo had picked up some furniture and left it in the house. They had a lot of shopping to do, but it could wait till the next day. They would stay at Angelo's house this first night.

Jessica's mother by nature was a prudent woman and unknown to her husband and Jessica; she had been saving money for this very move. Her husband had mentioned moving to America near his brother for a long time, so she knew it was coming.

It took only a few days for Jessica and her mother to shop for and buy the required necessary items for living in the big house. The smaller personal items, they could buy at their leisure and be sure to get just what they wanted.

Jessica's father applied for the job that Angelo had told him about and was hired on the spot at a good salary and the family was finally settled in for living in the United States of America.

They had all applied for Citizenship, and had the necessary papers to stay here.

Jessica's cousin Eileen worked for the Postal Service and knew a lot of people and she started to look for a job for Jessica. Jessica had not worked at any steady job. She had received enough money from her playing to keep her happy.

Jessica was now in a situation she had never been in before. She had no work experience and she was not well known enough to earn money playing the piano.

Eileen brought home a flyer that had been hanging in the post Office on a bulletin board advertising employment by the Federal Government. As Jessica read it, she came to a paragraph that said they were especially interested in people who spoke foreign languages.

She circled that paragraph and folded up the paper and put it in her purse.

The next day she located the address on the employment bulletin and walked in. The man behind the glass partition motioned her into a booth where his desk was and motioned her to a chair. She sat down. She took out the employment paper and handed it to him.

He said. "You should not have removed the bulletin, just copied the address. What is your name?"

"I had no paper and pencil so I took it down, I will put it back. And my name is Jessica Levanti." She answered.

"What type of job are you interested in?" he asked.

"It says you are interested in people who speak different languages, I speak fluent Italian, English and Tanganese with a little Chinese and a smattering of Spanish." She answered.

"You can speak fluent Tanganese?" he asked.

"Yes." She said.

"Wait here." he said.

He left the booth and returned a few minutes later with a small cassette tape. He slid the cassette into a small player and told her,

"Listen to this and tell me what they are talking about."

As the tape played, Jessica listened, intently at first then she relaxed and listened to the rest of the tape. After it stopped she said.

"In the first place, it is not all Tanganese, there is some Chinese in there also. It is a story about a boy and his dog playing in the yard."

Mr. Cavanaugh sat still for a little while then said, "You say there are some Chinese words in there?"

"Yes, there are two that are Chinese, They are similar, but not exact." Jessica told him.

Mr. Cavanaugh sat there for several minutes then asked.

"You are Italian, How long have you been in the United States?"

Jessica went back to two years before leaving Italy and told him everything leading up to their coming to live in the United States. She told him about her uncle Angelo and her cousin Eileen and where she worked. She told him they had all applied for citizenship. She told him about seeing the bulletin and then coming to him for a job.

"You say you are a well known Pianist." He said.

"In Italy." She answered.

"Do you have time to fill out an application form for me today?" he asked.

"Yes." She answered.

Mr. Cavanaugh came back and handed her some sheets of paper and motioned her to follow him to a table and chairs in an adjoining booth.

"Fill those out the best you can and bring them to me in my office." He said and left.

As Jessica filled out the blanks in the application papers she could hear Mr. Cavanaugh talking on the telephone. There were several pauses and several dial tones. He was evidently talking to several people.

It took Jessica over half an hour to finish the paperwork and take them back to Mr. Cavanaugh's booth and hand them to him as she sat down.

He picked them up and checked them over before he stood up and said.

"Thank you, Miss Levanti for coming in. We will review your application and let you know as soon as we can."

Jessica picked up the bulletin and left the office. She immediately went to the post Office and put the bulletin back where it belonged.

Nearly two weeks later Jessica received a letter from the Office of Personnel Management. It requested her to stop in at the office of Mr. Richard Cavanaugh at her earliest convenience.

The next day as she walked into the office of Mr. Cavanaugh, she noticed he had been waiting and motioned her directly into his Cubicle.

"Keep your coat on, we are going somewhere else." He said.

They went directly to his car and he drove to a rather large Park that was nearby. He parked in the parking lot and they walked out into the park. When they came near a comfortable looking wooden bench he motioned her to sit down. Jessica noticed he checked all directions to see if any other people were in the immediate area. There were none, so he sat down and started talking and asking more questions.

"First, how many people know that you can speak Tanganese? Second, do you like to travel?"

Jessica thought a few minutes, then answered.

"Very few, I can think of only two, one in Rome and one in London when I helped an elderly Tanganese woman at the ticket booth. I only saw them once. Not even my parents know, because I did not tell them. They would ask me when I learned to speak Tanganese and I do not know myself when I learned it. I had a very traumatic experience once when I was thirteen and since then I seem to know things that I do not remember learning, but they are in my memory and they all seem to be correct. If that sounds funny, it is and that bothers me sometimes. To answer your second question, yes I do love to travel. I traveled extensively all around Italy playing the piano for concerts and in Amphitheaters for recitals."

"Excellent." Mr. Cavanaugh said. "Almost exactly what we are looking for. Do you have a really close lady friend who could travel with you on round the world tours?"

"Why yes, I do, but she is still in Italy and I don't know if she would come over here or not. Probably she would, for she said she would like to come with me, but she had no finances to cover the move and she would also need a job for support." Jessica told him.

"Jessica, tell me truthfully, and give it some thought before answering." Mr. Cavanaugh said.

"Can she be trusted with other people's lives and secrets if the need arose?"

"I would trust her with mine anytime." Jessica answered. "She is two years older than I and very smart, a high school graduate and willing to learn more."

"Would you need help in getting her over here for an interview?" He asked.

"No, I think mom and I can do it." Jessica said.

"Jessica, you can consider yourself hired by civil Service, but tell no one and do not mention this conversation, not even to your friend until she gets here. Then we will explain all this secrecy and what you will be doing. When she gets here, come into my office and we'll go from there. If your friend turns out ok, she will be working with you for us also. And you can expect a call to ask you to play at a concert coming up soon, right here in Philadelphia."

He stood up and took her hand saying, "Welcome to the civil service crew, Miss Levanti. Call me as soon as your friend gets here." They walked slowly back to the parked car and drove back to the office. They separated and she took a cab back to the house.

Jessica had a lot to think about. Why all the secrecy and the need for a traveling companion. Of course it would be nice to have Terry along. She was used to that. Terry had traveled all over Italy with her and she was handy to have around and help with everything. That would be nice. They were really close friends, and she would be paid also. Jessica was full of a variety of emotions and Thoughts

That evening Jessica called her friend Terry on the phone and talked to her, friend to friend and told her that she missed her and ask her if she would like to come to America and visit for a week or two. Terry ask her,

"Jess, you know I do not have that kind of money, where would I get the money for a ticket?'

"Terry, do not worry about that, Mom and I have some money left after the move and we'll buy the ticket. We will try to arrange for you to pick it up at the Bus station. If you can get enough cash to buy a little food for while you are traveling, you can make it ok." Jessica said.

"Ok Jess, I can get that much together, let me know when the ticket will be there. I do miss you Jess and I would love to visit." Terry replied.

"Good." Jessica said. "I'll call you as soon as I can make the arrangements, bye now."

"Bye." Terry said and the call ended.

Jessica called the travel agency they had used on the move from Italy and explained the situation to them. They suggested she send a Western Union money order to Terry and let her pay her way as she traveled. They explained it would be a lot easier that way and faster too.

They even planned the route and estimated the total cost.

That evening Jessica called Terry and told her the situation and told her to expect a call from the Western Union when the money order was received. She sent the money order the next day and waited for an answer when Terry received it.

Terry called Jessica the next day and told her that she had received the money order and that she would leave for America in two days. She said that she wasn't sure just how many days it would take to make the trip and that she would call or send a cablegram before she left London if she could.

Three days later Jessica received a cablegram saying that her friend Terry would arrive at approximately 6:45 PM the next day at Philadelphia International Airport.

Jessica and her mother were there to meet Terry when she came off the plane and then helped her with the luggage. The two girls sat in the back and talked excitedly all the way to the house.

Jessica did not mention any thing about the new job, only that she had applied for it. Mr. Cavanaugh had said to not tell anyone till both girls had talked to him, and Jessica was good at keeping secrets.

Terry, whose real name was Teresa Santini, was tired after her trip so they talked little till bedtime. She was looking forward to tomorrow and seeing some of Philadelphia. She had heard a lot about the big City and was anxious to see some of it. Jessica was also looking forward to tomorrow, but she had something different in store for her friend Terry. She was anxious to get on with the Job she was going to be doing, whatever that was.

Jessica's father and mother had gone to the Automobile License Bureau with Jessica and all had temporary driver's licenses. Jessica received permission to use the car that her father had bought after they had arrived.

She and Terry told her mother they were going for a little shopping and they took off. Terry was a bit apprehensive as they stopped in the Civil Service parking lot and walked towards the Office doorway. She followed Jessica into the building and then to Mr. Cavanaugh's Office as he motioned to Jessica to come on in.

"Mr. Cavanaugh, I want you to meet my good friend Teresa Santini, recently arrived from Italy and a very good friend of mine." Jessica said.

"My pleasure." Mr. Cavanaugh answered. "I hope your trip was a pleasant one, I know they can be tiring at times, but they have improved quite a bit in the last couple of years since the War. Please have a chair, we must talk."

"Miss Santini," Mr. Cavanaugh started, "While you were on your way here from Italy, we have been checking on your background and we have found that everything Jessica said about you is true, of course we will check further if we need to, but we are quite satisfied with what we have found out so far. Miss Levanti is working for us now and in the role she will be playing she will need a traveling Companion. Your name came up and she told us about you and how you had traveled throughout Italy with her because of your friendship. So you see we had an ulterior motive for bringing you to the United States. We want you to work for us also and be her constant companion as she tours the European Continent and even to the far East to those countries. You will be paid well and all your travel will be taken care of. Do you speak any foreign language besides Italian?" He asked.

Terry answered. "Why yes I do, I took French in school and speak quite fluently and I have learned a little German."

Mr. Cavanaugh said,

"Great, we cover a large spectrum of languages and that is what we need. There is no one else here in the offices so do not be afraid of speaking about anything that bothers you. There are no bugs in these offices and nothing is being recorded. By the way Miss Santini I have some papers I would like you to fill out before you leave, just for our records."

Jessica spoke up, "What you are saying is that we are going to be spies and eavesdropping for information that you want. Don't spies get shot if they are caught? She asked.

"Don't be melodramatic; they do not shoot people like that anymore. We trade spies back and forth if they are caught and then release them back into society for they are no longer any good to us if they are caught. You Jessica are going to be touring Europe as a visiting Tourist playing at Piano Concerts all over the world. There will be do direct contact with the United States agencies of any kind. We will get into that after you two are finished the training you will receive." Mr. Cavanaugh explained. He continued, "Your friend Terry will be your traveling Companion and assistant The only thing we will do is to help set up some of the concerts in some of the areas we are interested in. We do not expect any trouble, but we will train you for any unexpected problems that may arise."

"What do we do if we hear something that we think you should know, Mr. Cavanaugh?" Jessica asked.

"Call me Dick, and all you have to do is remember it. There will be no hardware or recording equipment and no written words of any kind. That kind of evidence could get you in real trouble. You two were picked because of your intelligence level. You are both way above the average and there will be enough contacts that you will not have to remember for too long a time between them. We are setting up a two-week course for you two and a couple of others to take before you go into the field. Can you both be ready to leave for a couple of weeks at the end of next week?"

Jessica looked at Terry and Terry nodded, so Jessica said,

"Yes, but what will we tell our parents we are doing?"

"Just tell them you are going to work for Civil Service and there is a basic course in typing, and protocol that is required of all Civil Servants. That should cover it and let them relax." Dick said then added, "One of the concerts is coming up soon and we want you ready."

"Girls," Dick added, "One thing you must be very careful of, is letting anyone know how many languages you can understand and speak, you must remember you can only speak Italian and English fluently. Understanding a few words would not be a problem, but speaking fluently would mean you could understand an adjacent conversation and could be listening in for a reason. You will have to be real careful, especially in the Orient."

Terry spoke up, "We do not understand Oriental speech so that should not be a problem."

Dick looked at Jessica and Jessica said, "I speak fluent Tanganese Terry, and I will explain later she said."

Terry just looked at her little friend and said, "You never stop with these surprises do you Jess?" She looked at Dick and said, "I'm getting used to them now. Where are those papers you need filled out Mr. Cavanaugh?"

A few days later Jessica received a phone call asking if she could be available To fill in for a pianist that could not be there. Of course she said yes and was told where and when to show up and the type of music that would be expected of her.

The concert was to be at an outdoor theater and one of the weekly concerts that was held nearly every Friday night if the weather was fair enough. As it turned out the weather was beautiful and the concert was packed and very noisy. There was dancing on the concrete in front of the stage and even spilled over onto the grass as the evening progressed.

When Jessica was introduced, her name could hardly be heard above the noise of the crowd. After she started playing the crowd showed disapproval and she suddenly switched over to a faster melody and the drummer jumped in with a beat and the crowd quieted down to listen and dance. When that song ended, the crowd showed their approval with shouts and applause.

She selected another similar song and began playing. The drummer joined in and soon other instruments followed. The crowd was cheering and having a great time dancing. It was not exactly what Jessica had wanted but she really did enjoy the total sound.

Terry had been sitting in one of the front row chairs, but one of the young men that were there asked her to dance and now she was dancing almost constantly. Both of the Italian girls were having the time of their life and loved it.

After the next song, Jessica got up and bowed to the audience and started to leave. The crowd stood up and clapped until she turned and sat down on the bench and put her hands on the keyboard. They became quiet and she started playing again. The other instruments joined in and the dance started again. She played through four more songs before she could walk off the stage and down to Terry.

The crowd formed around her and Terry and they were kept busy answering questions, mostly if they would be back next week to play. Some of the other musicians came and talked to her also. The organizer of the concert asked her if she would be able to come back on the next Friday evening. Jessica gave her the phone number of the phone in the house and asked her to call on the next Tuesday and she would know then.

They had many offers of rides to their home but they declined and left

On the way home in the car Jessica ask Terry if she would like to join a health club. There was one on the street they lived on and it was just a short walk away from their house.

"Yes I would," Terry said. "I have thought about it a few times and never got the chance, so I'll be glad to join one."

"Good", Jessica said. "We will join the one down the street and we can go two or three times a week and keep fit." She added, "If we are here."

"Yes Jess, I've got to talk to you about all that one of these days." Terry said as she looked at her little friend.

Later that day, Jessica's parents had left to go shopping. Jessica and Terry were alone in the house and relaxing in the living room. Terry said,

"Jess, you knew most of this secret stuff when you first called me, why did you not tell me what it was all about. When you called?"

"In the first place, phone lines can be tapped and we could have been overheard, we do not want that, no one is supposed to know about us dong what we are going to do."

Jessica said, "That stuff about him hiring you and you taking the job was not sure until after he interviewed you and found out just what type of woman you were. I was not sure if you would want to work with me either. What we are going to be doing is not exactly the kind of job most people would want. I did not know how you would take it, so I let you think that it was just a visit. I really wanted to have you here to visit at least."

"Well it is a little sudden and scary, but I suppose I could get used to it and I do need a job that pays good. On top of that I will be working with you and nothing could be better. I will have to write my parents and tell them some story that they will believe. I will send them money every once in a while and that will keep them happy." Teresa replied.

Jessica spoke, "Terry, I am going to tell something that I want you to promise you will not tell anyone ever, do you remember that time I was raped and told you that after that incident I had knowledge that I did not remember actually learning. Well, some of the knowledge that I do not remember learning was how to speak Tanganese. I remember being a young Tanganese princess Named Li Chan, and one night with my two attendants I went to a hidden garden to see my lover, Chen Li. While waiting for Chen Li, bandits tried to kidnap me for a ransom. There was a fight. Both my attendants and I had been trained in the ancient art of Machedo. Machedo is a technique of last resort and is meant to kill your opponent quickly. There are other techniques that can be used to injure and put the attacker out of the fight also. We killed all but two of the attackers but as I killed the leader of the bandits, I was stabbed from behind as my attendant Su Lin killed my attacker. I died there in the arms of Chen Li as he came into the battle with his two men. The soul of Li Chan, my original soul left my original body and drifted off.

This physical body that I am in now, belonged to a thirteen year old girl, Jessica Levanti, as she lay unconscious in the grape vineyard her soul left her as she was near death. The soul of Li Chan came down and as Jessica was still alive, slipped inside the frail body. Once inside she absorbed the knowledge of Jessica and started controlling and willing her to fight to live and soon Jessica woke up and from then on you know.

I know it all sounds a little crazy, but it is the only explanation that will fit the situation I can speak fluently in Tanganese and English and I have never had a lesson in either, The Soul that brought me the memories of Tanganese must have been in another body that spoke English, for I also have memories of being in the body of a young man named Robert who played the piano very well and died of Cancer. That is where I learned the English and piano."

"I know how it all must sound. I have never told anyone else what I have just told you and I will not tell anyone else. I trust you and you have seen things happen that are hard to believe so you may start to believe some or all of it. They will put me in the nut house if I tell people what I have told you, so please forget it. It may help you understand some of the things I do."

Terry's face was half scared and half unbelieving. After a while she opened her mouth to say something, then closed it again. Then opened it again to say, "Could that be true." A few seconds later, "it must be, I saw you in action and you can speak perfect English. That must have been Tanganese that time in Rome when you helped that foreign couple at the bus station. I won't tell anyone, don't worry, they would just think I was nuts too."

The health club proved to be a fun thing. The two girls were in very good health to start with so they enjoyed the exercises and the first two times they went to the club the people there were very nice. The third time when they went in there were the usual members and then there were three that they had not seen before. They were young men and evidently thought they were better than anyone else for they were talking loud and watching for someone to argue with or start trouble.

As the two girls were going from one exercise machine to another, the young men were making remarks, some lewd and suggestive. The girls ignored them and continued their exercises. After half an hour of exercise they changed and left the club. The three men still making suggestive remarks followed them.

As they started up the street, one of them made a particular nasty and crude remark about Jessica. She stopped, turned around and walked back to them and said,

"You Idiots have been harassing us ever since we got here. It looks to me like you are looking for trouble. Make one more crack like that last one and you'll get it."

The youngest looking one on the right made about the same remark and Jessica moved so fast he had no time to move out of the way as her left foot caught him on the side of the head and sent him sprawling on the grass. He lay there nearly unconscious. She looked at the other two as they backed up to get away from her.

As she turned and continued up the street with Terry, the other two men went to help the fallen one up, still looking after them.

Terry remarked. "Machedo?"

Jess replied, "No, just a little Judo"

The girls continued on to the house.

Terry asked. :" Will you teach me a little of that stuff as we go along?"

Jess replied. "You got it"

The next Monday was the day they were to leave for training and would be gone for two weeks and tonight was Friday night again so she would be playing and Terry would be dancing again.

About an hour later at Mr. Cavanaugh's office, one of the men he had assigned to watch the two girls came into the office and walked in to talk to him.

"I don't think you will have to guard them two girls very much. They left the Health Club about an hour ago and three men followed them out and were harassing them. I couldn't hear what was said, but what ever it was, your delicate little Piano player had had enough. She suddenly turned around and approached the men. She said something and the youngest of the three answered her. Two seconds later he was on the ground and the other two were backing up and looking at her. She had spun and caught him on the side of the head with her heel so fast he never had a chance of ducking. She looked at the other two. They backed up and went to check on their buddy, keeping an eye on her all the time. Then the girls went on up the street. That girl is faster than anyone I ever saw fight that way."

"That girl is something different." Mr. Cavanaugh said. "I knew that the first time I saw her. She is full of confidence and a very intelligent girl. Working with her should be quite interesting and rewarding."

Jessica and Terry wanted to get there a little early so they could look the situation over and find out where they were to sit when they were not doing their show work. They were a little anxious too to see all the young soldiers that would be there to see the show.

They drove to the park for the concert and parked in the lot nearest the bandstand. They wanted the car where they could get out fast and get home. They did not count on meeting anyone they would be interested in except for the dancing. Jessica was hoping she would get a chance to dance if there was dancing. Sometimes they left it to the audience. If they were in a listening mood and the music was classical or just easy listening, the evening would pass as a concert of relaxing music.

As the night progressed, Jessica noticed that the crowd had increased over last week and the applause was louder. She understood that she had to feel out the audience likes and dislikes, so she slipped over to soft relaxing music that she liked to play so softly and listen to herself. To her surprise the audience became so quiet that the soft sounds of her playing could travel farther. She noticed the people at the back fringes of the crowd had stopped and were listening too. It was an old favorite she loved playing it. When she finished the song, it was quiet for a while, then the crowd broke out in applause and shouts. She understood that they wanted more and she ran her fingers over the keys and the crowd quieted down to listen.

Terry was having the time of her life again with a young man that had asked her for a dance, then would not let her go. It seemed that she was quite satisfied with him so he lucked out and danced with her the whole show.

It was a nice warm night and the musicians stopped for an intermission. Hot dog and popcorn venders, along with soda carts came through the crowd and every one was having a grand time. Terry and Jessica had been introduced to hot dogs and they loved them. Terry's dance partner had a friend that he introduced to Jessica and they talked and ate through the intermission.

Finally Jessica climbed back to the stage and went to the piano. The other musicians followed and the music started. The crowd kept them playing till nearly midnight.

Jessica came down off the stage and was met by admirers and was kept talking till midnight when she grabbed Terry and led her through the crowd to the parking lot and they finally left.

Jessica received a phone call the next Sunday evening and was told to report to the employment office on Monday morning at eight o'clock and be prepared for a two-week stay. Food and quarters would be provided.

During the next two weeks they were kept busy learning rules, regulations and procedures that all military and civilian intelligence personnel receive when they enter the government service. There was a restaurant at the training center and sleeping quarters as well. When the two girls were not in actual training they were studying for the next day's training session. They learned about the newest Electronic development and surveillance units, miniature cameras, transmitters etc.

They spent two days on the shooting range and instruction building learning to handle, take down, load, unload, aim and shoot nearly every type of pistol, revolver, rifle and even shotgun. Their shooting score was, to their instructor's surprise, among the highest. Both girls were very accurate with whatever weapon they were using at the time.

Mr. Cavanaugh came in the first day they were there and approached them.

"I hear you had a little trouble at the health club." He said to Jessica.

"Very little, some young kid got a little wisecracking, but he stopped." Jessica said.

"What would you have done if his friends had taken up the issue?" Dick asked.

"Put them both down, hard." Jessica answered.

Mr. Cavanaugh looked at her and smiled.

"I bet you would have too." He said, and continued. "That may happen once in a while. You two are a rare type and both are quite beautiful. Men are going to attempt almost anything. But I am sure you both know that. I will try to have some help available if you ever do need it."

"Thank you Sir." They both muttered.

They spent one day learning to drive all the military and special equipment and trucks of every description and were surprised at how easy it was to do. Moving that much weight around so easy surprised them and they enjoyed every minute of the day.

One day was in a classroom learning about the different bombs and shells that were being used by nearly every country. The names of all the different explosives, how they were used and how they were shipped.

Another day was spent on learning Key words to listen for. Many times the whole sentence was not necessary. Only the key words would be enough. Compass headings, north, south, east and west, were all key words to remember, plus many more.

When the two girls walked out of Mr. Cavanaugh's office at the end of the two weeks training session, their knowledge of the world's military and operations of said Military had vastly increased. Actually the knowledge was a little scary. Knowing all the ramifications and antagonistic feelings around the world could give anyone a reason to be scared.

Jessica and Terry were glad to be back in Philadelphia and they were ready for a little relaxing. Jessica's parents were a little concerned but Jessica explained it as typical Government indoctrination and paperwork.

They had stayed overnight on Friday after the training was finished so they relaxed and left for home on Saturday.

On Sunday Jessica looked in the Sunday paper for ads advertising Judo training. She wanted Terry to start learning the Tanganese arts of fighting. There were several different styles and combinations. If there was a Judo instructor close by she would go with Terry and watch. Jessica had never instructed anyone and did not really want to start now. If Terry could learn from an instructor the basics and all that could be taught, then Jessica could easily show her the advanced Machedo.

Jessica found one and the address was only five blocks away on the same street on which they lived. Jessica and Terry drove down and walked into the building.

The shop was called the Gung Ho Karate. The Chinese man inside was called Kuon and according to him he taught Judo, Karate and Kung Fu. He had one class that had just started one lesson ago and he said he would be glad to enroll both of the girls in that class if they would make up the first class. They said they would and he told them to come back the next night at seven o'clock for the second lesson.

It was two weeks before Mr. Cavanaugh called and told Jessica that she was to be one of the featured Musicians at a show at the Military base outside of Philadelphia. Hollywood was putting on a show for the military personnel and she was to be the pianist and would be expected to play a couple of solos during the show.

During that past two weeks Terry and Jessica learned a lot about Karate, kung Fu and basic Judo. Most of the moves that Kwon demonstrated to Terry brought memories of the same move to Jessica. A few variances, but all in all it was a refresher course for Jessica from a long time ago.

Teresa was a good and quick learner and at the end of two weeks she was very quick and accurate with her blows and had learned a lot. Of course she had not been in a real combat situation and a lot depended on how she would react to an actual life or death encounter.

Now that a show was coming up the girls were ready and full of enthusiasm and anxious to be on the job they were getting paid for.

The show was in the afternoon and was an outdoor show with an open stage with seats for several hundred people with much more standing room.

Jess and terry arrived a little early and met some of the stars and Jessica sat down and ran her fingers over the keys to play a favorite song to get the sound of the piano. When she did she played softly so as not to disturb any of the other performers. When she stopped and looked up there was a crowd of listeners who tried to talk all at once and tell her how beautiful she played.

Terry had arrived with her and had contrived to stay near her. The stagehands moved the piano around for her and knew just where it was supposed to be so there really was nothing for Terry to do. She found two seats in the first row with their names on and sat and observed the crowd. There was no room in the little stage building except the dressing rooms where anyone could sit down so most of the chairs in the front row were reserved for the performers.

The crowd started forming and soon the seats were all taken and soldiers were standing around talking and watching the people on the stage. The man from the MES finally walked out on the stage and tapped the microphone to get the crowds attention.

"Welcome to this afternoons performance." He announced. "We have several performers for your entertainment today. Most of them you have already seen, there is one new musician, a pianist, recently arrived from Italy. She is well known in Italy and Italy's loss is our gain. She and her family have applied for US citizenship. I understand a few of you have already heard her play, let's get on with the show."

It was a rather noisy show the people in the standing areas were continually talking it seemed, but even in those areas the music and the singing could be heard. There were dancers, singers, comedy routines and the solo musicians.

Jessica was introduced and played a song that many in the audience had requested even before they had heard her play. It appeared the right thing to do and she received a long and loud applause for her effort.

Terry had been sitting in the front row, but there were military people behind her and some walking past in front of her as she sat there. She was practicing her key word listening and she picked up what she thought was a few key words. She figured she would check with Jess to see if she was right. She did not want to get up and walk around because it would not be the thing to do. She was supposed to be enjoying the show. So she sat there like a good listener.

Jess looked at her a few times and winked then came down and sat in her chair for some of the dancing and comedy routines. When it was her turn to play again, the MES (Military Entertainment Service) producer motioned her to come back up. When she stood up and walked to the steps that led to the stage, the crowd started to applaud and shout until she sat down at the piano and put her hands on the keyboard. Then they really quieted down to hear her play. She was only to play one song, but when she got up to leave, the crowd made such uproar that she sat back down and played another selection. A female singer followed her and Jessica was the pianist that she sang with so Jess just waited for the introduction of the singer and continued playing. The crowd loved that and the singer had a really good voice also.

After the show ended, the crowd stayed around and talked with the performers and a lot of soldiers surrounded Terry and Jessica and were all trying to talk at once. The PX was only a block away from the stage area so the guys persuaded them to go to the PX with them and get a soda. Two officers soon monopolized them and the enlisted men had to back off. They entered the PX and found a table and sat there with the Officers and drank their sodas while the officers talked about themselves. All the girls had to do was nod or "ooH" or" ahh" a few times and that kept them talking.

A lot of the key words that Terry and Jessica had been told were heard and repeated. The young officers were good looking and the girls did not mind spending time with them. They were learning a lot of things that they did not know too. They learned the Officers names were Roger Neville and Robert Miliken both were Captains in the Air Force and had been in the service over three years. The girls both figured they were married and had wives at home but they did not say anything.

Nothing had been said about dating or getting a boy friend since Terry had arrived and Jessica had not given much thought since the rape. She was a little leery about approaching any boy or rather young man.

Of course she had thought about it. At her age normally it was on both young men and women's minds. It was a natural thing and not to be ignored. Jessica's experience had helped her to ignore it, but it was still there and really could not be ignored for long.

They had noticed two MPs keeping an eye on them so Jessica said to Terry, "Terry, we had better go, we're due at the health club in about an hour."

"Ok, Jess, I don't want to miss that appointment." Terry answered.

They thanked the two Officers for the drinks and walked out. The MPs followed and escorted them to their car. They left and went right home as they were both tired.

Each of the girls had her own bedroom and shared the upstairs bathroom. Jessica's father and mother slept in the only downstairs bedroom. When they were ready for bed, they usually sat and talked for a while. Tonight was no different. Jessica went into Terry's room and sat on the bed and they talked over the day's happenings.

Both of them had been listening for "Key "words when they were with the two Captains so they compared notes of what they had heard.

"I heard "Shipping out "once," Terry said, "and "Warm weather gear "twice".

"One of them said "Small outfit" once that I heard." Jessica said.

"I wonder how we are going to be contacted to tell them what we heard?" Terry said.

"I don't know." Jessica answered. "Bet it is soon. See you in the morning."

The next day as they were getting ready to leave on a little shopping trip, the MES van pulled up out in front of the house and stopped. Jessica walked out and the driver handed her an envelope. She thanked him and walked back into the house. It was a note from Mr. Cavanaugh. They were to come to his office on their way downtown.

When they walked into Mr. Cavanaugh's building, he was waiting and motioned them on into his office and said.

"Well, that was some show the other day at the base, what did you think of it. That is the sort of stuff you two are going to be seeing for the next month or more. I hope you like it."

"I loved it." Jessica said. "Terry did too, I think, but it would be nice if Terry could do something too."

Mr. Cavanaugh turned to Terry and asked, "Did you ever do any singing Terry? You seem to have a nice voice and if we send you to an instructor maybe we could put you in the show. What do you think?"

"I would be scared to get up in front of all those people and sing." Terry said.

Cavanaugh said. "We could put you up there with a singing group or another singer for a while till you get over the Idea of singing in front of people. Would you be willing to take a few lessons to see what you can do and what you would sound like?"

Terry thought about it for a while then finally said,

"I have never sung for any one, but I do like to sing, Ok, if you can find an instructor that will spend a little time with me I'll go."

"Did you two hear any key words that you thought might be important/" Dick asked them.

"A few like "Shipping out", "no warm clothing" "full combat gear", there was no time mentioned, but one soldier said that it was nice to see such a show just before they were shipping out. It would leave good memories for the ones leaving" Jessica said.

Terry said, "The soldiers sitting behind me were talking about the firearms training they had completed a few days before the show."

Cavanaugh said. "That's good. That is the kind of stuff we are interested in. We need to know what kind of stuff a spy would hear if he were in the audience listening."

"Your next show is in about two weeks. I will call you tonight and give you the name of a singing instructor and Terry, see what you can do in the next two weeks. If you want, I can get you a singing partner to start with so you will not be up there all alone. If either of you can think of anything that will help, let me know." Mr. Cavanaugh said.

The girls left and went to the local restaurant for a sandwich and to talk about getting Terry to become a singer. It left them a lot to say. Jessica said,

"We have a large living room at the house, why don't we buy a piano and we can practice your singing at home? I need one there anyway to practice new tunes on."

Terry said, "Good, let's get a phone book and find a good piano store."

The piano store they found was about three miles away, so they drove over to look at different Pianos.

Jessica was amazed at the variety of different Pianos. She finally saw a small Baldwin that she thought she would like and sat down and pulled the bench where she liked it while playing.

She let her fingers float over the keys and gradually let them increase the sound until she reached the level she liked. Then she played several of her favorite melodies.

Terry was standing behind her watching and listening as she played. Neither girl was conscious of their surroundings as she played.

The sales people as well as any customers that came into the store gradually walked up behind them and were listening as she played.

When she finished, she turned to talk to Terry and saw the group of people. She blushed and said.

"I am so sorry, I did not mean to play so long, but it is such a good sounding piano, I love the sound of it."

"Don't be sorry, "one of the Salesmen said, "That was the best music I have heard in a long time, and I did not know that Piano sounded that good."

"Why, thank you." Jessica said. "By the way do you know of a good singing instructor in this area? My friend would like to take a little instruction. I would like to talk to you about the price of this Piano too if you are the salesman?"

"Of course, just follow me into my office and we will discuss both of those issues." One of the men in the group said, and he started off toward the back of the store. The girls followed.

After they were seated in the gentleman's office, He introduced himself as Mr. Ashford, Owner of the music store. He turned to Jessica and asked.

"And you are?"

"Jessica Levanti. And this is my friend Teresa Santini." Jessica said.

"Oh yes, I recognize the name." Mr. Ashford said, "I have heard quite a bit about you and your Playing, and I am pleased to meet you Miss Levanti. Will you excuse me a moment while I make a call?"

"Of course." Jessica replied.

While Mr. Ashford was on the phone talking he interrupted his talking to look at Terry and asked her if she would be available the next afternoon for a singing lesson. Terry nodded yes and he continued talking on the phone for a few minutes then hung up. He wrote something on a note pad, tore off the top sheet and handed it to Terry. It was an appointment time for her first singing lesson the next day.

"Thank you." Terry said.

He then turned to Jessica and said,

"Now about the price of the piano, it is one of our smaller versions and I can make you a good discount price on it if you are sure it is the one you want."

"It is the one I want," she said. "I love it."

The Piano was delivered the next day and the men carried it into the house and put it where Jessica wanted. Terry wanted Jessica to go with her to the singing lesson, so Jessica accompanied her and provided moral back up for Terry.

Surprisingly, when Terry started to use her voice for singing, she had wonderful control and the lesson was mostly learning basics.

When they returned home and Terry could relax with no one watching she sang while Jessica played and they were both surprised how good she sounded. Terry did not know the words to very many of the songs that Jessica played so they had to go shopping for sheet music with the words in. She would have to memorize songs for a while,

Friday night came and they went to the concert in the amphitheater. Terry had met a singer about her age the first time they had played the theater that she liked.

The singer's name was Celeste Varden. She was a blonde and had a very good voice with a wide range.

Terry walked over to Celeste and asked,

"Hi, Celeste, I would like to ask you a question, have you ever sang in a duet or with a small group?

"Why yes." Celeste answered. "Many times, Why?"

"My boss wants me to learn to sing and I now am taking singing lessons and I don't want to get on stage and sing alone. I would like to sing along with someone else till I get my confidence up. That is if I ever become a good enough singer to appear on a stage to sing." Terry replied.

"Good." Celeste said. "Pick a song that you are familiar with and get Jessica to play and we can try you out right now. There is hardly anyone around yet and they can be critics when we are through."

Terry called to Jessica and told her what song she wanted played and Celeste heard the name and said, Good, that is a favorite of mine also."

Jessica started playing and when the time came, both the girls started singing and Terry automatically blended her voice where it sounded the best as far as she could figure. When the song ended, no one said anything for a while then suddenly the little crowd that had been standing around started clapping and applauding.

Celeste said. "Terry, that was beautiful, you have a wonderful voice, let's try another. Do you know "The white Cliffs of Dover"?

Terry said. "Yes", and looked at Jessica. Jessica nodded and sat down to play.

The crowd had grown and this time Celeste did not have time to say "Very good", before the crowd broke out with applause.

Jessica was really surprised at the way her friend Terry could sing. It had never occurred to either one of them that she would be able to sing like that. Terry's face was red from blushing with embarrassment. It was all so new to her. She was very happy and excited over the results and she had just started the singing lessons. She knew she would have to take more though to perfect the different techniques required of an experienced singer. She was looking forward to them now.

Terry did not sing anymore that night. She wanted to get more instruction before she started the actual singing in public before an audience. The audience this night was a mixed crowd of soldiers and civilians and they listened for the key words as usual heard a few, but nothing they thought important.

The next day Mr. Cavanaugh called them in and when they were through talking about the concert the night before, he said,

"You girls will be leaving in a couple of weeks on a tour, starting in Tanga, then into Asia, central Europe and into England." He looked at the girls and said, "I don't think we will be stopping in Italy this trip, sorry about that, maybe next time."

He hesitated a bit then added, "There will be about two shows a week and it will keep both of you pretty busy. We will work Terry into the routine as easy as we can. I need not tell you there will be danger, especially inTanga. There is still some hatred about the two cities that we used the bomb on. You must be alert at all times. You have been trained as best we can and there will be other agents around if you need them. We will be flying from place to place and you will be quartered on Military bases and eating military food, maybe not all the time."

Jessica's mind went to the thought of Tanga and it brought up the memories of Li Chan and then to Chen LI. Maybe, she thought. They had been close and the feelings were strong. She asked herself, "Would they still be strong if they came close again?" Maybe they would, it was a long shot to hope for, but she could not forget her first love.

During the next two weeks Terry and Jessica had been busy. Terry had turned into a very good singer. The two concerts that had occurred gave her a chance to get on stage and sing with Celeste and the two had been received with much applause. Terry was happier than she had thought possible.

There was to be a stop over in California for a show there, then on to Tanga. The show was of course a hit and the soldiers seemed to really enjoy the whole program. The crowd was a lot noisier and a little rougher, but the MP's kept order. The girls did not leave the base.

The flight took off early in the morning and it was a long flight to Tanga

They finally arrived at an American Military Base on the Island of Tanga and Jessica had mixed feelings and was somewhat mixed up between emotions. Her only childhood experience had been Tanganese, but that was centuries ago. It was the only childhood she could remember. Her name had been Li Chan and she had been a royal princess and at age of twenty she had been in love with a Tanganese military Officer named Chen Li. What had happened to him? Had he traveled as she had and now where was he? How had he died and at what age?
As she left the aircraft and walked out on the tarmac to the busses that were to take them to their quarters her mind was bringing back long forgotten memories.

She must not forget that she is on the job and her job is to listen to Tanganese and not speak Tanganese, for any reason. She is here as a spy and she had better not forget that. Dick had told her as well as Terry that the Tanganese that still hated the Americans were in small groups that are continually trying too get even with the Americans for the two big bombings. They were to keep their ears and eyes open and not let it be known that they could understand the Tanganese language, even a little bit. They would have to be careful, very careful.

The girls, including Celeste were taken to the Officers quarters building and given the end rooms, which had separate showers and dressing rooms. They settled in for the night and were looking forward to tomorrow.

The next morning the girls had breakfast, then left the Cafeteria and walked to the stage where they were to perform later. Jessica checked out the piano for sound and was satisfied that it would do the trick.

There were a lot of Tanganese, both men and women working on the Air Base. It seemed that they were everywhere. There was continual chatter in Tanganese, and Jessica soon was tuned in so that she was listening in on a lot of conversations. She was trying not to show that she was listening and it kept her wondering how good she was doing. She turned to Terry and in a low whisper she asked,

"Terry, how am I doing in pretending I do not understand what the people around are saying? I am trying to ignore them and I am still listening to what they are saying."

"You are doing fine, I couldn't tell it at all." Terry said. Then added,

"When someone says in Tanganese, "Hey American bitch, you wanna try Tanganese man on for size? Then you listen good, because if you don't get angry or show you heard them, they will believe you cannot under stand Tanganese and that they can talk safely. Keep a poker face."

They walked over to the PX to buy some girlie things and then went back to the barracks and their rooms to rest up for the performance that night.

Again they had names on the backs of the chairs for each of the performers to sit in while they were off stage. Mr. Cavanaugh had a small musical group of country western and one of rock and roll along for variation, so all of the members had a chance to sit and enjoy the show. If any of the other performers were there in the same capacity as Terry and Jessica, Mr. Cavanaugh did not tell them. They had to assume they were the only ones in the category and play it that way.

The Soldiers had not seen an MES show for a long time so the place was packed and very noisy until the show started. Jessica was back stage for a while before she was called to the stage and she had listened to the Tanganese attendants, both men and women as they talked among themselves. She could tell they were feeling the new Americans out to see and find out which ones could speak or understand Tanganese. The way they talked and the things they said began to grow more insulting as the night went along. They were watching for some of the Americans to get angry and say something to them about the insults, but no one did.

Not all of the Tanganese that worked back stage could speak English, but quite a few could at least understand what you were trying to say. The Tanganese seemed to like the different music that was being played. They loved the country Western.

They all listened when Jessica played the Piano solo and was tickled when she started playing again and Terry and Celeste sang. The applause from the soldiers was a Thunderous roar as they finished their songs.

That evening Jessica and Terry heard a lot of talking, both for and against the Americans being in their country. In all the talking there was nothing really threatening. Mr. Cavanaugh acted as their taxi most of the time so that they could tell him if anything important was heard. When he took them from the stage to their sleeping quarters after the show they told him all that they thought was important, they asked him if they could go off the base the next day for a sight seeing tour of some kind.

"Well." He said. "There is a lot to see, but there is also some danger in traveling around without an escort. So what I will do is arrange for a Marine escort to be with you all the time. Do you both have your weapons with you?"

""Yes." Jessica said, then added "She is really good at some of the things I do also."

"Some day I would like you to tell me about those things you seem to be so good at and where in this world you learned them?" Mr. Cavanaugh replied.

He dropped them off at their barracks and said goodnight.

Terry and Jessica noticed a military jeep parked a small distance from their barracks when they left in the morning. They walked to the cafeteria for a morning coffee before they hailed a cab to take them into Tokido. They noticed the jeep following the cab. The two Marines were doing their job it seemed. They told the driver to take them to a store to shop for dainty things. He stopped in a very busy shopping area and they stepped out of the cab, paid him and walked away.

They both went into several stores and bought a few things they liked and had seen a lot of different things they would like to have but it would be too much to take back.

They finally hailed a cab and asked him if there was a park in the city. He nodded yes and started off. He finally came to a beautiful rather large park in the center of the city and let them out.

They walked out into the park area looking for a bench to sit on and enjoy the scenery. Terry glanced over at a jeep at the edge of the park behind them and said,

"The marines have landed; they are parked over there by the water fountain."

"I've been keeping an eye for them." Jessica said. "Come on, there is a bench over there by that tree, let's rest a while."

They sat down and put their purses beside them on the bench, and started talking about the things they had seen so far.

Jessica did not tell Terry about her feelings and memories that were coming back to her. She had seen Terry look at one of the shawls she had bought in one of the stores. She knew Terry was curious but she did not say anything.

Half an hour later Jessica caught sight of four Tanganese boys of sixteen or so coming toward them. She did not know if the Marines had seen them or not. She whispered to Terry,

"Here comes some purse snatchers, you take two and I'll take two, use Machedo if you have to, but put them down."

They were sitting quietly and were ready when they heard the sudden rush.

They moved away from the bench and moved fast. They moved toward the attackers, timed their kicks and knocked the wind out of the first two, then spun and their heels caught the second two on the side of the head and they went down fast.

Jessica picked up the two purses, tossed Terry's to her and they walked away leaving the four young men on the ground. As they walked away they glanced back and saw the two Marines come running up to the four boys lying on the ground. Jessica giggled and winked at Terry as they walked on over to the cab stand and hailed one.

It was still early when they reached their barracks, so they took the stuff they had bought up to the rooms and came back down and went to the PX to sit and enjoy a cold drink and a sandwich. Jessica wanted to talk to someone that had been here for a year or two and would know where any museums or historical items would be. She told Terry as much and Terry understood, and was even very interested as well. Jessica had told her a lot more than anyone else knew.

They had not been sitting long before Celeste came into the PX and joined them. They were sitting at a long table and it was not long before some soldiers came and sat in the empty seats around it.

"Hey you guys up there, do any of you know if there is a historical museum or something of the kind in this town." Jessica asked.

One of the janitors, a young Tanganese boy had overheard Jessica and stopped beside her and said,

There is a historical museum about two city blocks the other side of the park on the left side of the road, it is a big building and you cannot miss it. Any cabbie will take you there. It is new building since War." And he went back to sweeping the floor.

A few minutes later Mr. Cavanaugh came walking toward the table they were sitting at and sat down. He glanced at Jessica and Terry and asked,

"Did you two have any trouble in the park today?'

Terry looked at Jessica and Jessica took the initiative and said,

"No real trouble, there were some teenagers arguing and it finally turned into a fight so we left and came back here."

Mr. Cavanaugh smiled and turned to the two Marines behind him and said,

"See, I told you there had been no trouble."

The two Marines did not know what to say, as they left it sounded like one of them said,

"I would hate to be around if there ever was trouble where they are concerned,"

Mr. Cavanaugh smiled and said, I'll see you girls later." And walked away

Later as they sat in the chairs in front of the stage talking Mr. Cavanaugh sat down beside them and they told him about the attempted purse snatching. They asked if the boys were alright and he said they were a little bruised but otherwise alright.

The crowd was beginning to fill the seats and it promised to be a busy evening. Jessica was looking forward to a visit to the Museum the next day. Her mind was in turmoil and she was remembering many things that she had forgotten over the decades since her childhood. The times and actions of the Tanganese people had changed so much. She could not put them together and make them fit. If the Museum was a large one and had been kept up to date she would be able to follow the change to a certain extent.

The show went well; Terry and Celeste were somewhat of a hit. The crowd kept applauding to get them back. Of course the fact that they are beautiful girls and were dressed in tight fitting long dresses did not hurt the appearance of them. The crowd was huge, the largest they had ever played for.

The show finally ended at nearly midnight. All the entertainers were tired and anxious to get back to their quarters and relax

Jessica had dreams that night most made no sense, just a jumble of visions. Tanganese soldiers in different uniforms. All resembled what she remembered of Chen Li. Her first twenty years of life as she knew it was coming back to her. She was also thinking of what she would find at the Museum the next day. The night passed without giving her much rest

The next morning after a visit to the cafeteria for breakfast, Jessica and Terry hailed a cab and told the driver they wanted to go to the Museum. They had already noticed the Jeep that was to follow them to the museum.

They noticed there were Tanganese guards at several different places around the huge building as they walked up the steps and into the huge open doorway. Directly ahead as they entered was a long wide hallway with several openings in each side.

The first few openings led to Historical Items and times, some recent and some happenings of long ago. Finally in the center of the building they turned to enter a room and Jessica stopped, then backed a step or two.

Terry was watching Jessica as she stepped back. There was an odd look on her face, not fear, but awe and reverence. Jessica and Terry had agreed to take small pocket size purses with them on this particular trip. In case of another attempt at purse snatching They wanted to be free to move fast and even run if the occasion called for it.

Now Jessica reached into one of her pockets and pulled out a shawl and oddly patterned headscarf. As Terry watched Jessica put the headscarf over her head and tied it under her neck, then put the shawl over her shoulders.

Jessica then put her hands together in front of her heart, bowed her head slightly and walked straight in toward an Idol at the back of the room facing the entrance.

Terry slipped inside the doorway and to one side so that she could see, but still protect Jessica from any attack from behind. She did not trust any of these people.

The floor of the Temple room had strange markings on it, at different distances apart and Jessica seemed to be reading them and their meanings. As she walked past each of the different signs there was a change in her action or look. There was no doubt about where she was going. She never raised her head, but she was gong directly to the Idol at the back of the room.

Unknown to either Jessica or Terry, there was another pair of eyes watching Jessica walk toward the Idol. The eyes were old and the small frail face and body were something out of the past. The eyes were looking through the slits in the curtain behind the Idol and were watching the slowly approaching figure of Jessica as she moved toward the Idol. They were seeing the slow even steps, the hesitations at each mark on the floor. The movement of the hands, hardly noticeable to an untrained eye brought a nod of approval from the aged figure watching. Each movement was correct and as the girl approached, brought a tear to the old eyes as they watched and remembered days past, long past.

Jessica came at last to the first level change and saw the new fresh blue satin pillow at the foot of the Idol on the first level. She slowly lowered her body till her knees came in contact with the blue pillow. Her head still bowed, she began to hum an ancient long forgotten tune.

A voice said. “You are from the past. We have not forgotten you, Li Chan. We have heard of the incident in the park. That is why I am here. We knew you would come here to try to connect to your past.”

The voice was speaking Tanganese so the old man knew that she could understand when he spoke. She hesitated before she spoke, then in Tanganese that she knew she said,

“You knew I have the memories of Li Chan, and you know of Li Chan, How? Why?”

The voice started speaking again and the curtain opened so she could see the old man.

“You were a Royal Princess, Li Chan. And when you died, your father the Emperor decreed that someday you would return to Tanga and that your memory be kept alive. We have your little jeweled sword in the next room waiting for you. When you are able to leave the physical body you are currently in, we will be waiting here in Tanga. What you have been doing has been done before, but by a man, many years ago. Perhaps you will know him. He came back."

Jessica spoke softly,

"I have wondered why I was given this gift and all the time I have been thinking of my childhood and wanting to go back to the place of my birth and first years of my life. Now I begin to understand and look forward to my chance to return here, my homeland."

"Princess, you have made me a very happy man," the old man said. "I have waited these many years on the chance that you would return to your homeland. I am a distant relative of your father and a very distant relative of you. I have lived a long time, I do not know how many years. I have forgotten. Now you know enough of the story and I am sure we will see you again."

The curtain closed and Jessica arose and slowly walked backward along the beautiful tile path that she had followed in.

Terry had walked out of the room as Jessica started back and was waiting outside the doorway. She had not been able to hear any talking so she knew nothing of the conversation. She had seen Jessica's lips moving, but had assumed it was prayers of some kind.

When Jessica was out of the little chapel, she removed her headpiece and shoulder shawl and put them into one of her pockets. She was happy and a tear rolled down a cheek as she thought about what had happened. Whether the tear was of happiness or of sadness was the question. Being between two places that she loved just wasn't where she wanted to be.

Now she knew she could eventually be back where she had been as a child, and with the people she had been originally borne to. Meanwhile she would enjoy the life she was living as an Italian American and know also what the many memories were from and not have to wonder what they were and where they came from.

Jessica turned and walked to the next doorway and walked in. There were three glass enclosures, one straight ahead along the back wall, one to her left and one to her right along the two sidewalls. They were actually display cases; the one on the right, held clothing, the one on the left held bedclothes and floor covering. The one straight ahead held personal things.

As Jessica slowly walked into the room, her memories recalled the room in the Palace where she had slept when she was a child and where she lived till the night of the kidnapping. There was her sleeping mat of woven wool, her many beautiful little pillows, even some slippers to cover her toes as she walked. On her right in the glass case were all her beautiful Kimonos of silk, her shawls and the many different head coverings to wear to the prayer sessions. There was an area of beautiful beaded and jeweled sandals, Displayed on a blue satin background were her jewelry, a beautiful collection of rings, bracelets, necklaces and pins.

As she approached the back wall and the smaller glass case in front of it she could see that it held the little Ninja sword that her father had made for her and that she had dropped when she died. It was lying on a black velvet pillow in the center of the case and it was simply beautiful. The knife was out of the case and lying along side of the sheath of dark brown leather of some kind.

Jessica stood still, transfixed, not scared, but astonished and surprised at what she was looking at. It seemed she was standing in her own little bedroom in the old castle and her father would walk in at any time. She turned to Terry, took her arm and pulled her closer to help stop the shaking that her body was starting to do.

She opened her mouth to say something, but nothing would come out and she turned back around and looked at the startling assembly of memories that came to her. Tears came to her eyes and Terry handed her a handkerchief and put her arm around her. The rush of memories, held back for so long came forward and the tears streamed down her cheeks as her body shook with sobs she could not suppress.

Jessica could not turn her back on the room, so she backed out slowly with Terry helping until she could turn and walk toward the entrance of the Museum. With Jessica still sobbing, Terry kept her arm around her and walked slowly toward the doorway.

Jessica managed to stop the sobbing and they halted just inside the entrance for a while for Jessica to compose herself before going outside to face the public. At the age of twenty she had been too busy doing the things a teenager does and thinking of boys, she had gave very little attention to being the daughter of an Emperor or what it meant to the populace to have a beautiful princess in their country. Her role never entered her young mind.

Now it appears that she had been very important to the people of Tanga and that she had meant so very much to them. For Jessica to look at the way they had revered and kept her in their minds was simply astonishing, unbelievable. Yet she had seen it all back there in those two little rooms.

Jessica looked at Terry and said.

"Did you see that last room, terry?" then added, "That was my Bedroom with all my things almost as I left them that night I went to meet Chen Li." The tears started again.

Quite a few tears later she composed herself again and they were nearly ready to face the people they might meet on the street.

A few minutes after Jessica had left the sacred prayer room where she had seen the old man, Terry began to notice tall Tanganese women, all dressed in white, with a short sword, appearing in the Museum. They kept equal distance apart, but were not in any kind of pattern.

Just before the two girls were about to start through the entrance to the streets outside, one of the women in white approached them and said in perfect English,

"Do not pay us any mind. We are here to protect Miss Levanti and will not be a problem. No further contact is needed." She bowed, turned and walked away.

Terry watched as the woman walked away and thought; boy would I hate to get her mad at me. Jessica looked at Terry and said.

"They don't need to do that, but it will do no good to say anything. The old man probably set that up. Come on Terry, let's get out of here, I want to go somewhere and think about all this."

They hailed a cab and told the driver to take them back to the air base. The first thing they noticed was the tall Women in white. The short swords were hidden, but they figured they still had them. The women ignored Jessica and Terry, but the two girls knew they were not missing a thing.

When Terry and Jessica went into the cafeteria for lunch Mr. Cavanaugh must have been watching or waiting for them. Within minutes he showed up and sat down to eat with them, and of course talk. He looked like he was bursting at the seams.

'What have you two been up to?" He said, then, "Are these women in white connected in any way?"

Jessica spoke up. "We can't talk here, are you sure you want to know everything or just about the women in white?"

"Just about the women in white." Mr. Cavanaugh said. "That seems to be all that the military is concerned about. They have not seen them before."

"If that is all." Jessica said. "That is easy, they are my personal body guards and they will die trying to protect me. If you ask why, we will have to go somewhere private. It is a long and unbelievable story, but true as the Sun."

"They are worth their weight in gold to our aircraft and all the people who are with us, for nothing will slip past these women while I am with them." Jessica said.

Mr. Cavanaugh sat for a time and ate some of his food before he said; "That sounds like a political Hot Potato. They will not give us or the military any trouble will they?"

"Not unless you or the military approach me too close." Jessica said, then added in a whisper "To them I am sacred material, untouchable to mortals, without my personal permission."

Mr. Cavanaugh looked at Terry. Terry nodded, then asked, "Where did you pick them up?"

"In the Museum." Terry said and Jessica nodded.

Mr. Cavanaugh stood up, and said. "I'll see if I can calm down the military, they don't know what to think, "and he walked away.

The two Marines that had been watching Terry and Jessica did not know what to do but just stand by somewhere close and watch the proceedings. Mr. Cavanaugh convinced the Military Commander to just sit and let things be till his plane left. At that time the trouble would be gone, or so he hoped.

The Entertainment people were scheduled to leave the next day. They had one more show to do before they left.

The show went well and the soldiers showed their thanks by applause.

It was nearly midnight. Jessica and Terry were sitting in there chairs near the end of the first row of seats watching the show. One of the tall Tanganese girls, now dressed in total black suddenly appeared behind Jessica and whispered in her ear.

"Tell your MP Captain to look under the big Airplane," and she disappeared into the darkness.

Jessica immediately went backstage and told Mr. Cavanaugh, who turned and left.

After the show, when they were in the cafeteria talking, Mr. Cavanaugh came and sat down with them. He looked at Jessica and said.

"We have your tall women to thank for saving our lives. Someone dressed like a mechanic tried to place a bomb in the baggage compartment of our plane. They found out about it, killed him and left him and the bomb under the aircraft for us. Whoever they are, they do not fool around."

As a precaution only, they went over the plane to make sure there were no other unknown packages on the plane.

Jessica slept well their last night on the Island of Tanga. Her emotions were at a high level, but they were rather satisfied emotions and she knew she would straighten them out ok. Connecting her past as she had done in the last two days eased the tensions and thoughts that she had been having. Not knowing a lot of what had happened after her childhood, and she had almost forgotten who she was. Those two rooms had told her a lot. She was someone really important and she really had a place in life.

She had seen no reference to Chen Li, but she felt that she would find out more about him soon. The old man had not mentioned him, but he had mentioned that a man had made the same type of journey she was making and that he had came back. The old man even had said that she, Jessica might know of him. She asked herself, "Who could that be and where was he today?"

She had seen many nice looking Tanganese men around the city of Tokyo but she had felt no interaction. Perhaps the old man of the chapel would tell him and maybe he would show up before the plane left.

Jessica knew that in the physical body of an Italian American she was just another American now and not a princess and that she would act the part. She liked it that way for now. She could be a princess when the time came, meanwhile she would live the life of an Italian girl in America. She even liked working for the American Government and getting paid for it too.

She even liked the idea of the tall Tanganese Women protecting her. Of course they would stay in Tanga, wouldn't they?

When she and Terry were in their rooms later, Terry asked. "Jess, do you really remember all those things in the room you said were like your bedroom when you were twenty?"

"Yes," Jessica said. "It is funny, when I search my memory and I come across something and then I think about it, other things keep coming in that are associate with it. I seem to have lived part of several other lives. My childhood was the first memories that I had and I guess they are the strongest.'

"Well," Terry said. "You certainly are an interesting person to know. You have proven to me that when you say something it is true and you mean it, but you must admit that most of it is a little hard to accept, let's get some sleep, we've got a busy day tomorrow, we are leaving."

They were up and packed early and the civilian workers had picked up their baggage. The tall women in white picked up Terry and Jessica's. The other workers seemed to accept them and said nothing. The girls then went to the Cafeteria for Breakfast. The other Entertainers were there by then.

While Jessica was drinking her last cup of coffee she felt the presence of someone she should know. She looked around, but could not center on any one particular person. The presence was strong and she got up and walked around the Cafeteria to get closer to the feeling. She sat back down and finished her coffee.

The feeling was still there as they left the Cafeteria and entered the busses that were to take them to the aircraft. As they left the busses the feeling was stronger and Jessica looked around to see what was close.

A Tanganese Security van was pulled up on the other side of the huge aircraft and three Tanganese officers were standing outside of it talking and looking at it.

Most of the Entertainment equipment had been put on board and now the last of the crew were closing hatches as the last of the entertainers boarded the plane.

Jessica had dropped out of the line to see if she could locate the source of the feeling. She was looking at the Tanganese officers and was about decided that one of them was the source when the crew motioned her aboard.

The feeling that Jessica had felt was not unlike the feeling she remembered having when Chen Li was around. It had been so long ago that she was somewhat confused about it. It might just be that one of the Tanganese officers was a relative of Chen

Li. Besides she was an American now and was about to take off for Europe. This was not the time for her to meet Chen Li again, if it was the Soul of Chen Li.

Jessica sat back in her chair and relaxed to enjoy the ride. She looked at Teresa, her very best friend sitting beside her and at Mr. Cavanaugh, her boss, a good friend, and thought how lucky she was. Later if something happened to her and she left this body, she would then go back to Tanga and see what she could find. I really wanted to look a lot longer at the stuff in those two rooms in the Museum, she thought, especially the little Jeweled short sword, I think I can open it. She had no Idea what her father had told the Jeweler to put inside the secret mechanism. It could be anything from Jewels to silk or money. It had to be small though because the dagger was only a few inches long overall.

She did not remember seeing any drawings or pictures of herself. Although when she thought about it there had been no known way to take anyones picture in those days, only hand painted portraits or drawings were available. She knew there were paintings but she did not remember seeing any in those two rooms.

CRASH

On board the huge plane, chartered by the military to carry an entertainment company around the world to stop at the military bases and entertain the troops, were two young women. Both women were Italian borne and in their low twenties. One, "Jessica Levanti" was found near death by the Lost Soul of Li Chan at the age of thirteen and kept alive by the strong will and control of Li Chan.

Jessica Levanti now has the knowledge and power that Li Chan had picked up on her travels. She was an expert in the art of Machedo, an ancient art of self defense that could kill as easily as put down an assailant. She could play the piano like a professional. She knew the meaning of Love and had felt the feelings of passion and wants in some of the bodies she had entered in her travels.

She was well known in Italy, her home country and had moved to America with her family to advance her career with the Piano. She had brought her close friend Teresa Santini over a little later to be her traveling companion.

Both had been retained by the Government to work as spies as they traveled around the world. Li Chan could speak fluent Taganese and she had learned English from the first body she had entered. When she had saved Jessica she had the memory of Italian Her close friend Terry could speak fluent Italian and she had learned German in school. Between the two they could listen in on a lot of conversations and learn a lot.

They were now returning from the round the world trip and had been gone from America for nearly two months. They were both tired from the time changes and lack of sleep that they incurred.

The huge aircraft finally touched down outside Philadelphia and two hours later they were in their apartment relaxing for the first time in their surroundings. Their boss had told them to take a few days off and enjoy the rest. He would call them when he was ready for them to take on another job.

They had been talking for several minutes when Terry said,

"You know Jess, you have probably noticed that Mr. Cavanaugh and I have been together a lot during the later half of the trip. You also know that we went out a couple of nights together. I think I am falling in love and he thinks so too. I know, he's my boss and all that, but this is different. This is personal and we both feel the same way."

"Well, what is wrong with that, a lot of girls would like to marry their boss, and if you love each other, so much the better." Jessica said.

"I knew you would understand." Terry looked at her and added. "You are my best friend and always will be you know that."

'I know that Terry, I love you like a sister and always will, what say we go out tomorrow and do a little shopping before your new boyfriend calls us to work?"

Terry said, "OK, let's get some sleep now"

Both Jessica and Terry had their own cars and this time it was terry's turn to drive. They had made their own breakfast at home and left right afterwards on their shopping trip.

Every thing went well until they were entering the suburban area and Terry rushed a caution light. As she was about to leave the intersection another car came in from the right and hit her car broadside with terrific force causing a larger crash by pushing her car into another car coming toward them in the intersection.

Both terry and Jessica were crushed inside the car and glass was everywhere. Jessica's body and head were forced behind the steering wheel and there was blood on everything. Terry was screaming and yelling for help. People were coming from all around and many people were out of their cars walking about and waiting for an ambulance and police.

Terry looked at Jessica and was talking,

"Jess, Jess can you hear me? Please answer me, Jess."

She was trying to lift Jessica's head up and see how bad she was hurt, but the car was so badly bent in that the door on Jessica's side was driven into the center of the vehicle. Terry could not move enough to help herself or Jessica.

It was several minutes before a wrecker came and the police used the mechanical jaws to pry the door off of Jessica and lift her out of the vehicle and into an ambulance. She had not regained consciousness.

Terry was still conscious and was bleeding where her head had been struck by glass and she was in severe pain as they moved her into a second ambulance and followed the other ambulance to the hospital.

Mr. Cavanaugh went quickly to the hospital and had an hour or more to wait before he could see either of the two girls. Finally the doctor came out and took him into the office to talk to him.

"Mr. Cavanaugh, I am sorry to say that one of the girls did not make it. The crash crushed her rib cage so badly that both her lungs were punctured and she was practically killed instantly.

Her name is Jessica Levanti, I believe. I am truly sorry, but there was hardly anything we could do to save her."

"The other girl, Miss Santini, I believe will be alright in a few days." he said, then added. "You may see her in a few moments."

When Mr. Cavanaugh entered the room and saw Terry lying there on the white sheets looking so pale he nearly broke out in tears. He rushed to her side and took her hand. As he did so her eyes opened and she tried to smile. The first thing she said was,

"Oh Dick; How is Jessica?,"

Dick Cavanaugh did not know just how to say what he had to say. He just kneeled there and looked at her trying to figure out just how to say it.

That is all Terry needed to see. She burst out crying and Dick took her head in his hands and put his head down beside hers and cried with her.

"I am so very sorry." he whispered. "I know how close you two were, but there was not much the doctors could do, her body was so crushed. She did not suffer much they said she must have died almost instantly." The tears continued.

When Jessica's life giving flow of the red blood began to weaken and the Soul of Li Chan could not maintain control of any of the body parts, especially the brain, the Soul of Jessica and Li Chan collected all the memories and slowly slipped out of the physical body of Jessica and drifted above for awhile. She had really received much pleasure and enjoyment while in the physical body of Jessica.

As she looked down on the scene of the accident and saw Terry crying and trying to get her to talk, she remembered all the good times she had with Terry and remembered that she had told Terry about her past and how she had been the soul of other physical bodies. Terry would know that she, Li Chan would look to enter another physical being and must know that she would try to look up her old friend Terry. That would be interesting.

The Soul of Li Chan had followed the ambulance with Terry to the Hospital and was now hovering over Terry and Dick as they cried and held on to each other. She was glad that Terry had a lover now and they would be good together.

Oh well, she thought as she let herself drift off into the universe, what now. I will probably come across another being along the way that needs help. Maybe I can go back to Tanga. I am rather anxious to see if I can run across Chen LI.

RICHARD

The boy, about eight years old was sitting on the porch swing in a sitting up position Just looking out over the edge of the railing at nothing in particular. In his hands he had a little pocket knife and he was whittling on a small piece of wood. Just what he was trying to make could not be determined yet from the looks of the piece of wood that was left in one piece.

The boys name was Richard and of course they all called him, "Little Dickie." His arms and head were the only part of his body that was moving as he whittled. He was paralyzed from the hips down. He had no control of any part of his legs. It had been that way since his birth and though he was growing at the normal rate, he had never felt anything in either leg as they grew with the rest of his body. When he was held up, his legs would drop down normally and looked natural, but he could not move them.

All sorts of doctors had tried to find the reason for the lack of control over the leg muscles, but to no avail. He had learned to talk like any child and was or seemed like a little above average in intelligence. The only problem had started six or so months back when "Little Dickie" had began to look a little depressed and talked less and less. He gradually became quieter and quieter until he was hardly talking at all.

His parents had become more depressed as well as time went along. His father worked but did not make enough money to purchase the available mobility equipment that "Little Dickie" needed. They had become tired of having to carry him every where they went, so they stayed home more, which added to the frustration.

On this day, they had wanted to go shopping. If they sat him on the porch swing on pillows and placed them right he could sit and look out over the yard and into the woods. He liked that and had spent many hours that way. The pocket knife was a present from his father and he kept it with him all the time.

About thirty feet from the edge of the porch, where the wooded area started there was a small ravine. Dickie had looked at that area a lot because he had seen some of the squirrels and even a woodchuck come up out of there and eat the grass that began there. The squirrels did not eat the grass, but they ran around looking for something to eat. He liked to watch them. He wondered what was down in the ravine.

He sat there thinking and suddenly came to a conclusion that he was going to go look over the edge of the lawn down into the ravine. His arms were very strong for he used them to move whenever he did move. He put a couple of the pillows on the floor of the porch and lowered his legs and then his upper torso out of the swing and onto the pillows.

Then using his strong arms he pulled himself over to the steps and down onto the lawn. He rested there a little before pulling himself out into the yard toward the ravine. A few minutes later he was peering over the edge of the ravine down into a bunch of leaves, limbs and even some holes in the sides of the ravine. There were small trees growing along the top of the ravine and Dick reached out and grabbed one to hold on to so he could raise himself up to sit on the side of the ravine and look it over. He pulled himself up until he could reach back and pull his legs around in front of his body. As he did so, with his legs coming round to the edge of the ravine, the little tree he was holding on to collapsed and his body fell into the ravine. He rolled down to the bottom of the ravine and on the way there his head hit a large rock very hard. His body came to rest at the bottom of the ravine and he lay there nearly unconscious. He just relaxed his upper muscles to rest a while.

LI CHAN ENTERS

After drifting aimlessly for days, months or weeks, time was unimportant to The Soul of Li Chan. She was drifting low over the surface of some beautiful landscape and as she passed over a small cottage near a large wooded area she noticed the pattern of a small human physical body lying in a small ravine at the edge of the wooded area. Curious she dropped lower until she could examine the body closer. She looked first for the action of the large air sacs that provided the life giving oxygen for the heart to keep working. She now knew that the young body was alive.

Slowly she entered. At first she felt some resistance, but it was a very young and inexperienced soul and she quickly absorbed it and took control of the brain and all functions thereof. Absorbing all the memory, she immediately knew the boys situation. She quickly willed him to wake up and try to roll himself over so he could pull himself up to a sitting position. This action took a lot of will power and she used all her willing power to accomplish it. Soon he was sitting there in the bottom of the ravine looking up the bank to the edge of the lawn. Li Chan could feel how strong he was in the arms and she willed him to grab the small tree trunks that covered the bank and pull himself up to the top where he could lay down on the grass and rest until he was again strong enough to drag himself back to the porch.

The process was tiring and it took some time for him to get to the porch and to a sitting position on the bottom porch step. It was there that his parents found him a few minutes later. His father noticed the drag marks in the grass and looked toward the ravine, but he said nothing.

He carried "Little Dickie" back into the house and sat him back on the chair where he could rest. He looked up at his father as he was being lowered onto the chair and said,

"You know Dad, that woodchuck has a hole in the bank in that ravine out there, I seen it."

"It is probably a young one that liked our grass and decided to make his home close by." his father answered, smiling at him.

"I like that." Dickie said.

Dick's mother looked at him when he first spoke. There was a change in his voice, nothing weak or unsure. No note of fear, just fact and a hint of pride. She asked herself why, and wondered what had happened to her son who for the last few weeks had hardly spoke at all. She said nothing of what she thought and went into the kitchen wondering what her son had done while they were gone. She was glad he had not been hurt in the process.

Things went well for the next few weeks and "Little Dickie" was almost constantly heard talking or moving about the house. One day, a few weeks after the incident, Dick was lying on his bed just thinking about something. He suddenly called to his mother.

"Hey Mom, will you come here a minute."

As his mother entered the room, she saw him roll over on his stomach, his legs straight out.

"Mom." he said, "Are you doing something in the kitchen that needs you or can you stay here and do something for me for about five minutes?" He took off his t-shirt exposing bare skin.

"No Son, I can stay here for five minutes or so," she said. "What would you like me to do?"

Dick said, "I have been remembering something that I heard or saw somewhere that might help my legs come alive. I will lay flat and you open your hands so that the Palms are flat and move them slowly up and down my spine from the bottom to my head and around my head. Keep them as close to my body as you can, all the time you are moving them"

His mother did as she was ask moving her hands up and down his back. To herself she thought what does he think this will do for him. About that time he began saying "Aw-w-w

That feels good", and when she came to his head he was quiet, but he turned his head from one side to the other each time she came near it so that she could cover both sides with her hands.

After a while he said, "That's Ok for now, Mom, will you do it again tomorrow, please?"

"Of course Son, get a little rest now." she said and kissed him on the forehead before she left.

The next morning after they had eaten breakfast and Dickie was still in the chair they used to tie him in while he was at the dining table. Dick had been looking at the old upright piano standing against the living room wall. He looked at his mother and ask,

"Mom will you move me over to the piano and let me play it a little, I will be real careful and not do anything to hurt it?"

It was an old upright with some of the ivory broke off of the keys, but his mother seemed to love the old thing and she often sat down and played some of her favorite songs on it. It seemed to give her great pleasure and Dick knew that. He had watched her many times and he liked to listen to her play. She looked at him curiously and said.

"Yes Dickie, you may play a little if you like, I know you have wanted to get up there and play, but you never asked before, why now?"

"I don't know, but I seem to think I know how you do it when you play soft music, and I thought I would like to try." He answered.

It was relatively easy for her to move the chair on the linoleum floor and soon he was sitting in front of the huge piano. He sat for a while just looking at the keys and then slowly he put his fingers on the keyboard. He sat there thinking for a while then moved his fingers beside certain keys.

His mother, watching from the kitchen door, was wondering what he was thinking. He was only a little over eight years old, what could he be thinking? She asked herself.

Suddenly his fingers ran up the scale on the old keyboard, first one hand then the other. Then silence for a few minutes as he sat there and stared at the keys.

The Soul of Li Chan brought the memories of past piano players to the active area of the brain of little "Dickie" and used her willing power to start the fingers of the young boy moving across the keyboard. The melodies were a favorite of hers. The music seemed to calm the Soul and induce a quiet happy atmosphere wherever it was played.

His mother stood there in the doorway. She was afraid to move for fear of interrupting the mood her son was in. Suddenly the soft sounds of a piano came into the room. She stood there entranced and listened as some of her favorite melodies were played as she had never heard them played before. Tears began to roll down her cheeks as she listened. She nearly fell to the floor as she tried to grasp what had happened.

Where she was standing was not in the visual range of the boy at the piano so she moved slowly into the room to a lounge chair that was somewhat behind the boy at the piano. She sat down and sat quietly and listened to her eight year old son play some of the melodies that she had tried to play, but had never quite succeeded. The hands of the boy were not big enough to play properly but however he did it, the music was beautiful.

The boy played for nearly an hour before he finally stopped and lifted his fingers off of the keyboard. He had played some of the melodies more than once as his thoughts ran through his new found memories. There were other things that came to his mind and he wondered at them. Not remembering ever learning some of them. There were tears in her eyes and she had to keep wiping them away as the boy played.

Once his mind went back to the time in the ravine out back when he had felt like he was dieing and then he decided he wanted to live. He remembered the sudden rush of things he thought he should do to get up out of the ravine and get back to the house before his parents came home. His mind had thought of a lot of things then and he wondered where they had come from. Then his parents had come and he had forgotten about the incident.

Richard turned to his mother and said,

"Ok Mom, it is time for you to give me the hand healing treatment now if you will move me into the bedroom."

"What do you mean, the hand healing treatment," his mother asked.

"Well" Dick said, "I read somewhere in those books you brought me that before a lot of medicines were invented they used to do what they called "laying on of the Hands", and it seemed to help a lot by reducing the pain and speeding up the healing process. The book said that the human body has an Aura around it and when the aura around the hand is moved back and forth or around in a circle over the damaged area it will speed the healing and take away a lot of the pain. I thought we should try it on my legs."

"Well it certainly is worth a try." His mother answered and moved him and the chair into the bedroom where he crawled onto his bed and removed his t-shirt.

After the five minutes of hand moving, Dick stayed there and rested. His mother went back to her daily routine. Only this time she could hardly contain herself. The piano playing had so excited her that she could not concentrate on any thing. Where in the world had he learned to play like that? She finally decided that he had not learned it. There was too much to learn to be able to play like he had played. That knowledge she could tell as he played, had came from deep in the Soul of the boy. How it got there she did not know, but it was deeply implanted. She remembered then what he had said about the ravine. That he felt a rush of thoughts and knowledge of things that he did not remember learning come to him as he lay in the ravine after the bump on the rock. She thought, there must be a connection. She went to Dickie and said.

"Dickie, lets not say anything about the Piano playing until we can figure out what to tell your dad. I am sure we can think up something that he will believe. Tomorrow we will have enough time to think of something.

His mother had been home teaching him since he was about four years of age. She knew that he probably could not go to a regular school and so she had elected to start teaching him at home. He was a good and eager student and she kept using actual examples to teach him. At the dining room table he was always tied in his chair for safety's sake and he did not seem to mind.

She thought she knew him better than anyone else, including his father and he had never shown any bitterness toward the situation with his legs.

He knew a few of the boys that were about his age in the area, but they never or at least hardly ever came to the house to see him. Even that did not seem to bother him. He had accepted his condition and enjoyed the outdoors from the porch swing or just sitting on the porch steps where he could hold on to the hand rail his father had put there for him to hold on to.

His mother had made a few trips to the nearest Library and borrowed different books to take home and teach him or just let him read them himself. He enjoyed reading different things and always remembered them.

When Richard passed his eighth birthday a few months ago, they had taken him to town with them when they went shopping. As usual he was left sitting in the car as they shopped. Unknown to his parents, there was another cripple in the village that day.

His father had parked the car so that the view from the back seat where Dick sat was right up through the center of the village. As he sat there, another car came into the village from the other direction. Dick watched as the other car parked about a city block away, pulled up parallel to the sidewalk and stopped. A man got out and then turned and opened the back seat door. As Dick watched the man pulled out a wooden ramp and a girl in a chair with wheels on rolled down the ramp and onto the sidewalk.

Dick had seen pictures of wheelchairs and read about them, but this was the first one he had seen. It was a surprise. The man then closed the door of the car, walked around behind the wheelchair and pushed the chair and girl down the street and into a store.

Dick started thinking. The first thing that came to his mind was that she probably went to school in that fancy chair too, and she could also be with the other kids her own age. He wondered what they would think of her in that chair, a cripple.

He knew that both his parents loved him and he also knew that they very seldom had enough money to buy food, let alone a wheelchair. Wheelchairs must cost a lot of money, he thought.

He was quieter on the way home, which caused his parents some silent concern. He did not want to trouble them and he knew that if he said anything they would probably try to find a way to get him a wheelchair. He was convinced that his father could not afford the cost of even a used one so he kept quiet.

That was the reason that he had been so thoughtful and did not talk so much. He could not forget the wheelchair and yet he did not want to give his parents any more trouble.

She was sure that if she talked to Dick they could come up with a story that his dad would believe to a certain degree.

The next day after his father had left she gave Dickie the hand healing treatment and then they talked about how they could tell his father about his ability to play the piano so well. They decided to tell him that she had been teaching him for a long time and he did not play after his father came home because Dickie did not want to disturb his father when he was relaxing after a hard day at work.

The Healing Hand treatments went on daily and so did Dickie's playing the piano. He loved to play and he wanted to get familiar with the piano.

One day he got started a little later than usual with his playing and his father came home a little earlier than usual. When his father came into the living room. Dickie was at the piano and his mother was sitting in the chair listening. Neither had heard the car come into the driveway or the door opening as his father entered the house.

His father stopped and stood still just listening. Dickie's mother, sensing another presence looked around and saw him. They both waited till the song ended before they spoke.

"How in the world did you learn to play like that?" His father asked as he walked toward his son.

"Mom has been teaching me in the afternoons and I been practicing, It seems so easy to learn and I like to play it soft and easy." Dickie said.

"That's great." His father said, "That sounded really good, can you play any other songs?" and he named a few.

Dickie turned to the piano and softly played the requested songs while his father stood entranced and listened. When the songs ended his father said,

"Boy, son you're pretty good, that must have taken a lot of practice."

"I know Dad, but I like it and mom likes to listen to it too, so I don't mind."

Dick and his mother exchanged looks and smiles. Their plan seemed to have worked.

Days, then weeks and finally a couple of months went by until one day Dick's father came home and asked Dick if he would like to play for a play at the school.

Dick was silent for a while and then asked.

"Will there be a lot of people there?"

"Only the school kids and some of the parents." His father answered.

"Well then," Dick told him. "I guess I can do it. Will they say anything about my chair?"

"I don't know, but I will talk to the school principal and make the necessary arrangements and your mom and I will take you over to the school to see and test the piano before the play night." His father told him.

It was now Tuesday and the play was on Friday night. Dick's father arranged for Dick to go to the school on Wednesday after school was out and took his chair with them for Dick to sit in while he checked out the piano.

When they arrived at the auditorium the Principal was there to meet them and show them in to where the Piano was. He did not know the family well and he wanted to see if the boy could play good enough for the required music.

The chair was carried in by the Principal and Dick's father carried his son. The principal had not been aware of a child in the area that had no use of his legs and looked a bit perturbed at the situation. There were two pedals on the piano and he could see they would not be used.

He did not know enough about music to know whether they were needed or not. He said nothing and let the boy's father and mother do the setting up.

After Dick was comfortable and tied securely, Dick's father and mother sat down in the front row where the Principal joined them. A few students gathered and sat a few rows back of them and waited.

Dick sat there for a while. The piano was nearly like the one he had at home only a later model and in better shape. As he ran his fingers over the keys and listened to the sound. He knew that it had been tuned recently, it sounded so much better.

As he began to relax by running his fingers over the keys getting the sound levels, he suddenly started playing one of the school songs that he had heard them playing on the radio at home. He had heard it playing many times and he knew the tempo they liked. As he came to the end of the song, he hesitated a few seconds and at that time he heard the students shouting.

Now he started playing the soft melodies he liked so well and everyone quieted down and listened, A few minutes later some more of the students and some of the teachers came into the auditorium and sat quietly down with the other students.

Dick was so engrossed in his playing that he forgot time and even what he was there for so when he did stop, he had been playing for over half an hour. After he stopped, everyone stood and clapped and hollered their appreciation. The principal turned to Dick's father and said.

"Well, you were certainly right when you said he could play the piano pretty good. That was beautiful music. It appears he will do nicely for the play." He turned and addressed Dick.

"Young man that was a beautiful performance, thank you. Will you come back on Friday evening and play for us? I will give you a list of the music required."

"I will be glad to Sir, and thank you." Dick answered.

They took the chair and went home.

The principal of the school called Dick's mother the next day and ask her if it would be alright if he brought out a wheel chair that they had in the storeroom, for

Dick to use. He explained that the chair had been donated years ago and no one was using it and that Dick might as well be using it.

Dick was delighted too get it and really had a lot of fun getting used to riding around in it. He finally told his mother about the time he saw the girl in one in the village.

The principal had delivered the chair to the boy's house in a van that he drove. The only way Dick's father could take the chair with them was to leave the trunk lid open and tie the chair into the trunk. On Friday they decided to get to the school a little early and let Dick roll himself into the auditorium and over to the piano to see how many pillows would be needed to position Dick at the level required to play the piano. Once they had him at the right level, they just sat in the front row and waited.

There was much activity then as the players and the audience came into the auditorium and readied it for the play. Richard was a little excited, but he was confident that he could do his part. He had practiced all the music that the Principal had given him and all he needed was for the card holder to put up the right cards at the right time. He had not seen the play or even read the script, but he could read the cards and tell what music came next.

The play proceeded well and was a complete hit, judging from the reaction of the audience. There were several standing ovations and much applause.

Richard and his mother and father got home about midnight and were rather tired; it had been a long and pleasant evening.

Many months passed. Richard was well adjusted with his wheel chair and was progressing well with his home teaching. As the school year was about to end, they asked the principal if they could register Richard for the next school year. They wanted to know if the wheelchair would be a trouble for the school. The principal said the wheelchair would not be a problem.

Richard and his mother had kept up the "Laying on of Hands' therapy and it seemed it was about to pay off when the summer vacation for the school children started. One morning when Richard's mother went to his bedside to wake him, she found him sitting up in the bed and he was rubbing his upper leg muscles and looked rather puzzled. She spoke up,

"What is it Dickie?" She was afraid to ask any more.

"Mom, I can feel my hands rubbing my leg, I never could before." He said.

"Can you feel it in both legs Dickie? She stammered, trying to keep her anxiety in check.

Richard put one hand on each leg and slowly rubbed them up and down his thighs as he stared at them wonderingly.

"Yes, mother and it feels so good." he told her.

"Do you feel like you could wiggle your toes? She asked him.

"How do you do that?" He asked her.

"Never mind, that can come later, just do what ever you think you can do without making them hurt". His mother told him.

Richard ran his hands up and down his legs feeling the muscles as they moved. HE finally leaned forward and felt his toes as his mother watched. When she saw the smile as his fingers touched his toes, she almost burst out in tears. She could hardly contain herself she was so happy.

She kept telling herself that it might not be as she was hoping and to not be too sure if what she thought was happening. She must wait to be sure before she said anything.

Richard had never stood on his two legs with any amount of weight on them and she was half afraid to let him try. She asked him if he could slide over to the side of the bed and put his legs over the side and let them hang down. She watched as he did what she asked. He had done that before but he had to use his hands to move the legs before. This time she noticed that the movement was slow but he did it without using his hands to move them. She nearly cried out with joy, but managed to just hold her breath until his legs were hanging straight down.

"Now just sit there for a little while and see how they feel, then I will hold you as you slide off of the bed and onto your feet." She managed to say, a little shakily.

"Does your body hurt anyplace now, or feel funny?" His mother asked.

"It feels a little funny at the bottom of my backbone, but it doesn't hurt." he answered.

"Richard." She said, "I will hold you and lift you like I usually do, and I will keep you straight up as you put your feet on the floor. If you feel any pain as I lower you so you can put more weight on your legs, you tell me right away, will you?" He nodded.

"You have never learned to walk so if your legs are getting better, you will have to learn to keep your balance and learn how to walk at the same time." She told him. "Here we go."

As she lifted him, she felt him holding back and she could feel him trying to hold his legs up. When she finally had lifted his body high enough to let his legs hang straight down, she felt him relax and let his legs straighten clear out. They she gradually lowered him so that he could touch the floor with his toes.

Slowly then she lowered him so that his feet were flat on the floor.

"I can feel the floor." he nearly shouted.

His mother lowered him slowly down a little more.

"Now I can feel the load on my legs and my leg muscles are tightening." He said.

His mother gradually lowered him till his full weight was on his two legs. She watched his face as she lowered him and she saw no sign of pain, only wonder. The leg muscles were weak, she knew, so she still had a good grip on the upper part of his body.

"Mom, my legs are starting to hurt a little, put me back on the bed, will you?" He stammered.

"Alright Son, that was great." She said. "The process of getting strength and balance will take a while, but I am so happy for you. It looks like you may be walking in a few weeks or so.

Richard's mother was is such a sate of mind that she could not settle on one thing to think about. Oh one hand she was so happy for what she thought was going to happen with Dickie, and on the other hand she wondered what had happened to make his legs work. Could it have been the hand movements over his spine, with her body Aura penetrating the nerves and helping the healing process to complete the healing of the nervous system? She probably would never know, but she was so very happy that it looked like both his legs would be normal after a few weeks of exercise and practice walking and balancing.

She started to call her husband a few times but decided to wait. He would be happy to hear the news but she did not want to jeopardize his job in any way. Jobs were hard to find anywhere close.

When he came in the door after work, he saw the expressions on his wife's face. He looked over to the bed where his son was sitting on the edge with a happy smile and a tear or two rolling out of his eyes.

The father rushed over to his son, then stopped short as he saw his son slide off of the bed and was standing upright on the floor saying, "Look Dad, I can stand up."

As dick started to fall, his father caught him and held him as they both burst into tears and held on to each other. Dickie's mother put both arms around them and joined in the crying. It was a release of years of holding back and now filled with joy. How many times had she sat and looked at him and wanted to cry but did not. How many prayers had she said and asked for Devine help. How many nights had she cried herself to sleep quietly. Maybe, just maybe that crying was nearly over. She would cry herself to sleep again this night, but they would be tears of joy and prayers of thanks.

It appeared that Richards leg muscles were responding a little to the willing of the soul of Richard. The nerves must have been slow in forming and then, maybe the laying on of hands had something to do with it too. We will never know. Whatever the cause, the body had apparently healed itself and was now becoming a normal body.

Two months later, Richard was walking around the yard without the help of his mother. It was a slow process. Learning to keep his balance and use the necessary pressures on his feet to walk was a very hard thing to learn. His legs were still quite weak and would take many weeks of exercise to bring them up to the strength needed for a boy of his age.

During this time of recovery, Dickie still spent his resting time at the piano. It was bringing out the memories of all the songs and happenings of both Robert and Jessica which had been instilled in the memory banks of Li Chan's Soul.

Richard began to receive requests for playing at plays, and concerts at the different schools and finally at one of the local Colleges. In some instances he received reimbursement for his time and travel cost, which helped the family keep him in clothes and food.

At one of the concerts, the Leader of a small band that was asked to perform, came over to him and asked him if he would consider joining them and forming a larger band with a drummer and some wind instruments. He told them he would think about it and call them, he was still pretty young.

At the age of nineteen, Richard had been back and forth across the country many times. The band that he was with were well liked and most always in demand He liked to travel and was earning more money than he ever thought he would see in a lifetime. He was always sending money home to his parents. He often thought of the first eight years of his life and was now realizing how hard it must have been for his parents. He was glad that he could send money home; he figured that he owed them a tremendous amount and he was determined to make it up to them. They had a new car and now had nearly enough to buy a bigger house and move into it. He was happy and really having a good time. Sometimes he was requested to play just the piano at a piano concert and it gave him a chance to be alone and enjoy the soft sounds of just the piano.

His legs were perfect and had made him a very healthy and good looking young man. He had finished school and Graduated with honors. While at the school he had spent some time in the Gym and had practiced boxing and had found out he knew something about an ancient type of Tanganese fighting. It was not the Judo that some of the kids were learning, but a more deadly version involving using the foot and various other parts of the body. The name Machedo, came to his memory, but he was not sure. It was a little vague, and when he was practicing it there were a few moves that came to him automatically that he figured might come in handy, for they were very fast. His upper torso was developed a little more than the other boys and was much stronger. That, he knew was due to the early eight years of his life. He often wondered how he would react in a real life fight. He was soon to find out.

One night in a large Midwestern city they performed at a concert in the local Convention center. Like most large cities, the convention center had been built in the near center of the city, but after several years the slum area of the city had crept up to the Convention Hall and it was safe to enter by the front, but the back could be dangerous.

It had been a long night and they had played late. The Audience had all left and band had packed up their instruments and carried them out the front doors and put them on the steps to await the buses that were to take them to the Hotel for the night.

Richard felt the need to relieve himself and did not want to go back into the Hall so he told the guys that he was going around the side of the Hall for a minute. As he left, one of the band members joined him and the two walked around the corner of the building and disappeared in the darkness of the alley they had entered.

As they were finishing their business, four dark covered figures loomed out of the darkness and the leader approached Richard.

"Alright pretty-boy, Hand over your wallet and be quick about it!" he said, and the open switchblade in his hand was supposed to back him up. Richard noticed that he was the only one with a knife shown. As the knife came closer, Richard moved forward, grabbed the knife hand, turned and brought his hip around as he pulled the would be robber up and over his body. It happened that he was close to the concrete building, so the robber hit the side of the building and dropped to the ground. One of the other figures came at him and he sent his right foot into the stomach, hard, and the man fell sideways moaning. As one of the other dark covered figures came at him, he moved in close and brought his knee up into the mans' groin with all the strength he could muster. The man screamed and fell to the pavement. The fourth man, a younger slimmer boy was backing away into the darkness.

The first man, the one with the knife was trying to get up. Richard approached him. Looking down at him, he asked.

"You planning to try that again?"

The young man on the ground looked up at Richard standing there looking down at him and muttered,

"No" He did not even look at the knife lying on the pavement.

Richard and the other band member walked back to the front of the Hall and helped put the instruments into the busses.

The other band member that had went into the alley with Richard, looked at him in an odd sort of way and said.

"Boy that was fast."

As we have found out before, the Soul of Li Chan wastes no time fooling around when there is trouble. She seems to want to act first and ask questions later. She had always figured that the first move had the advantage, so her willing to act was quick and decisive.

Richard had noticed that there was one of the band members that evidently had a dislike for him. It was a bass player on one of the Guitars. The young man had never been friendly with him and even ignored some of the other members of the band.

The band practiced in the local school auditorium. One evening after practice, the young man whose name was Bob Haden, approached Richard and said,

"Red said you are a pretty tough character, he said you laid out three guys the other night at the convention Hall. What did you have to pay him to brag about you that way? I don't think you are that tough at all."

Richard just looked at him and said.

"That is your privilege, think whatever you wish. It don't matter to me what you think."

"Don't get smart with me." Bob answered. "I'll show you what tough is."

Richard had been putting sheet music back into the bench he sat on to play the piano. He slowly put the music in the bench, lowered the lid, and turned and walked over to Bob. As he walked up to Bob, he timed his steps. When he was the right distance away, his right fist came out and hit the bully just under the rib cage, doubling him over as Richard's left hand grabbed his hair and brought his head down as Richards right knee was coming up. The knee hit the bully's nose hard enough to break it and blood spurted out as he was slammed backward to the floor of the stage.

Some of the other band members had heard the exchange and were watching. Richard then turned and walked back to the piano, picked up his jacket and walked out.

The other members went to Bob and helped him up and one of them took him to the emergency room for treatment. Before he left he said to one of his friends.

"I guess he really is that tough."

Richard's mother and father had moved into a new house that Richard had bought for them. It was not a new house but was one that they had always wanted one like. Richard had insisted that they accept it. His father still worked and they had sold the old house that Richard had been borne in. Dickie would not take the money from that sale. He told them to bank it and keep it for future needs if they came up. He was happy and he told them so.

A month later as they were traveling south for a concert in one of the larger cities they decided to stop at one of the larger restaurants for an evening meal. It was an Italian restaurant on the outskirts of the city. Richard was one of the first to enter the Restaurant and find a table. He and his friend Red sat down and picked up a menu.

As the rest of the young men came into the restaurant, a voice, speaking Italian said,

"Hear comes a bunch of those loud mouthed punk rockers, I wish they would go somewhere else to make trouble, not here."

Richard, sitting that close, understood every word and was shocked for a minute as the fact that he understood Italian words became clear. His memory had not brought up different languages before and it was a surprise. As the memory became clear he suddenly realized that he could speak fluent Italian easily.

When the rest of the band came closer and was preparing to sit down. Richard stood up and said.

"Don't sit down guys, the owner of this Restaurant over there," and he pointed to the Italian man who had spoken the phrases, "Just called you all a bunch of loud mouthed Punk Rockers and wished you would go somewhere else." and he added. "So let's go somewhere else."

There was a very pretty young lady standing beside the Owner of the Restaurant and as the band members turned and started out the door she said, "Oh no."

Richard turned to the Owner and said, in perfect Italian.

"Mister, you get your wish, pardon us for bothering you."

Richard then turned to the young lady, bowed, turned and followed Red out of the building.

The band members then proceeded in their bus to the motel where they had reservations and were to spend the night. The concert Hall was only two blocks away from the motel. The motel also had a restaurant and they ate the evening meal there.

As Richard walked away, his mind was still on the beautiful dark haired girl that had been standing beside the Owner of the restaurant. He thought, "Boy was she ever pretty". He wanted to turn and go back, but he knew he could not do that. Maybe he could come in to the restaurant later or something.

The Concert was to be held in the College Auditorium and was to start at eight o'clock that evening. The bus that carried the musical instruments had gone directly to the college and was probably already unloading the instruments. The crew knew how and where to position them on the stage for the opening Number.

By seven o'clock the crowds were already arriving and taking their seats and a large section near the stage had been roped off as reserved seats.

The piano was usually positioned on the left side of the stage near the front with the pianist facing the center of the stage.

At seven fifty-five the band members entered the stage from the rear door and each walked out to their instruments. They had become well-known and had become more sophisticated as they grew in popularity and now it began to show. They were all dressed in black suits and ties, with white shirts. As they walked out the crowd buzzed with excitement and began clapping. As they took their positions and looked ready to play, the huge auditorium became quiet.

As Richard sat down and put his hands on the ivory keys, ready to play, he glanced out at the audience. He almost missed his cue, for sitting in the front row with probably her family, was the beautiful Italian girl from the restaurant they had walked out of.

The band members had discussed earlier what the routine was to be. As this was more or less an Italian concert, they decided to play an Old Italian favorite from the homeland of Italy. Richard was to play through it first in a soft solo with the piano, then the band was to come in for the second playing of it with all the instruments. Richard had long ago decided that it was one of his favorites and he knew it by heart and loved to play it.

He looked down at the girl as his fingers softly touched the keys and the soft sounds of the old favorite reached the people in the audience. It was so quiet in the auditorium that only the soft melody of the song could be heard. She was looking at him with surprise and rapt attention as his fingers ran through the music of the song. When the song ended, he continued and the band came to life and the hall was filled with the music of the Italian homeland and the audience burst into applause as they showed their appreciation.

As Richard looked down again to the girl in the first row, it appeared that she had moved, but he would have seen her do it out of the corner off his eyes, she was that close. Then he looked again and found the girl, but she was closer this time, then he saw the problem. There were two girls the same in the first row. They sat about four seats apart and were in the first row. He looked at one then the other. They were Identical in every respect, even their clothing. Twins he thought.

During the first half of the show he glanced down a lot of times and wondered at the similarity of the two. They were completely identical in every respect. He decided he would go down during the intermission and talk to one of them. They sure were beautiful, he thought.

When they stopped for a short break and stretch, he stepped off of the stage and walked over to the first one of the girls. He was hoping it was the one he had bowed to in the restaurant.

He stopped in front of her and then spoke,

"I hope your father likes the music us "Punk Rockers' play."

"I am so sorry he said that." she answered. "He made a terrible mistake in judgment. He had no idea you were the band that is so well known for its music. You are all so very young to be playing music like that. It was very beautiful."

"Permit me to introduce myself, "Richard said. "My name is Richard Balantine and as you saw, I play the piano."

"And you do it very well, I would like to say. My name is Angela Delgado and I have never heard such softly played music like the first song you played, it was beautiful" Angela said.

And her smile simply glowed and he blushed as she looked at him. Suddenly another voice spoke, "And I am Angelina Delgado and it is a pleasure to meet you, Mr. Balantine. My sister is right. That music was beautiful and you seem far too young to be playing such old classics. You do not look Italian, and you speak it so well. Are you from Italy?"

"No, but I have traveled a lot. It seems you two are Identical twins. How do people tell you apart? Richard replied.

"Most people can't," Angela said. "We sometimes wear different jewelry. It helps some of the time. We do have different moods and habits though and people soon learn."

The band members were returning to their instruments and Richard excused himself and climbed back on the stage and to his piano. The concert continued.

Richard glanced several times down at the girls. He had never seen twins before, let alone twin girls that were almost exactly alike. The only difference he had seen was in their eyes. Angela's eyes were soft friendly and carried a hint of a smile, while Angelina's were calculating, cold and competitive. They were Identical outside but after seeing their eyes, he was willing to bet they were very different on the inside.

After the concert, as the band members were putting their instruments away. Mr. Delgado approached Richard and spoke,

"Mr. Balantine, I would like to apologize for my behavior the other day at the restaurant. You see, there is a bunch of young men in this town that have a small band and they are a rowdy bunch that has caused a lot of trouble. Please forgive me and I would be pleased if you wish to drop in for lunch or dinner sometime." Also, hc added. "I truly enjoyed the concert, it brought back a lot of memories for me; I hope you can be brought back another time."

"Well, thank you." Richard said." I thought as much, we have seen a lot of those small groups around the country. I do hope we can come back another time."

Richard looked around for the twins, but they were not in sight. He imagined that he saw a lot of interest in Angela's.

The band members slept on the bus as it headed back to their home town.

Richard had seen a lot of different girls in the traveling they had been doing, but he had never seen that certain something that he had seen in Angela's eyes, it was not in Angelina's. His thoughts were of Angela as he went his way. His inner self was against getting involved with Angela because of what he had seen in Angelina's eyes as she looked at him. He was not sure just what it was that he had seen, but his Soul was against it, whatever it was. He sensed a strong rivalry between the two girls and did not want to be in the middle. It would be jealousy and rivalry between the twins and he did not want to be the cause of it. It would probably come to the surface with any guy that displayed any interest in Angela, and not Angelina.

Before he went to sleep he had decided that he would see no more of the Delgado twins, they were trouble in the waiting.

Two days later he could not get the thought of Angela out of his mind. He had tried but each time he tried to think of something else a picture of her face and those eyes came back in his mind. The band had no immediate dates so Richard decided to drive to the city with the Italian restaurant and the Delgado twins. He kept thinking that he should not see them again but he also longed to see Angela again. It was nearly a hundred miles one way to the city, but he had nothing else to do, so he started out alone.

As it happened, the restaurant was on the opposite side of the city and when he came to the city he did not know his way around it so he decided to drive straight through the center of the city.

The state route he was on did not go through the center of the city, but through the lower half of it. As with most large cities it seems that the slum area is usually on the south side. As the buildings turned from residential to empty houses, then warehouses and factories, he noticed that people were scarce and there were homeless people on the streets and the hookers were beginning to show themselves.

He was driving along slowly and wondering when it would end when he saw a young woman sitting on the curb crying. No one else was around so he pulled over to the curb and stopped in front of her. When she looked up at him, wiping the tears off her cheeks, a young man about her age approached from between two buildings and stopped beside her.

"She is not working right now." He said. "Move along, and come back later."

Richard got out of the car and spoke to the girl. "Are you alright young lady?"

The young man stepped up to Richard and said. "I said move along, now get out of here, now."

Richard moved fast, a right fist to the stomach and followed up by a knee in the face as the young man bent over forward. He fell backward to the cement and lay there trying to get his breath.

Turning to the girl he saw that she had been beaten about the head and face and there was blood around her mouth. She started to say something, then looked toward the alley between the buildings. When Richard looked that way he saw two more young men coming toward him. Turning to the girl he said, "Get in the car, I'll take care of this, then we'll get you fixed up."

As she started around the car to get in, Richard turned to the two oncoming men and stood waiting. As they approached he stepped out away from the car and the man on the ground. He saw one of the men pull a knife from his pocket and open a blade. That made it a deadly weapon and he decided to play accordingly. The man was right handed. Richard grabbed the knife hand and pulled himself inside the man's arms. At the same time he brought his right hand down in a chopping blow to the side of the man's neck. The man fell to the cement and lay still as Richard swung around and caught the third man hard in the face with his foot. He also fell to the cement and lay still.

The first man had sat up and was holding his nose as Richard got into the car and was pulling away. He looked over at the girl and asked her if she wanted to go to the hospital or to her home. She started talking, trying not to cry.

"I want to get out of this town and I don't have enough money. They would not let me keep any of the money I made so I could not do anything but what ever they said."

"Where do you want to go?" Richard asked.

"I want to go back home in Wisconsin, I should not have left." She replied.

"Do you want to go to where you were living, for anything?" Richard asked.

"No, I have nothing there but old clothes and there may be someone there to stop me from getting anything anyway, but I have no money, I can't go anywhere without money." She started crying again.

"Don't you worry about that now" Richard said. "Right now I want to know how badly you are hurt. Do you want to see a doctor or go to the emergency room?"

"No, I just need to clean up and wash my face and fix my hair." She said. She did not mention the fight or the young men that they had left on the cement.

Richard did not mention them either. He knew what had been going on, but he wondered how he knew. To his knowledge he had never met a hooker before, but he seemed to know just what the situation had been back there. Young gang punks had played up to a young girl and told them how they could make a lot of money, and have fun doing it. Then she became a sex slave for the gang. She earned the money and they kept it so she could not run away. If she tried she would be beat and told what to do. Fear kept her in line and she was trapped.

Forgetting about the two Delgado girls, Richard turned the car and headed back the state route he had came up. At a clean looking gas Service station he stopped and let her go to the ladies room and clean up. He still did not know her name, but that was not important anyway.

Richard was sitting in the car wondering what to do next when the girl returned. When he did look up he got a very pleasant surprise. He was looking at a very beautiful girl. Where she had got a comb, he did not know, but her hair was beautiful and was a beautiful reddish brown. Her face was clean and but for a couple of bruises was quite beautiful to look at.

His face must have shown his surprise for she asked,

"What is the matter, you look surprised, I had a comb in my pocket and I used a napkin for a wash rag to clean my face. Do I look ok?"

"You look wonderful, how do you feel? He answered. "By the way", he continued, "What is your name"

"Edith, now what shall I call you, Knight in Shinning Armor." She asked.

"Richard Balantine, and knock it off. My friends call me Dick. Get in, we are going someplace to buy you some clothes. Then we'll ship you off to your mother, where you belong." Dick answered.

About half way back the way he had came up the state route there was a smaller city that had some department stores. Richard pulled into the parking lot of one of the largest. They left the car and walked into the store and Richard said "Edith, I want you to go to the girls' clothes section and buy yourself two or three outfits that you like and try them on, and I don't mean the type of clothes that you are wearing now. No more of that stuff. Got it? Your mother will see you in what ever you get, so do it right." He continued "I'll be in the luggage department when you are finished."

More than half an hour later Edith walked into the luggage department with her arms full of clothes. Dick told her to pick out a suitcase big enough to hold what she was going to need. She selected a medium size pretty light blue one.

After going to the shoe department and then the cosmetics and finally the outer wear for a jacket, they were ready to go for lunch. The little suitcase was about full. She had picked up a little purse in the process somewhere.

Richard was in the habit of carrying emergency money, usually large bills, in his wallet. So he was prepared when the clerk rang up the cash register. Edith looked a little ashamed when she saw the total. She said nothing as they walked to the car and put the suitcase in the back seat.

There was a restaurant next to the department store so they just locked the car and walked to it. They picked a table away from people so they could talk.

"I am so sorry to have caused you so much trouble. I really had no way out of the situation I was in. You have no idea how cruel those guys were. They were selling me to get them money. They only gave me a little food and clothes if I really had to have them. If I said anything, they would slap or hit me. I am so glad to be away from them. They don't know where I'm from, so if I can get back there I will be safe." She said and the tears started again.

"We are going a lot farther south before we put you on a bus or train and send you back to Wisconsin." Richard said. "We'll put you on something that does not go through or stop in the city you just left. Now let's eat, I am hungry."

Two hours later and over a hundred miles further south, Richard bought Edith an airline ticket to a large city in Wisconsin, the closest one to the town in which she had lived.

"I can call someone from home to come to the airport and pick me up." she said, then continued. "Richard, I don't know how to thank you. I was in an awful mess."

"Don't try", Dick said, "Just go back to your family and live, it is a nice life there. Be happy."

Richard took her hand and put some twenty dollar bills in it and folded her hand around it. She smiled, then kissed him on the cheek before turning and boarding the plane.

Richard, really feeling good about what he had done, turned and walked out to his car to go home. The day had been an odd sort of experience. He never gave the young gang members, if that is what they were, a second thought. Those kinds of people were no good to Society as far as he was concerned.

As he was driving back the way he had come, his thoughts were on the day's happenings and the beauty of the girl had been very appealing. Several times the thought of getting a motel room had entered his mind, but she would be obligated and he did not want that kind of situation. He knew enough about girls to know that a person never could be sure what they were thinking. She sure was a beauty though, and he could still picture those breasts. He sure was glad that he had kept that extra money in his wallet and that she was now on her way home and away from those guys.

Night had fallen and he was at the upper end of the speed limit alone on the highway. It was a long stretch of open road through what was to be a designated forest preserve. As he sped around a long curve, two Deer suddenly appeared coming onto the road from his right. He hesitated, trying to figure which way to go to avoid hitting them, then swerved to his right to go behind them as they came onto the road.

A third deer appeared in front of the car, bounced over the hood, and crashed through the windshield into the car. The car left the road and crashed head on into a large tree at the side of the road. The movements of the deer in the car could be heard for a while, then quiet.

The soul of Richard knew that the physical body was badly damaged. The breathing had been stopped by the way the steering wheel had been pressed back against Richards chest and now the heart that pumped the life giving blood was stopping also. The willing and controlling power of Li Chan, as strong as it was, could not maintain life in the body it occupied, so slowly and somewhat reluctantly it was forced to leave the physical being it had really enjoyed for so long.

As Li Chan hovered above and watched, another car appeared and seeing the headlights of Richards's car off of the road, slowed down and finally stopped a few yards away from the wreck. A man stepped out and walked back to the crash site. After a quick look at Richard, he ran back to his car and sped away at a high speed, evidently to get help.

The Soul of Li Chan knew that help could not do anything so she let herself drift off into wherever. Maybe she could go look at those two rooms in Tanga again; again came the memory of Chen Li.

Li Chan's Soul drifted for an unknown time. Her memories were intact and she was reviewing them and enjoying the thoughts that came with them as she drifted. She was in no particular hurry and was wondering if she could come across another physical body she could enter and save. She was unaware now of where she was so she would have to drift lower and see if she could recognize any of the terrain. Then maybe she could control the drift a little and go toward the Islands of Tanga, she still had the memories of Chen Li.

THE CRASH

The twin engine shuttle plane was about halfway between the two large cities that it shuttled back and forth between carrying passengers. The Captain had noticed a change in engine temperature and was watching anxiously to see what would come of it when it suddenly started smoking. He pulled the engine fire handle and cut the engine power switches. He knew that by now the passengers had noticed the smoke and would be apprehensive. He reached for the communication switch and switched to the intercom that went to the passenger compartment and said. "This is the Captain speaking, do not be alarmed. We have had to shut down one engine, but this aircraft is capable of flying on one engine safely, so please follow the instructions of the hostess, stay in your seats and fasten your seat belts."

The aircraft was not as heavy as it normally was. Only about half of the seats were filled and there had not been a lot of luggage The Captain knew that the one engine left operating could maintain the present altitude.

As the pilot glanced again at the No.1 engine, he was surprised to see a small stream of white smoke trailing behind it, then suddenly a burst of flame. He immediately slowed the No.2 engine and headed for the ground. The Co-pilot reached down and turned off the valve that controlled the flow of gasoline to the No. 1 engine to stop the fuel that evidently was burning. They had to land the aircraft before it was too late.

They had been flying at the eight thousand foot level and they quickly dropped to the two thousand foot level where the pilot could pick out a good enough landing area. The captain picked out a long field that looked good enough and lowered the landing gear as they approached a spot over the area he had selected. Unknown to him, the flames had stopped shooting out the rear of the engine nacelle of the No. 1 engine. The fuel shutoff valve had stopped the flow of the gasoline. He had been concentrating on the landing spot and making a safe landing and had not noticed. He was committed now to keeping the aircraft safe. He cut power to the aircraft to stop fires if there was a crash and waited for the craft to come to a stop.

Unknown to him there was a ravine ahead; it had not been visible from the air. It was about four feet deep and had large rocks covered with green underbrush. The aircraft, traveling at only a little less than flying speed dropped into the ravine and hit the rocks tearing the nose and cockpit area before coming to a halt. The nose wheel had collapsed and the nose section had been pushed back into the cockpit area, shattering the windshield and side windows.

Both the pilot and Co-pilot were in a twisted mass of metal, control column, glass and instruments. There was smoke and dust, but no fire as yet. The tail section and fuselage was pointing up out of the ravine at a high angle. Screams and shouts were coming out of the passenger area. An escape door was thrown open and people were starting to drop out. It was a short fall to the ground and finally someone pried open the main entrance door and jumped to the ground. One young man ran toward the front of the plane to see if he could help the pilots get out of their seats.

It happened that at about this time the Soul of Li Chan was drifting above and became aware of the plane crash below. She drifted lower and saw the young man running toward the front of the aircraft.

The area above the Captains seat was open and as the young man came up he saw the Captain. Li Chan dropped beside the captain's body and, not sensing any movement, slipped inside the body and took over control. In an instant she grasped the situation and as the young man rushed up, she willed the body to move a little. When the young man saw the movement he turned and shouted to the other people from the plane. A few minutes later the Captain lay stretched out on the ground away from the plane. He was still alive but was losing blood and there seemed to be no way to stop the flow. Li Chan had absorbed the knowledge of the Captain's brain and memory banks and knew all about him and his abilities and his life.

The young man and the people that had removed the captain now tried to get the co-pilot out of his seat. A quick check told them that it would do no good. The co-pilot's body was so badly crushed that there was now no life to save. They did finally get the metal out of the way, remove the body, and cover it with a blanket.

After a check of passengers it was found there was one person still in the aircraft. Two of the men that had helped with the pilots went back inside the aircraft and found a young man had been thrown forward in the crash and was beneath some of the seats that had broken loose in the crash. Together they carried him out and lay him on the ground. He was still breathing and they felt a heartbeat, but there was no way they could tell if he was damaged inside.

Li Chan, now the soul of the captain, knew that the captain was dying and when the time was near she slipped out of his body and hovered above watching.

When they brought the young man out of the plane and put him on the ground. She sensed that he was still alive, but he was not moving, so she dropped down and sensing no opposition, slipped inside the young man's body. Entering the brain and absorbing the knowledge there she knew that the body had not been hurt very badly and that he would be alright. She immediately took over control and was ready to be the Soul of a new body. Now there was really nothing to do. The young man, whose name was Ralph Nelson, had received a hard bump on the head when he was thrown forward in the crash. He was just unconscious and would only suffer a headache when he woke up. The memories of the Captain, whose name was Douglas Wetherby, Li Chan put aside for a while so she could concentrate on the present and take care of the young man. As she reviewed his memory banks she discovered that he was a lead guitarist in a small band. He was on his way to meet them in the next town for a show this night.

The Captain had been too busy trying to get the aircraft to the ground when the fire broke out to call in an emergency; the co-pilot had managed to call in a "Mayday" just before the crash, so that there would be someone on the way by now. In all probability there was a helicopter on the way and the crash site was not that far away. The chopper should arrive within minutes and would have medical personnel on board.

A few minutes later the chopper settled to the ground and the medical people jumped out and checked the two pilots to see if there was a chance of saving them, but to no avail. They then proceeded to check all the passengers. They found a lot of little cuts and bruises and a broken arm but nothing more serious. The young man, Ralph Nelson, was soon conscious and felt a pretty bad headache which the nurse said would last a while but was not permanent.

A bus soon arrived and all but the two pilots were taken on to the airport. The helicopter took the two pilots to the hospital.

The Soul of Li Chan was more or less just amused at the things that she had learned from the brain and memory banks of the young man she had taken over. He was a twenty one year old High school graduate, high in intelligence and a very good athlete, excelling in basketball. He had learned to play the guitar during his high school years from an instructor his parents knew.

A few months ago he had joined a small local group of musicians that had advertised for a lead guitarist in the local paper. They were playing at local clubs, bars, and parties. Their next gig was a private party tonight. Li Chan, now Ralph Nelson, did not know for sure if he would feel like playing at a party, which he knew from past experience would be noisy, but he would show up and see how he felt at the time.

The passengers had to wait nearly two hours for their luggage to get to the airport. One of the band members was waiting there for the plane to land and he was still waiting when Ralph arrived. After the luggage wait they were finally on their way to the motel room they had reserved for Ralph to stay the night after the party.

Ralph's friend, Henry Waring, said to Ralph. "John and his wife want us all to meet at their place before the gig for a chat. We've got about an hour before we go. Do you want to get a sandwich or snack first?" Ralph answered, "No Henry, that medicine the nurse gave me should stop the headache before long, I just want to lie down for a while and then I'll take a cab over to their place. You go ahead, I'll see you there." Henry left and Ralph stretched out on the bed and relaxed after locking the door.

Two hours later the phone rang and woke Ralph out of a sound sleep. It was Henry wondering if anything was wrong. Ralph answered. "No, I'm ok, just dozed off for a while, I feel much better now. See you shortly" and he hung up.

After a shower and some clean clothes, Ralph uncased the guitar and checked it over and ran through a few of the notes to check the tuning before he put it back in the case. He called a taxi service and waited.

About a half hour later he knocked on the door of John's apartment. John's wife opened the door and motioned him in. He noticed that the other band members were there and nodded to them as he entered. There were lots of questions about the crash and was he hurt and he shrugged them off and told them he was feeling sorry for the families of the two pilots. They all gathered in the living room to talk about the crash and the coming party.

Ralph was always the quiet one and usually went along with whatever the rest of the band wanted. Some of the band members were now drinking beer but Ralph had taken a well known soft drink and was enjoying the moments, thankful to still be alive. The gang had noticed a change in Ralph and had figured it was from the crash.

The drummer for the little band was a young man twenty-five years old and a little overweight, his name was John Cameron, his wife Lucy was sometimes the singer for the band. The little bass guitar players name was Angelo Vincenti. The last man was a man from the hills and he had brought along his Banjo, his name was Seth Parkins.

When the drinks were about gone, John disappeared into another room. When he came out he cleared off the low table in the center of the room. Ralph wondered what now, as he watched John take out a little packet of white powder and lay some straws on the table. He then put the white powder in little strips a couple of inches long on the table. Then he stood up and looked at the other band members and said. "This stuff will make us feel good at the party tonight, come on now, you know what to do." Angelo was first to take a straw and suck up a string through the short straw into his nose. Then Seth took a straw and did the same. Lucy said. "I need this stuff to get up there on the stage and sing to the crowd." as she snorted a string. John looked at Henry and Ralph then took a straw and inhaled a string of the stuff.

When he stood up he looked at Ralph and Henry and said. "Ok you guys, you're next, get with it, we've got to go in a few minutes." "Not me," Ralph said. "I'm not putting any of that sh—t in my body, it is the only one I've got and I'm going to take care of it, how about you Henry?" "I'm with you Ralph, none of that stuff for me, I've got better sense". Henry said.

"Are you saying I don't have good sense"? John bellowed as he turned to Henry. Ralph stood up and stepped between them and said "If you think taking that stuff is showing good sense, you sure don't".

Ralph was thinking to himself, why am I doing this? All the time I have been with this group, I have never stood up to John for anything. I have always said "Ok, I'll do it." Why now do I stand up and confront him? Why am I not afraid of him now? The only thing different is the plane crash. Now that I think about it, I do feel different since the crash, what happened to make me feel this way?

"You both are going to take some of this stuff if I have to pour it in your mouth." John said as he reached for Ralph. A second later he felt a hard punch in the stomach that doubled him over and before he could take another breath he felt a hard blow to the side of his head as Ralph's foot came around and hit its target. He fell backward across a chair and rolled to the floor, nearly unconscious. The others sat there stunned while Ralph said to Henry. "Come on Henry; let's get out of this dope hole." Henry got up, grabbed his Violin as Ralph picked up his guitar and they both walked out to Henry's car and left.

As they were leaving, Henry said. "Boy, for a quiet guy, when you move, you really do it fast." "I've wanted to do that for a long time. I guess I just got tired of waiting." Ralph replied, then added. "How long have they been on that stuff? I kind of suspected they were using something but I wasn't sure till today. I wonder what made him think we would go along and become users."

Ralph was thinking, I wonder where and when I learned to fight like that. It just came to me and I reacted instantly. Other thoughts came to him and he thought he had better start getting some exercise and tune up his muscles. His punches had not been as hard as they should have been and his legs hurt a little.

Li Chan was in control of Ralph's brain, but the healthy brain of the normal Ralph was doing its job and remembering the current and everyday things to do under the steady willing and controlling of the Soul which now had the memories of a few other people other than him. If occasions arose that were above the regular daily routines, then Li Chan's Soul would quickly move her memories into the forefront and take control of what action was required.

Now she was willing him to think of what was to be done now. Both were surely out of a job, so they would have to figure out the next move. They were both free to do as they wished. Neither had a steady girlfriend, or family ties that would prevent them from going anywhere they chose. Ralph had often dreamed of the north woods and thought that someday he would go there. He liked the out of doors and spent as much time as he could hiking in the local wooded area near where he and his parents lived. It appeared that now was as good a time as any to take the leap and go there and see how it was. They both had save a little money and he turned to Henry and said. "Hank, how would you like to take a trip to the north somewhere and find a job? I would kind of like to see those tall trees and some thick wooded mountains?" "Sounds good to me Ralph, now is as good a time as any. Spring is coming and we'll have the whole summer to see if we like it." Henry said. "So let's go." He added.

They spent the next few days storing some of the things they did not want to take with them and closing out some of their accounts. They did not buy any new clothes as they wanted to see what they would need and they would not find that out till they were there. They just put their essentials in luggage and as Henry's car was a station wagon they had plenty of room. They could even sleep in it if they so desired or if the occasion called for it. They finally said their goodbyes and hit the road headed northwest. Of course they took their instruments with them. They were planning on playing in some night spots as they went to earn some traveling money.

The first two days were spent in traveling. Near the end of the second day they began to see hills and higher hills in the distance. They had not tried to find any place to play their instruments as they were enjoying the sights and the freedom.

The second night they stayed at a smaller motel that had a restaurant at one end. They stopped early and relaxed at the evening meal.

As they sat there looking around they discovered that there was a raised platform at one end of the dining area. It seems they were in luck if that was where a small band played occasionally.

As they sat down at a corner table, a young girl appeared from what was evidently the kitchen and walked toward them with a small pad in her hands.

"Can I help you?" she asked as she came to the table.

"Why, yes," Ralph answered, "We would like dinner, do you have a menu or is that it on the wall by the door?"

"Well, that is it by the door, it is what we have prepared and it is very good and is ready to serve. If you would like something else it will take longer to prepare" she replied.

The sign by the door listed;

Meat loaf, with mashed Potatoes, gravy, with side dishes.
Beef noodles with side dishes.
Side dishes were: French fries
Coleslaw
Applesauce

They both ordered the ready prepared dinners and sat looking around as the waitress left and prepared their orders. They were both curious about the raised floor at the end of the dining room, but they wanted to eat first.

The food was country style and well done and seasoned just right. They both were hungry and did not talk much during the meal. The waitress stopped by to see if they needed anything else. They had both ordered coffee and she kept the cups full.

As they sat there talking about how good the meal had been and sipping the coffee, the waitress came and took away the empty plates and dishes. When she came back with the coffee pot to keep their cups full, Ralph asked her:

"Have you got time to answer a couple of questions for us?

"Sure have," she said, "Ask away"

"Do you have any empty rooms, we would like to stay a couple of days and rest up?" Ralph asked.

"They are all empty, take your pick" she told him. "Next question?"

"Is that raised floor over there for the use of a small band?" Ralph asked.

"Why yes", she answered, "We have music on Friday and Saturday nights for three or four hours, depending on the size of the crowd. It varies according to the weather and seasons. Sometimes it gets crowded in here and sometimes there are only the local people, within a mile or so."

"Thank you very much; we'll take the first room, where do I sign in?" Ralph said.

"Follow me, I'll sign you in." and she led him to a small office just outside the door of the restaurant under an overhanging roof.

They had parked the station wagon right in front of the No. 1 motel room, so they just took their stuff into the motel and relaxed.

"I didn't ask about the band because I figured we could wait till Friday night and find out for ourselves." Ralph said as they sat down to rest and talk.

"This is already Wednesday and we can look the country over tomorrow, I "d like to walk out into these woods, I love the outdoors." Henry told him.

Henry discovered a radio on the chest of drawers and turned it on, finding a station that they liked was a problem but he finally found one they could listen to and they both fell back on the beds and relaxed.

The next morning, after they had showered and put on a change of clothes, they walked into the restaurant for breakfast. There was a new girl waiting on tables, and to their surprise nearly half the tables were filled. They picked a corner table and sat down.

The waitress soon came and handed them a breakfast menu, then left. It was a few minutes before she returned for their orders. They both picked the No. 2 which was eggs, home fries, toast and coffee.

While they were waiting, they noticed that several people were looking them over. They figured that it was because they were from out of the area. Most of the looks were curious, but there were a few that were antagonistic and Ralph wondered why. He thought "Oh well, we will find out sooner or later". He supposed it had something to do with some of the dark looks he had seen between some of the other customers

They were both hungry and were quiet till after the meal was consumed and they were enjoying the coffee when the waitress from the night before approached them and sat down in one of the empty chairs at their table.

"Well, "she asked, "How did you sleep, you both looked pretty tired when you left. Hello, my name is Virginia, I am the owner's daughter and I want to thank you for stopping here"

She was looking and talking to Henry, with an occasional glance at Ralph so Henry answered,

"Hello Virginia, I am Henry Warring and this is my good friend Ralph Nelson. We are traveling thru, but we are taking our time doing it. We wanted to see some of these mountains so we thought we could start here. It is so beautiful."

"Well you couldn't have picked a better place. I love it here." She said.

"We would like to do a little hiking today if we could," Henry told her, then asked, "is that logging road down the road a piece ok to hike on?, we saw it when we came by."

"That would be ok, we own that property, I've walked back that road a lot and it is very pretty and has some very large trees that they left." she told him.

About that time the on-duty waitress approached and Virginia said, "Karen, I want you to meet these two travelers. This tall dark haired one is Ralph Nelson and this handsome one is Henry Warring. They stopped over to look over the sights for a few days. Boys this is my best friend Karen Williams, the best waitress west of the Mississippi."

"Good, it is a pleasure to see some new blood around here for a change." Karen said as she turned back to her work.

"Well, I'd better get into the kitchen and to the business at hand, see you guys later for dinner I hope." Virginia said as she got up and turned toward the kitchen.

Henry and Ralph finished their coffee, leisurely and talked about the food and then the girls. Henry kept looking toward the kitchen where Virginia was and Ralph saw it was with a little more than casual interest too. He kept saying, "Boy, she sure is pretty." and Ralph would answer, "You got that right."

Karen came with the check and Ralph gave her a large bill and she went to the cash register and brought back his change. He put a tip on the table and they returned to the cabin.

"Let's take a little hike down to the logging road and go into the woods. I need the exercise and I would like to see some of those big trees closer ". Henry said as he put on some boots that was worn and comfortable. "Good," Ralph said, "I am with you on that exercise bit, I've been neglecting it lately."

As it was still early in the spring, the air was a bit chilly and they both picked out a light jacket for the walk and they left the cabin and headed down the road they had came in on. When they came to the opening that was the entrance to the logging road they turned in and were a little surprised at the way the road had grown over. There was not much to block walking for the last years growth had died and was flattened by the snows of winter. The new spring growth was just starting and made the walking very easy for them.

There were a lot of tall stately trees that were unmistakably of the pine variety and the limbs extended out over the narrow road which was then covered with the dead needles that were continually dropping.

Under the big trees there was very little underbrush and visibility was really good and they could see for quite a good distance. It was very quiet and as they walked they became aware of the stillness and did not talk, and when they did it was barely a whisper. It seemed like a different world; they were enjoying it.

They walked slowly, enjoying the quiet stillness of the woods and noticed that there was no movement what so ever. They saw no movement of birds or animals and wondered about that.

Ralph had always loved the woods and knew that it was because they were new and strangers to the area and that the things that lived in the woods had seen them coming and had hidden until they were sure that the strangers meant them no harm before they would show themselves, and even then they would be cautious. Their lives depended on that cautiousness.

Occasionally they saw huge stumps where some tall pines had been cut down, probably to build the houses in the area. They were scattered, indicating to the men that they did not want to clear any area of the tall trees, and preserve the beauty of the area.

When they had walked for what they figured was about half a mile or so, they stopped and sat down on one of the huge stumps to sit and talk. Henry said,

"Boy, this is some country. I've never seen anything so big before, those trees are over a hundred feet tall and so big around."

"More like a hundred and fifty," Ralph said, "and it took a lot of work to saw it down and drag it out of here to the sawmill."

"Look up ahead, Hank, ", Ralph added, "It looks like there is a lot of underbrush close to the ground. The trees are not so thick there and the sun has gotten through and caused the underbrush to grow. Next time we come this way we'll check it out. I am getting a little tired for now and I'm getting hungry again. It is a long walk back and we'd better turn around now."

"Ok" Hank said, and they started back the way they had come. The little road was easy walking and they headed back toward the main road.

When they neared the restaurant they noticed that there were a few cars parked outside. It was about noon now and they figured that people were stopping in for a sandwich and a cup of coffee. As they walked in and looked for a table they were surprised at the number of people sitting around having coffee and talking.

Virginia was sitting at a small table with a young man about their age. They found a table in a corner away from the gathering, which seemed to be having a meeting of some kind. Karen was waiting tables and was working with the group.

As they sat down at the table, Virginia got up and came toward them, and sat down at the table with them.

"Did you guys have a good walk?" she asked as she sat down and looked at Henry, smiling.

"We sure did," Henry told her. "That is the biggest bunch of trees I have ever seen. It was beautiful back in there"

Ralph looked at her and asked, "We saw a couple of stumps that had been cut fairly recent. Like maybe a year ago, is somebody building around here?"

"Why yes", Virginia said "Mister. Reynolds, from a little town a few miles on up the road is going to build on a piece of land he bought at the edge of our little village when the wood was cheap enough. He did not have any trees of his own so dad sold him some of ours."

Karen came up to the table to take their order, and as she left, the young man who had been sitting with Virginia approached and took Virginia by the arm and said.

"You have talked long enough, come back and sit with me, I wasn't through talking to you."

Virginia tried to take her arm from the young man's grip, but he was strong and when he tried to pull her up out of the chair Ralph spoke up and said,

"Take your hands off of her and leave us alone."

The young man dropped both his hands to his side and said loudly "What did you say, little man."

Ralph stood up facing the stranger and replied "I said take your hands off of her and leave us alone, now get out of here and stay away from us. She has a right to talk to whomever she chooses."

"She is my girl and she will do as I tell her to do." the young man replied as he reached for Virginia "I do not want her talking to strangers."

The next thing he felt himself being lifted off of the floor and thrown onto the table next to theirs. He landed on the table and then crashed onto the floor. Surprised and stunned, he staggered to his feet and looked at Ralph. He tried to figure out what had happened. No one had done anything like that too him before. He was bigger than any of the men around the town and had been bullying his way to anything he wanted. He thought he was in love with Virginia and therefore she was his. Slightly mentally handicapped he usually got what he wanted. This was s surprise to him and he could not figure it out. He had worked hard around the lumbering and building that went on and he was very strong and solidly built.

Now he stood looking at Ralph, trying to figure out what to do. Suddenly he came at Ralph, arms outstretched and fast. Ralph grabbed one arm and pulled as he through his hips under the big body and lifted. The added momentum sent the huge body nearly two tables away and against the wall with a loud thud, scattering chairs and tables.

Ralph sat back down and sipped his coffee. Hank just looked at him with an odd grin on his face. Virginia's father came out of the kitchen and came to the table.

"I was watching the whole thing, that should have happened a long time ago, but most of the men around here could not handle him. He had us all scared to say anything" he said as he went to the man lying on the floor.

Virginia, still sitting in her chair at the table, had mixed emotions. She knew the big man but she did not feel anything other than friendship for him. She had tried to tell him many times that she did not want to be his girl friend, but he would not accept it that way. Because he thought he was in love with her, that she should be in love with him.

"I feel sorry for him, but if I go to him now he will take it wrong and think it is because I care for him. I will let dad handle it. He needed that to happen to make him think a little. He is a very slow thinker and it will take him a while to figure things out." She said, mostly to herself.

Mister Braddock went to the man on the floor that was nearly unconscious and helped him up and into a chair. His head had hit a table or something and his nose was bleeding. He looked toward Virginia, but she would not look at him.

The young man's name was Junior Hathaway. His parents lived about a quarter of a mile from the restaurant to the north and he was an only child and due to his condition had been spoiled all his life.

As Virginia's father led him into the kitchen, he glanced toward the table where Ralph sat talking with her and his friend. He had not said a word, even to mister Braddock.

Virginia's father must have treated him and then took him out the back door, for they did not see him the rest of the day. There was no way to tell if he was planning anything or just what he was thinking. He probably was still stunned at what had happened and didn't want to believe it

After a few minutes and the people in the group at the other end of the restaurant were sure that Junior had left and probably would not be back, one of the older men left his chair and came over to Ralph's table and sat down on the one empty chair. He introduced himself, to the two young men.

"Hello Gentlemen, "he said. "Let me introduce myself. My name is Jack Henderson, I own the big house a quarter mile north of here. I own a lot of property across the road and further west of here on that ridge. I wish to thank you for what you just did, although I saw it and still have no idea how you did it. That boy has been hard to control and has had his way around here for a long time. We have thought about ganging up on him to make him behave but we like his father and mother and did not wish to hurt them. The boy has a mental problem and no doctor has any idea what to do or just what is wrong." He turned his gaze to Virginia and continued. "We've felt sorry for the position he put you in, but we did not know what we could do to help."

"I know, Mister Henderson." Virginia said. "I have tried to tell him several times to leave me alone, but he kept saying that I could learn to like him if I tried. I was at my wit's end. I hated to see him hurt, but he has hurt a lot of people. Now that he has been hurt himself, maybe he will think a little and stop, but I am afraid he will try to get even with Ralph." Turning to Ralph she said. "You be careful and watch behind you, he will probably try to approach you and want to fight or try to get in the first punch, he is very strong and has broken some bones in the other boys that he fought."

Jack Henderson turned to the two young men at the table and said "Are you young men staying around for a while or are you moving on?'

"We would like to stay around if we can. We are both musicians and would like to play some evening if there is someone to listen, and we would like some work if there is anything we could do to earn some money. We have enough for a short while, but it will run out eventually." Ralph told him.

"Well that sounds good, we have a small group here that play on the stage over there sometimes on week ends, maybe you could join them this weekend. We'll wait and see. I think you can find work too, soon. Some of the land owners are talking about clearing some land of the trees to do a little farming and they will need men. It is hard work but good for the soul, if you know what I mean. I'll pass the word to the other land owners". He stood up and went back to the group

Henry was talking to Virginia quietly and Ralph now heard him say;

"Virginia, I am sorry that we have brought this on for you. We did not mean to cause any trouble for anyone. Do you think he will blame you or cause you trouble?"

Virginia answered. "He may, I have no way of knowing what he will do, he is very unpredictable. He has been in control for so long, and with his simple mind, it is anybodies guess as to who he will blame or what he may try to do. He will confront you again, only he will be more careful next time. He will try to get hold of you and squeeze you to break your ribs or maybe just come at you from the front and try to box with you, He thinks he is a good boxer, and has hurt several of the boys and men around here pretty bad."

She was looking at Ralph as she was talking.

"You made him look like a fool and he will surely watch for a chance to catch you off guard, so you keep your eyes alert. I don't think he will resort to a weapon yet, he thinks he can't be beat in a man to man fight."

"Is there a lawman in this district, close?" Ralph asked.

"Yes." Virginia answered. "I'll have Dad call him and explain what is going on. He won't want to come alone. I think he is afraid of Junior, so he will bring some help, in case it is needed."

The Sheriff came the next afternoon. Ralph and Henry were in the back yard at the restaurant splitting wood for the restaurant furnace. They followed the sheriff and the two deputies he had brought with him into the restaurant and they all sat down at one of the larger tables.

Mr. Braddock came to the table and introduced the two boys to the sheriff and his men then sat down to tell them what had transpired. He had been watching nearly from the start and knew the whole story.

When her father was finished, Virginia, who had been sitting at the next table, came over and pulled up a chair and looking at the sheriff, said;

"Sheriff, I have been hoping you would show up. Junior has been taking over control of my life and I haven't been able to keep away from him. He has been getting more and more demanding and I was getting really scared. I could not do anything with out getting his permission. I could not go anywhere without him following along. When these two strangers came in, I had to come over to their table to take their order. When they started asking questions I sat down in a chair to answer them. That is when Junior came over and the trouble started.

"Is that when you interfered and stood up for Virginia?" The Sheriff asked Ralph.

"Yes," Ralph answered. "When he grabbed her arm and tried to take her back to the table he had been sitting at, I told him to leave her alone, she could talk to anyone she chose."

"When he came at me, I used my hip to throw him over the next table. He stood for a minute or two to figure out what had happened, then came at me again, fast. I grabbed him and pulled and used my hips again to throw him farther that time and he slammed onto the wall and some tables. That time he lay there till Virginia's father came and helped him up and out. I haven't seen him since." Ralph finished.

The Sheriff looked at Ralph and asked, "Do you think he will leave you alone now?"

"No, he thinks I haven't been fighting fair and he will try to come at me face-to-face" Ralph answered, "He knows now not to rush at me, it seems to give me an advantage. He will want to box, where he can use his fists."

The Sheriff asked Ralph, Can you use your fists."

"Yes," Ralph told him, "but not as a boxer. I don't know how to box, fists are used a little in an ancient type of Marshall Arts that I am familiar with. There are several ways to put down an opponent, some will render them unconscious and others will kill them instantly. I will have to be very careful, but I can not be sure, it is a very fast procedure."

The Sheriff looked carefully at Ralph and sat a while thinking as he sipped his coffee.

Finally the Sheriff looked at Ralph and said, "Well you will have to protect yourself, Junior will probably try to kill you. He has nearly killed a couple of the young men around here. We will be around for a day or two and will be watching."

It was nearing the dinner hour and Ralph and Henry were getting hungry so they excused themselves and went to the motel room to freshen up. When they reappeared they went over near the raised platform to find a table. It was Friday evening and they were expecting a little music and maybe a chance to play a little music themselves.

As they sat down and looked around, Ralph noticed a blanket covered object at the back of the stage that looked like it might be a piano.

When Karen came to their table to take their order, Ralph asked her,

"Karen is that a piano over there under that blanket?"

"Yes," Karen answered, "I don't remember just where it came from, no one here can play one so it is just there"

As Karen walked away, Ralph got up and walked over to the stage and uncovered the Piano. Dust filled the air for a while as he folded the blanket and pulled out the bench and wiped off the dust. He sat down on the bench and slowly raised the lid that covered the keys. He was half afraid to touch the keys, but his memory was bringing it all back to him as he sat there.

Henry was watching him as he was doing all the dusting and studying the old upright piano. As far as Henry knew, his friend had never had any interest in a piano. He had noticed a change in Ralph since leaving the old group back in the city. And he wondered now at more change.

Henry watched and wondered when his friend sat down on the bench and put his hands on the keys and started to make the soft sounds as he ran his fingers up and then down the keyboard listening to each note. Then he sat back and looked at the keyboard a few minutes.

Ralph was confused. He did not understand how he knew what he was doing, but it was coming to him now, but slowly as he kept trying to think where he had learned the piano playing. The name Robert kept coming to him and was mixed up with a girl named Jessica" He tried to concentrate on the piano playing and separate the names and soon he remembered the songs and the titles and how to play them.

Henry listened with amazement as his friend put his hands back on the keyboard and started playing some of the old songs that were still favorites. He played softly and other people sitting at some of the tables turned and listened as the soft music found its way around the open area and into the kitchen.

Some of the people at the other end of the large room picked up their coffee and brought it with then as they moved closer to the stage. Suddenly, Mr. Braddock came out of the kitchen and slowly walked toward the stage, he looked shocked as he approached the source of the music.

No one was talking, the only sound was the soft notes of an off-key piano, but no one noticed, the music was so pleasant sounding.

Virginia had been left alone in the kitchen and finally she came out to get Karen to help fill the orders and get them to the people. She stopped, surprised to see who was at the piano and making such soft music. She finally took Karen back into the kitchen and started filling the dinner orders and taking them to the tables. She brought Ralph's order out last, then walked over to the piano and tapped him on the shoulder and said "Hey Maestro, your dinner is served. You can play for us later."

Ralph was startled and sheepishly got up and went to his table and sat down, saying,

"Oh, I am sorry; I was engrossed and trying to remember some old songs to play".

Henry had been watching him all this time with a look that was both surprise and wonder. He had known his friend for a long time, since school as a matter of fact and he had never in all that time ever showed any signs of knowing how to play a piano. Now, how in the world did he ever learn how to play, and so beautifully too? It must be that he was one of those children born with special genius knowledge of music. He certainly could play a guitar. But a piano? He wondered.

"Don't ask me". Ralph said as he looked at his friend Henry after he had seen the look on his face and interpreted it correctly. "I am trying to figure it out myself. Lets eat, I'll tell you about it later, I really enjoyed playing that old piano. It needs tuning though."

No one else in the room had said anything. The two boys were new and they were waiting to find out more about them before judging them.

There were now people at all the tables around them as they ate. Mr. Braddock came over to the table next to them and sat down with an elderly man and his wife. Ralph heard the other man say to him;

"Well Harry, Are you ready to sell me this place and move back to town yet?"

Harry Braddock sat for a while then looked over at his friend and said

"I've talked it over with Martha and we are considering it, that's a lot of money, and we are not making a lot with this business". He said and then added "We like it here though and Virginia likes it, her friends are here and she loves the country."

"Young people can always find new friends and I am anxious to call a lumber company in to take out some of these big trees for lumber and I'd like to take some off this property at the same time." Jack Henderson told him. "Just sell me the acreage and keep the business he added, "It won't take much off the money I'll pay you."

"That might work out, with the money Martha and I could take a vacation and see the world, then come back and run the business" Harry answered, but he did not sound too anxious or enthusiastic. "We'll think on it, Jack."

Harry Braddock excused himself, got up and returned to the kitchen.

Ralph Nelson, sitting at the next table wondered why it sounded to him as if Henderson was pushing a little hard. If he was Harry's friend why didn't he sound a little more like it?

"Oh well" he thought. "Not my problem"

The next morning as Ralph and Henry were eating breakfast, Ralph said.

"Hank, why don't we take another walk down the logging road? I'd like another look at those big trees. I'll take my camera along and we can take some pictures. The folks back home might like to see where we are spending our time."

"Good." Hank said, "I love the woods and this is certainly a beautiful area."

After they had eaten they returned to the room and put on light jackets. Ralph got his camera and they started out on their hike into the woods. They had seen no sight of the bullyboy, Junior, but they were keeping alert, just in case. Hank was thankful for Ralph being with him. Junior looked awful big to him.

It being early spring, the air was fresh and just a little chilly as they headed into the wooded area. The new grasses were starting to show and here and there were greener sprouts that indicated a possible flower, like the early spring beauties in the eastern woods back home. Some of the earlier flowering shrubs and smaller trees were already starting to show the start of leaves and the lower visibility was beginning to cut off the distance you could see ahead. The huge evergreens were really something to see, standing so tall and stately. A few had been taken down and used for lumber, but they had been selected so that they were not so thick in any one spot and it was not noticeable. Now and then they could catch a glimpse of a squirrel, high up in one of the trees ahead, but it would be gone in a few seconds when it caught a glimpse of them coming toward it.

The two young men did not have any way of knowing where the property lines were and so they did not know whose property they were on. Virginia had told them about a half of mile from the road was where her father's property ended. It didn't really matter; there would not be a problem if they did wander onto some other person's property.

They noticed they were nearing an open area where none of the huge pines were growing and there was a lot of underbrush over a fairly large area on the left side of the logging road. They decided to investigate and check it out to see what was out there and what had caused the brushy area and stopped the tall pines from growing.

As they started out into the low brushy area Henry spoke;

"There are no big trees out here at all. There must be something in the ground that won't let them grow in this area."

Soon the ground became clear of trees and brush and was just a form of rough grass and weeds. They stopped and looked ahead. The ground had become softer as they walked and now it was mushy and was turning black. Ralph muttered, "What in the world would cause this kind of thing to happen? It must be some kind of chemical. It is not rocky or clay."

Henry had walked on ahead of Ralph and was studying the ground intently. He turned and said, "Look here old buddy," and he pointed to the ground. There was a small pool of some kind of black liquid and the ground around it was soft and mushy. Ralph stood beside him looking down at the black stuff and said "OIL".

The ground ahead was even blacker and barren with spots of liquid and soggy looking dirt over a large area. Henry was busy checking the wet spot and touching it and smelling it. Looking at Ralph he said "My dad told me about places like this, but I've never seen one before. He works for a company that drills Oil wells and he knows a lot about them. I think I'll call him tonight and tell him about this and see what he says. Let's not tell anyone about this until we know for sure. If I am right there is a lot of oil under us and Mr. Braddock is sitting on a gold mine and don't know it."

"So I bet that the reason for Henderson wanting to buy this property is that he already knows about this and will not tell his friend Harry" Ralph said, then added "Some friend".

The area was relatively level and surrounded by thick forest and an unlikely place to get into by just taking a walk. Surrounded by thick brush on the ground it would be unlikely any one would walk into it. They walked back to the logging road and headed back toward the main road and the motel.

As they approached the motel Ralph became alert and was watching for any sign of Junior. He knew in his heart that the young man was planning something and he wanted to be ready. As they were approaching their cabin Junior appeared coming from behind the building, directly toward Ralph.

"I've got you now, little man" he practically yelled as he closed with Ralph.

Henry jumped away from his friend to give him room to move. It was a good move for Ralph spun around and drove his right foot into the stomach of Junior as he came toward him. Junior doubled over and suddenly was hit in the face by the left foot of Ralph's hard enough to break the nose bone and send Junior up and backward to the ground.

Suddenly there were people around them and the sheriff was looking down at Junior.

"Junior, I was watching from the restaurant and I saw you start this fight." He said, "But the next time you start something, my deputies and I will haul you off to jail."

He turned and went back into the restaurant and sat down where he could see the area.

The other people had followed the sheriff back into the restaurant, but were sitting so they could see where Junior lay.

Ralph and Henry went into the cabin and left their jackets then entered the restaurant to get lunch.

No one stayed to help Junior.

Ralph knew that he had not seen the last of Junior.

Junior lay where he had fallen, nearly unconscious, trying to get his breath back. The pain from his broken nose was not registering as yet. He was concentrating on breathing again. It had all happened so fast he was still trying to comprehend what had happened. One moment he was aiming his fist at Ralph, The next he was hurting something awful and he felt like his nose was broken and he could not breathe right. He was lying on the ground and people were standing around looking at him. Then he heard some talking before the people left and went into the restaurant.

He straightened his body a little more comfortable and rolled onto his stomach then he managed to move to a sitting position. His nose was bleeding and he reached and pulled a huge bandana from his hip pocket and held it to his bleeding nose. He was breathing better now but his stomach was still hurting.

He looked toward the restaurant, trying to see Virginia, but she was no where in sight. He could see some faces, but did not recognize anyone through the reflective glass. He started to get up then, slowly and carefully. He turned and started toward his parents' house on the edge of town, walking slowly and his mouth was moving as though he were talking. He was thinking and talking at the same time.

"I'll kill that stranger," he muttered. "I don't know what he did but I hurt something awful and I'll get even, only this time I won't get near him, and give him a chance to do something. I'll get my shotgun and sneak up to where I can get a clear shot and blow him in two".

Junior's parents did not know what had happened so they just waited to see what he wanted them to do. They were as scared of him as the townspeople. His mother got a damp washcloth and went to him to clean his face off and try to stop the bleeding. They did not talk and waited for him to say anything if he was going to talk at all. They had learned a long time ago that he had sort of a one track mind and way of thinking, so they kept quiet.

When the bleeding had stopped, he got up and went to his room to lie down and rest. His parents suspected that it was the stranger that he had fought before and received the first bloody nose. Maybe this time he would stay away and leave the stranger alone. No his mother thought he will look for revenge. He had never been beaten and he would not stop now. She wondered what he would think of now to get even. She thought now of his favorite gun, a double barrel twelve gauge shotgun that he kept in his bedroom. I hope he don't use that, she thought as she listened for his movements.

In the restaurant, the sheriff was sitting where he could watch Junior and still have lunch. When Ralph and Henry came in he motioned them to chairs at his table. The two Deputies were together at another table close by. When they sat down, Karen came to the table and took their orders and left. The Sheriff looked at Ralph and said;

"It looked like you knew he was coming, did you? He asked.

"Not for sure, but I sensed it and was watching." Ralph answered.

"For a young man you move awfully quickly when you need to, I've never seen any one move that fast before and land their blows so accurately. You must have practiced a lot. You did not use your fists either." The sheriff said.

"I did not want to get that close with him." Ralph said. "The killing blows come when you get close and have to end it fast."

"What do you think he will do now?" the Sheriff asked Ralph.

"He will probably get a gun and try to shoot me from ambush. The good thing is that he will want me to know he's going to do it, so I will have a little warning". Ralph answered then added "I also think he may try to shoot Henry as well. He's the one that Virginia was talking to the most and seemed attracted to."

They watched as Junior got up and walked to his parents' house.

After they had all finished their lunches, the sheriff assigned each of his deputies to an advantageous spot and took a spot where he could watch Junior's house and relaxed with a cup of coffee.

As Ralph and Henry sat drinking their coffee, Mr. Braddock came to their table and sat down to talk.

"Ralph, are you going to play the piano again? It was sure great to hear that thing making music again. If you are going to be here for a while and will play it once in a while I will have it tuned. It was my mother's and I have been keeping it for old time's sake. It was sure good to hear it again. He said.

"I would like to play it some more. When does the guys that play here come in to play, maybe we could join them and make some good music." Ralph told him.

"Tonight is Saturday night, maybe they will come tonight and you can get together with them. I sure hope so. We need something to cheer us up." Harry said.

Karen came over to the table and said to Ralph,

"Ralph, they tell me you can play a mean piano, why don't you go play awhile so I can judge for myself."

"I'll just do that." Ralph said as he got up and headed toward the piano. He turned to Henry as he left and said, "Keep an eye out Hank; I'll be pretty much occupied."

Soon there were the soft sounds of music in the air and all talking stopped as the people relaxed and listened to the music that came from the old upright box at the back of the stage. As Ralph played one particular old song he happened to glance at Harry Braddock and caught the glistening sight of a tear in his eye.

He was enjoying the sounds and melodies and played for over an hour before he stopped for another cup of coffee. Karen brought it and sat down at a separate table with him.

"That was wonderful Ralph, you must have been playing for a long time to be able to play like that," She said. "I thought you said you played the guitar, are you that good on the guitar too?"

"You'll have to judge that for yourself when you hear me play." Ralph told her.

Ralph really looked at Karen now and saw that she was actually a very pretty girl, the blue eyes went nicely with the dark blonde hair and she had a most enchanting smile that came easily for her. Beautiful, Ralph thought as he looked at her. The smile came as he looked at her and her eyes told him she was reading his mind and he blushed a deeper red and suddenly became interested in his coffee.

Virginia had sat down at the table with Henry and her dad as Ralph played. They were only a table away from Henry and Virginia. Ralph looked at Henry and said.

"Come on Hank we'd better go split a little wood. The weather is nice and we need the exercise."

The Sheriff said to them as they passed his table;

"You boys keep your eyes open," Then added, "the ones in the back of your head too."

They nodded as they went out the door and headed out behind their cabin toward the pile of wood.

The Sheriff turned to his two men and gave them some instruction. The both got up and took positions where they could see Junior's house and the street in front of it. Then the Sheriff went to a room in the back of the house where there was a window that he could see the area behind the cabins and the restaurant without being seen.

It wasn't long before the sound off splitting wood could be heard. Ralph and Henry both had axes and were hard at work. They would split for a while then would take a break and stack the stove ready wood in neat racks beside the restaurant. It was good exercise and they needed the muscle action for their own good.

Nearly two hours later one of the sheriff's men went to the sheriff and told him that a figure had crossed the road by Junior's house and went into the wooded area carrying something. A few minutes later the sheriff caught a glimpse of Junior ducking from tree to tree and working his way toward the two young men chopping wood. He was carrying his favorite shotgun and the sheriff was sure it was loaded.

Junior was sure no one knew he was in the area but he was very quiet and careful as he moved from tree to tree. Moving only when he thought they were looking the other way. When he was within less than two hundred feet of the two men, he checked the gun again, and then he stepped out and slowly walked toward the unsuspecting men raising the gun to a level position as he shouted;

"Now I'm going to kill the both of you,"

He had the gun pointed at Ralph and he pulled the trigger. When Ralph heard the word "now", he dove to the side and Junior's first shot missed him entirely.

Junior was flustered as he saw Ralph move as he pulled the trigger. Henry was still standing there and Junior moved the gun toward him as the sheriff shouted from the back of the restaurant;

"Drop the gun Junior"

As Junior's gun settled on Henry he shouted;

"Got you"

The sheriff shot an instant before Junior pulled the trigger and Junior tottered backward. The gun went off into the air and Junior fell to the ground, kicked a few times and was still, dead from the sheriff's bullet.

Henry was a little dazed. It had all happened so fast that he was still standing with the ax in his hand. He could still see that gun pointing at him and hearing the sound as it went off. The sheriff came out of the back of the restaurant and was walking toward him. Ralph said;

"Hank, you OK?"

"I, I guess so, that was close, wasn't it?" he stammered as he put down the axe and sat down on a large piece of wood.

"Did any of that first shot get you?" the sheriff asked Ralph.

"No, I'm OK lets go inside and sit down a while." Ralph answered.

The sheriff went to Junior and checked for a pulse, but there was none. He walked into the restaurant and sat down at the table. They had put two tables together to form a large table and all sat around it for conversation.

"That's too bad about Junior, but it was bound to happen sooner or later. His mind was not right and he was way too strong for his age. I'll call the county coroner after I talk to his parents. He'll come and pick him up." The sheriff said.

"I am awful sorry for all this trouble. We meant no trouble when we stopped here for the night." Ralph said. Then, "It is about dinner time so Henry, let's order some food. I am hungry"

After Karen took their order, they sat quietly, each thinking their own thoughts and enjoying the food. When Henry finally reached for his coffee he said,

"I was scared there for a while. Then I was sure glad when the sheriff shot, I had forgotten he was around. I should have known he would be watching for Junior to do something. He knew him a lot better than we did."

The Sheriff took Junior's body to his parents' house in one of the watching men's truck and carried it into the house of the crying parents. The father of the dead boy just looked at him and then said,

"I knew it would happen some day, but I did not expect it so soon. I could never control him and he was always making trouble for someone. Did you call the coroner?"

"Yes," the sheriff said. "He'll be out in the morning, early,"

There was more chatter and several people who had heard the shots came to see what the problem was. The restaurant was soon filled with people. Ralph and Henry wanted no part of the talk so they quietly left the restaurant and went to their room.

Henry finally got a chance to call his father and tell him about the oil seepage and ask him if he could come out to the place and have a look at it. He asked his father to keep it quiet until he could be sure of the situation. His father told him he would come out but it would be a few days before he could get the chance. The next day, being Sunday, a lot of the local people turned out at the little church in the center of the little village for services. Ralph and Henry stayed in their little room till the middle of the morning and then went to the restaurant for late breakfast. They did not want to be cause for conversation at the church.

The county coroner came early, just a little before eight and took the body of Junior and left.

People stayed in their houses till he had come and gone. Then the daily Sunday routine started and people followed their routines, there were a lot more of them it seemed to the Braddock's. The restaurant was busier than it had been in weeks.

After they had eaten they decided to go for another walk in the wooded area around the town. This time they crossed the road and entered the wooded area owned by Mister Henderson. They found a well traveled path that led into the large grove of tall pines that covered the hillside for what looked like miles. It was an awe inspiring sight as they entered the quiet and beautiful area beneath the huge trees. The sun was completely held out and the bed of brown needles on the ground was like walking on a blanket. As they walked they came across places that looked like someone had had a picnic. There was no mess, as such, just a bit of paper or piece of napkin along with some sign of disturbed pine needles. It looked like what it was, pure virgin forest.

Ralph had been thinking and he found a nice area of soft needles and sat down on them. Henry stretched out near him as Ralph said.

"If Mister Henderson is so anxious to get Braddock's land for the lumber, why hasn't he been?"

"If Mister Henderson wants to cut timber so bad, why doesn't he cut it from his own land? He has enough here to keep him busy for years."

Henry was thinking and now he spoke up and said;

"He knows about the oil and he is trying to buy up all the land or mineral rights to as much land as he can get before someone finds out about it. When dad gets here and looks it over we'll tell him just how good a friend old Henderson is. I wonder if he has bought any other land from unsuspecting people."

When they were ready to leave they followed a little path down the side of the ridge, just to see where it led. As they were about to turn toward the little village they came to a spring on the side of the hill that looked like it had been used for fresh water for a long time, so they stopped and took a drink of the fresh cool water. Then they headed back toward the village and dinner.

It was a little early for dinner when they reached the village so they just had a cup of coffee and sat and talked.

Mister Braddock came over to their table and joined them. Looking like he might be relaxed for a change. The problem with junior and his daughter must have kept him in a state of frustration and worry. He was smiling when he said.

"I hope the boys with the musical instruments will come over tonight. They were going to play last night but the happenings of yesterday did not promote a musical evening so they stayed away. By the way." he added. "The piano tuner will be out sometime this week. I hope you are sticking around for a little while longer."

He was looking at Ralph as he finished.

"I don't know." Henry said. "Our money is slowly disappearing, so if we don't find work soon, we'll have to leave."

"I'll pay you to split wood and stack it if that's what it takes to keep you here for a while longer. I want to hear some more of that piano playing before you leave." Harry Braddock said.

"Mister Braddock," Henry said. "Has Mister Henderson bought or tried to buy any other properties around here in the last year or six months that you know about?"

"Why yes." Braddock answered. "He bought the farm of a small beef rancher down in the foothills. The man just couldn't make ends meet so Henderson bought him out, cheap too. He made two of my other near neighbors an offer, but they refused. Why do you ask?"

"No specific reason, only why does he want your woods and property to cut lumber off of when he has those big woods across the road. That doesn't make any sort of sense to me." Henry answered, and then he added "It looks like he's trying to buy up all the land around here."

Harry Braddock got a serious look on his face, and looked thoughtfully at Henry. Then he said,

"You know, you might be right. I haven't thought about it for years, there is a spot of ground at the back end of my property that I stumbled across when I bought this place and logged out the lumber for these buildings that looked like oil was coming up out of the ground. I had never heard of anything like that happening so I immediately put it out of my mind. You don't suppose it is anything like that do you?"

Ralph and Henry looked around to see if anyone was listening. There was no one at the tables around them, so Henry said,

"Mister Braddock, Ralph and I have been to that place you saw and my father works in the oil business and that black spot is a lot bigger now and means that you are sitting on top of millions of dollars worth of Oil. I have called my father and he will be coming out to take a look. And tell us the true story. That is why Mister Henderson, your "Friend" is trying to buy your property. Whoever owns this property will be a millionaire in a few years and a very good income will be coming in just a few months from a land lease. We had better not let the news out till after my father gets here and has checked it. That kind of news will cause a big change in this place as you know it, so let's wait."

Mister Braddock looked stunned and just sat there staring at first Ralph then Henry, when he looked at Ralph, Ralph just nodded in affirmation. Harry Braddock just sat there looking at the two young men, then down at the table, not saying a thing. His mouth opened a couple of times and then closed. The scope of things to come was just too big for him to comprehend. One practical thought did come to him "I guess I'll have to build a couple new motel cabins."

Ralph was looking ahead also, he said

"We had better wait till Hank's father confirms our findings, then call for a meeting of all the Landowners within five or ten miles of here and then break the news to them all at the same time. He should be here in a day or two."

Harry Braddock finally said, "And I thought I had problems before. This is really going to be something. in this town. I think you guys are right though, we had better keep it quiet and tell them all at the same time, to be fair."

Ralph got up and walked over to the old piano, sat down and started playing softly as a few customers came into the restaurant and sat down

Virginia came out of the kitchen and sat down with her father and Henry.

"I thought I heard some music faintly." she said, "good, I like the way he plays, it is so soft and the old songs are very pretty."

"Virginia," her father said, "How are you doing after all that has happened. I am sorry that I couldn't do more about Junior. I was hoping that you could hold him off and keep things quiet. I don't know what I was thinking. I just didn't know what to do. You are looking better than you have for a long time."

"I feel great; better than I have felt for quite a while. I shouldn't say this I suppose but I am glad that Junior is gone. I was deathly afraid of him and he was getting quite demanding. I didn't know what to do about him. He wouldn't listen to anything I said. He wanted his way about everything. It was awful. Thank goodness it is over."

Ralph kept playing and the tables began to fill up and poor Karen was kept busy just bringing coffee. It was not yet the dinner hour and Ralph wondered hw the people found out he was playing. Then he noticed that the phone was nearly in constant use. He guessed people were calling their friends and telling them about the music. He was certainly enjoying it himself. By dinner time the tables were all full and the five stools at the little bar were filled. Then four men of different ages came into the restaurant carrying musical instruments and walked toward the raised platform to put their instruments down.

One of them went to the back of the platform and brought out four folding chairs and gave one to each of his friends. They glanced at Ralph occasionally, but went ahead and set up the chairs and sat down, and soon the sound of a little band blended in with the piano and Ralph altered his playing to match theirs and there was a loud applause from the listening audience.

Virginia looked over at Henry and with a cute smile said.

"When are we going to get a sample of your playing? I have heard that you play the violin pretty well."

Henry had been listening to the small band play and thought that it sounded very good. The group now had a violinist and he sounded very good.

"I have only been playing for three years and not all the time. I am not really good but I do ok." Henry replied. "These guys sound pretty good and with the piano they should make a good combination. And they could use another violinist, different key."

The drummer, had only a couple of drums, but they were the two that were most used and did quite well. His name was James Harrison and, a young man still in school and nineteen years of age, full of youthful ideas and thoughts. They now had a wind instrument, one of the older men had a Saxophone and he seemed to be a very good player. The other and last of the four was a lead guitar player and he sounded perfect.

They played for about half an hour and then stopped to get acquainted with Ralph and Henry.

It was close enough to dinner time that the customers decided to start ordering their dinner so Virginia got up and headed for the kitchen to help her mother take care of the orders and help Karen if need be. With a crowd of this size, Harry Braddock knew that he was also needed in the kitchen so he joined his wife in the kitchen and could hardly contain himself with the new news he had to hold in secret till the time was right, but he managed because he knew it was necessary.

They soon heard the music and the evening was off to a fantastic start. The addition of the piano was an incentive to play and it seemed to fit in very good for the people responded graciously as the evening sped by. Henry got his violin and joined the boys on the stage a little later and the added Violin seemed to please the patrons.

Unknown to both Henry and Ralph, the only pay received by the old band was what ever the patrons put in a "TIPS" labeled cardboard box on top of a small table in one corner of the small stage. Ralph noticed it as he was glancing around as he played and watched as people danced by and dropped something into it. He hadn't seen anyone put it there and he wondered.

Harry Braddock had put it there because he could not afford to pay a decent amount for a band to come and perform at the restaurant on Friday and Saturday nights. He needed the income from those two nights to keep the restaurant in supplies. The food and well being for his family came from the proceeds of the restaurant and the motel rooms he had. The latter was not productive much during the winter months as tourists were not out and about. The money collected from the patrons on Friday and Saturday nights, kept the band coming back each weekend. He had never seen how much they had put in the box, but it must have been enough for the band kept coming back and seemed satisfied with the amount.

Harry Braddock was so happy he could hardly contain himself. For the last year he had been thinking about his situation financially. He was headed for trouble unless he did something. Just what, he did not know. The restaurant was his only source of income and it was not enough. This he knew. He was getting farther and farther behind in their car payment and he was having trouble keeping the stock of food required for the restaurant. He was not paying the medical bills that his wife had accumulated and the doctor was complaining.

He had been about to sell the property to Jack Henderson when the boys had told him about the Oil. Now there was some hope. If it would just come in time. He was now anxious to meet with Mathew Warring and hear what he would have to say about the Oil seepage.

If this little village was sitting on top of a large lake of oil there would be a boom town here for a long time to come. The little plateau that the village was built on was nearly covered now with houses, except eastward toward the location of the seepage. That area was all heavily timbered and would have to be cleared to build anything, but no one would want to live close to a working oil well. Building in that direction would be limited. He could sell building lots for a half mile or so. First the lumber would have to be taken off then the land could be surveyed and divided into reasonable size lots, for building. He could hardly wait. Several thoughts were going through his mind and he was trying to figure out whether he should tell his wife or not. He finally came to the conclusion that it would be best to wait, so he put is mind back to satisfying the customers in the dining room and went back to work.

Both Virginia and Karen were kept busy, all the tables were filled and the little bar was also filled. They brought out a makeshift long table and some folding chairs and seated most of the standing customers. Both of the girls would like to be free for a while, but it was impossible with a crowd of this size so they just kept working.

By Eleven O'clock, everyone was tired, and the band stopped for the night. The tables were still nearly full, but they were nearly all through eating and were mostly drinking and listening to the music. With the music stopped they were beginning to get up and leave. The band found seats at some of the vacant tables and sat down to order a sandwich and a drink. When the leader took down the "TIP" box, he was pleasantly surprised and divided it up, not just between the original four, but among the final six players. There did not seem to be any dissention among them, and they were glad the evening was over.

The girls and the kitchen people worked nearly another hour before they could relax and sit down. When the kitchen was cleaned and the girls had all the tables cleared and cleaned. Mr. and Mrs. Braddock put two tables together and the six of them sad down to have coffee and talk. All of them were very tired and were glad the day was over. None of them had anticipated the crowd they had needed to take care of. It was a pleasant surprise for Harry, they really needed the money and he was anxious to count the daily take, which he would do in the morning. It was entirely too late to do it tonight. They all agreed it was time to get some sleep. The subject of oil was never brought up, the women did not know of it so it was left out of the conversation.

The next day was Monday and was usually quiet at the restaurant. They opened but did not expect much business. The two boys knocked at the back door of the restaurant and were let in to have breakfast. Karen knocked and was let in a few minutes later and joined them. After a good breakfast they walked outside to talk. It was such a beautiful day that they decided to go for a long walk. Mrs. Braddock could handle the restaurant alright herself. Arm in arm the two couples started walking along the road out of town and soon found themselves walking back the logging road that led them to the oil seepage. There was an old log a few feet from the open area of the seepage so they sat down on it to talk and rest.

It wasn't long before one of the girls asked, "Why aren't there any trees growing over there?" And she pointed to the open area of the oil seepage.

"Because there's over a million dollars under the ground there" Henry said, then looked at Ralph, who nodded. Henry went on and told them the whole story as he and Ralph knew it. He added, "We'll know in a few days, after my father gets here and confirms what Ralph and I think. We have told your father," He said as he looked at Virginia. "But we all thought that we had better wait and keep the secret till we are sure, before we call a meeting of land owners and tell them all at the same time."

"We want you girls to keep the secret too. It might cause a lot of trouble if we don't." Ralph added.

"Dad only bought a few acres." Karen said "But it could make us millionaires, too." then added, "Oh, I hope it's true. Can we go out and see it closer?"

The girls wanted to walk out into the area to see the oil, so they got up and followed the boys out to a spot where they could look at raw crude oil slowly oozing up out of the ground in a slow thick black mess. On the way back out of the area, both of the girls were quiet with thoughts of their own.

They were suddenly back on the logging road and arm in arm they headed for the restaurant, each couple separate and talking to each other. There was much on their minds and no one could be sure of anything except that there was a rough road ahead for everyone in this area if what they suspected was true.

When the four came together again, Ralph and Henry noticed the girls were altogether too quiet. Ralph said.

"You girls will have to fake it. You are too quiet to be your normal selves, come out of it or you'll give it away. Say you don't feel good or something. We should not have told you."

Henry spoke up and said "My father should be here in a day or two and he can give us the news, good or bad, but I think it will be good news, I am all most sure of it, and in a few months most of the people in this town will be rich and the rest of us will all have good paying jobs if we want them. Until then we should keep quiet about it or we could cause panic."

"Oh I am so glad and I hope it is true," Virginia said. "Dad has been worried sick. He hasn't said anything, but I know he has been worrying lately. The restaurant has not been doing well enough for him to keep up on the bills. Most of the money has gone back into the restaurant to keep it operating. I know he was getting close to selling to Mr. Henderson". She gasped, and added "Do you suppose Jack knows about the oil and was trying to get the property away from dad?"

Henry took her hands and said.

"We're sure of it Virginia, there is no other reason to buy the property. He has plenty already but he was getting greedy. Friendship means nothing to him where money is concerned."

She went into his arms and he held her close.

"Oh Hank" She said. "I am so glad you are here" and she looked up at him as he lowered his had to kiss her.

They clung to each other for a while as they began to feel what a first true love felt like as it became nearly all consuming. Arms still around each other they slowly turned and followed Ralph and Karen slowly back toward the main road and the restaurant. A lot had happened on this little short walk into the woods. All four were in an altered frame of mind, with much to think about.

When the four young people returned to the restaurant, they sat down at the double table they had put together a few hours earlier. Virginia's parents came out of the kitchen and sat with them. Harry Braddock could tell by the way the two girls were acting that the boys had told them about the oil so he looked at his wife and said;

"Martha, we have something to tell you and I don't want you to faint or get hysterical about it.

Do you remember when we bought this place years ago? We walked back to the east end of the property to look it over and you said how beautiful it was, with all the huge trees and the evergreens, flowers and even some of the wild creatures. Do you remember the black dirty spot we saw about half way to the property line?"

His wife looked at him and said. "Yes what about it?"

"Well." Harry said. "That spot is a lot bigger now and there is thick dirty and black Oil seeping up out of the ground. It now appears that we are living above a huge lake of crude oil, if so it will be worth millions of dollars." He hesitated, then continued "This whole town will be worth millions of dollars and it is bound to become a boomtown, which I really don't look forward too."

"Harry, are you sure? Nobody has drilled around here for miles. How do you know there is oil down there?" She asked.

"Henry's father is an oil man and Henry knows a lot about it and he thinks there is Oil there. He has called his father and his father is probably on his was up here now. He may pop in at any time." Her husband replied.

"That would solve all our problems" His wife answered.

"We decided that we will not let the word out till Henry's father gets here and confirms the theory, then we will call all the landowners within ten miles of here and tell them the news at the same time." Harry told her and she nodded in agreement.

From the look on her face as she walked away, she might as well have said, "I'll believe it when I see it". As she walked into the kitchen to make some sandwiches, she wasn't about to believe anything like that until she saw it with her own eyes. It was too big a deal to believe without proof. No one goes from rags to riches that fast without a lot of grief and she did not need any more grief She really did not have much to begin with, but it was building up and there seemed no way to stop it unless she could talk Harry into selling the place and then he would have to look for work and she did not want that. If it were true it would sure change things, and for the better she would just wait and see.

Karen had not told her parents and they decided to let it remain that way.

The sandwiches came and they sat and enjoyed them as they talked more about the oil. There was no one else around to hear, so excitement built up as they imagined all sorts of monetary amounts and thought how it would affect the small community. The bank would have to enlarge; it was now only a small branch office, so Harry decided to include the Banker in on the meeting coming up. Construction would start and all sorts of improvements would need to be done. It would mean prosperity and plenty of work for everybody would probably get into the act. There was money to be made and everyone in the town would want to get some of it.

"Now let's not get carried away." Harry said "Let's cool down and keep it that way until we hear what Henry's father has to say. If he brings leasing contracts and is sure there is really a lake of oil under us, then we can get excited and throw a few parties and look forward to a lot of exiting times ahead. Meanwhile, cool off, and be your old selves till the truth comes out."

They all tried, but the people who knew them real well were looking at them with a kind of curiosity that told them they were not dong too good a job of covering it up. They knew that something was up but could not say what, so they waited.

Monday was usually a quiet day with very few people coming in for breakfast, of course the two boys were captive customers and they slept in till nearly noon before they showed up for any food.

After a good meal they went out back to the wood pile and spent the afternoon splitting and stacking wood for the Braddock's to earn their keep, so to speak. There was not much else to do. It was nice spring weather and they were enjoying themselves and getting needed exercise as well. Occasionally some of the local residents would stop by and talk awhile, and they had several offers for their wood cutting services, which they accepted. They figured they might as well make hay while the sun was shinning, as the saying goes.

Henry figured that his father would be anxious to see the oil seepage and would probably arrive the next day, probably in the afternoon. The day passed and they became aware of the difference they had caused since their arrival. Every time they stopped for a minute and went into the restaurant for a drink or a sandwich they were immediately aware of the attention they were getting. When they entered, all talk ceased and all eyes were on them. It became annoying and they stayed out longer, and they asked the girls to bring the drinks out to them.

When it was time for the evening meal, they left the woodpile and went into the restaurant and picked a table near the piano. Karen took their order and then sat down to talk to them. There were very few customers and she wasn't really needed anyway. Virginia came out of the kitchen and joined them for the meal.

After they were finished and the dishes were carried away, Karen asked Ralph if he would play the piano a little. Karen knew that Harry wanted to hear more of the soft music he so remembered, and so did she, she thought.

The Sheriff was one of the few customers that were still hanging around and he thoroughly enjoyed the piano music. He came over to the table next to theirs and sat down and ordered more coffee. Henry turned to him and asked,

"Are you going to be around for the next few days, Sheriff?"

"Wasn't planning on it." the Sheriff said. "Why, you got something going on I need to know about?"

Henry glanced around him to see if there was anyone close. Ralph was still playing the piano and the other customers were listening to the music. The sheriff noticed the gesture and slid his chair closer to Henry's. He leaned a little closer to the sheriff and said.

"Not sure yet, but I think we'll know tomorrow, If it is like I think it will be, you will probably be needed, so it might be wise to stick around at least one more day. Do you know most of the people that live around here?"

"No," The sheriff said, "I know a lot of them, but I've only been here about five years. As County Sheriff I moved to the county seat about twenty miles from here. A town called Pineville. I can stick around another day if you think I should. I like the food here anyway. I feel an undercurrent and the people are not acting right. It is a feeling I got."

"Good." Henry said." I hope you're not needed, but we'll see."

Henry knew his father pretty well and he felt sure his dad would arrive tomorrow and things would change by tomorrow night. The landowners could be here in a few hours for the meeting so tomorrow should start things hopping.

Henry's father drove up to the restaurant just a few minutes after noon. Henry and Ralph were down the first village block splitting wood for missus Woodward. Her husband was in bed with a bad case of sore throat and she needed wood for cooking and washing clothes. Ralph and Henry offered to do it for exercise as they still had some money left and was not really in need. She had gone to the local grocery store and had seen a car pull up in front of the restaurant and noticed an out of state license plate on the front of it. She had heard the two boys talking about Hanks father coming so she immediately assumed it was his father so she went behind the house to tell them about the car. Upon hearing that news the two boys put down their axes and headed for the restaurant.

When they entered the restaurant they found Henry's father talking to Harry Braddock.

He was saying,

"I understand there are a couple of wayward young men wandering about and one of them is my son Henry, Hello, I am Mathew Waring, are they about?"

Before Harry could say anything Henry shouted,

"Dad, you made it". And he grabbed his father and hugged him. With his father holding him close he added." Gee dad I am glad you made it ok, let's sit down to talk".

Tuesday was an average day at the restaurant and there were a few customers in the restaurant so they picked a table as far away from people as they could and sat down. Harry Braddock looked at his daughter Virginia and motioned her toward the table they had chosen. She immediately approached and took their order and returned to her duties. He would wait till they called him if they wanted to talk.

Mr. Warring was really hungry and so were the boys so they all three ordered a good meal and talked very little, mostly about the food. Nearly an hour later, near the middle of the afternoon the customers were all gone and the restaurant was empty except for the boys and Mr. warring. The boys decided it was alright to talk. There was no one about to hear so they signaled to MR. Braddock to join them at the table.

As Harry sat down, Henry said. "Mr. Braddock, why don't we start off by you telling father about you buying this place and the black spot on the back end of the property, then bring him to date on the situation."

"Well," Harry said, "I bought this place twelve years ago from a bank foreclosure and had it surveyed and marked. During the surveying I came across an open spot in the forest where nothing but low brush would grow and the ground was just black dirt. I did not think much about it at the time. And as time went by I forgot all about it until the boys came to me and told me what they had found back there."

He looked at the two boys and said,

"Now Henry, you tell your part."

"Well I did not want to say too much over the phone but Ralph and I were walking back an old logging road and we came to the place where no tall pines would grow, just low underbrush and some weeds. We decided to walk out into it and see if we could find out why nothing would grow there. We found spots where the earth was literally black and then we discovered that a thick oily liquid was coming up out of the ground in several spots and spreading out over the ground."

Mathew Warring sat for a moment then looked around the restaurant, then back at his son.

"Can you take me to the place?" he asked.

"Yes." Henry said, "It is only about half a mile and easy walking. We can go now if you wish. Ralph and I will be glad to show you the spot."

Ralph spoke up. "If you don't mind, I think we had better go out the back door and go down to the logging road back off of the road out of sight of the villagers that might see us leave. That way we can get there and back before anyone gets curious. It is all easy walking."

"Good Idea, let's go." Hank said.

Harry Braddock joined them as they left by the back door of the restaurant headed toward the logging road through the tall trees. They reached the old road and headed deeper into the deep forest. No one seemed interested in talking; it was so still and peaceful.

When they reached the spot where the girls had sat on the big log and then wanted to know what caused the open area, the two boys sat on the log and let the two older men walk out into the brush to look at things. The men took nearly a half hour looking before they returned to where the boys sat. Mr. Warring looked at Harry and asked.

"Are you sure this is on your property, Mr. Braddock."

"Yes, more than a hundred yards. Harry replied.

"We will have to drill several wells to be sure." Mr. Warring said." but I think there is a lot of oil under these trees and just how much, we will have to drill to find out. This is virgin territory and oil here will change the whole landscape and the little village where you live, a lot of trouble but also a lot of pleasure. It all comes together."

Harry Braddock looked at him and asked.

"Do you think we should tell the people of this area there is oil under these trees now?"

"We'll tell them just what I've told you. We think there is oil under here, but we will have to drill several wells to find out for sure. It is bound to cause problems, but it is the only way we can do it. Has anyone been trying to buy up property around here in the last year or so? Some one may already know about it and is trying to get as much property as he can, if so he will be pretty angry about us telling everybody."

Harry Braddock looked at the two boys, then told Mr. Warring about Jack Henderson.

"He will be pretty angry when he hears the news, but he will deny knowing about it, you can bet." Mr. Warring said.

They entered the restaurant through the back door and sat down at a table. The sheriff was sitting at the front of the restaurant where he could see the road. He looked up as they entered and sat at a table. Harry caught his eye and motioned him over to their table.

As he sat down he glanced at Ralph and asked.

"Is this going to be what you were talking about last evening?"

Ralph nodded, then said "Sheriff, this is Mr. Warring, Henry's father." and he indicated the stranger. "I'll let him do the talking."

"Sheriff," Mr. Warring said. "Something has came up that will shake this town to the roots, cause a lot of greediness, hate and distrust between friends as well as enemies. The boys here discovered Oil on the Braddock property. I think there will be a lot of it too. Probably under the whole area, only drilling the whole area will prove anything. There will be trouble when

We make the announcement. Friends will become enemies and Greed will become the hot item of the day."

The sheriff was quiet for several seconds, then said,

"This will cause a mess of everything. There will be a lot of money, a lot of trouble, a lot of greed and best of all a lot of work for anybody that wants it. This town will double or triple in size. When will you make the announcement?" and he looked at Harry Braddock.

"There is plenty of time yet today for me to call all the landowners within five miles of here. And tell them to come to an important meeting tomorrow. Here at the restaurant. I will tell them to be here for a one o'clock meeting." Harry replied, then added "Let's keep it quiet till then, Ok sheriff?"

"Of course, by all means, we do not want any more trouble than is necessary." The Sheriff answered.

Ralph and Henry excused themselves and went back to the widow's house and continued chopping wood for the rest of the afternoon, then went to their cabin for a little rest before the evening meal.

Refreshed after a quick shower, they walked into the restaurant a little after five o'clock and sat down at a corner table for a cup of coffee. There were only a couple of people sitting at tables so when the girls came over to their table they asked them if they could get away for a quick walk into the woods. There was a sort of path where they had taken Mr. Warring down to the logging road and did not want to be seen from the highway past the restaurant.

The two couples then walked into the woods holding hands and talking the way only the young and in love talk to each other. The subject this afternoon though was not of love but how much it would mean to the town if there really was oil under the ground beneath them. The girls of course were thinking about the new dresses and clothes they could get and how tickled they would be shopping for new pairs of shoes.

They soon turned and headed back toward the restaurant, not really wanting too but they knew that the evening dinner hour was coming fast and the girls had to be there. The girls went to the kitchen and the boys went back to the corner table which was still empty. Henry sat at the table and Ralph went on to the piano, sat down and started playing the way he liked to play, soft and easy.

A few people came in and sat down and ordered dinner and some of them went to the phone and called someone. Henry noticed and suspected that they were telling someone about the piano playing. It wasn't long before cars started pulling up outside of the restaurant and people came in and sat down.

Ralph was getting used to the people looking at him and talking. He could not hear what they were saying but he knew that he was the subject of the conversation. Ralph had noticed that he and Henry were being talked about most of the time they were around people. They could not do anything about it so they just ignored it and went on about their business. There was no nasty looks or talk that they could feel or hear so they did not worry about it.

When they were with the girls they received some nasty looks from some of the eligible bachelors and two or three of the older young men looked antagonistic a few times. Maybe they were friends of Junior and did not believe what they had been told about the fights. Ralph had had with Junior. There was nothing they could do to change their minds about that either, so they just ignored them.

Ralph played for about an hour before he stopped for dinner. When he stopped and stood up, the crowd applauded and he stopped, waited for quiet before he thanked them and told them he would be back after he had something to eat. Then he walked toward the table where Henry waited. As he passed the second table where four older young men sat eating, a foot came out to trip him. He was expecting something and saw it coming. Timing his steps, as the foot come out he brought his right foot forward fast and hit it hard on the shinbone, knocking it back into the leg of the table. He walked on by, keeping his stride and went to the table where Henry waited, and sat down to order.

The sheriff was sitting only two tables away and had seen the whole thing and smiled as he looked at Ralph and gave a slight nod. Ralph gave a slight nod and smiled back.

By now the restaurant was filled to capacity and some were waiting outside where it was cool for someone to leave. As Ralph sat down he looked at his friend and said;

"Did you see that? That guy at the second table tried to trip me. He must be a friend of Junior's".

Henry said, "You better keep an eye on him, he means trouble, and he is big enough to give it"

It seems a few of the people sitting at some of the tables near the trouble maker had seen what happened and were waiting to see what else would come of it. They did not have long to wait. About half an hour later, Ralph got up and walked back toward the piano to continue playing.

As he approached the bully's table, the bully got up and stepped out in front of him and stood there, hands on hips. Ralph timed his steps and at the right time moved forward quickly and rammed his right fist into the bully's stomach just below the rib cage, knocking the wind out of him. At the same time, Ralph's left hand grabbed him by the hair and pulled his head down to meet Ralph's right knee coming up. The crack was loud enough to hear a few feet away as the nose bone was broken and blood spurted out of it. Ralph lowered him back into his chair and then pushed his face down on his plate, before walking on to the stage and sitting down at the piano.

It had all happened so fast that people could not believe it. Only the few that had seen the bully get up and face Ralph really knew what had happened. Ralph moved the piano so that he could keep an eye on the bully. All eyes were on Ralph now and people were talking and looking at the bully, whose head was now coming up off the plate with blood running slowly down on the plate.

The sheriff was watching intently and it looked like he was ready to get up in a moments notice if anything went further. He was watching both of the boys and was thinking if he was the bully, he would stay in his chair, that Ralph was entirely too fast to mess with.

The bully finally got his breath back and slowly got up and walked toward the entrance. His friends followed and they left the restaurant.

The remaining people, it seemed, were all trying to talk at once, and look at Ralph at the same time. Some of the people at a table near where the bully had sat were just looking at each other but not saying anything. Just looking at Ralph with an odd look and keeping quiet.

Ralph was quietly enjoying the soft music he was making and his mind was wondering where the name "Li Chan" had came from and as he was thinking this, he wondered who "Jessica" and "Robert" were. He was going to think on this a while to recall things.

The sheriff was the first to get up and walk outside. He wanted to see where the bully had gone and what he would do now. He would be angry and would want to do something. His nose hurt pretty badly and he just wanted to get home for now and get his nose fixed. His friends must have gone with him. There had been only one car leave the parking area. He went back into the restaurant and sat back down at his table. Some of the men nodded as he went past their table.

Harry Braddock had not seen the encounter but he finally came out of the kitchen and looked around. He spotted a few of the land-owners so he walked around past them and told them of the meeting set for the next day. They were curious but he just told them to be sure and come.

The sheriff wanted to talk to the boys and thought about talking to Henry, but he did not want to show favorites now that there had been an encounter. He knew there would be more trouble and he wanted to stay independent. His two men had left the day before and he decided he had better call them back for tomorrow's meeting. He went to the pay phone and put in the call, then returned to his table.

Ralph played for nearly two hours before he finally stood up and lowered the cover over the keyboard and joined Henry to wait for the girls to get off work. They planned for a little walk after the restaurant closed.

The next morning after a good breakfast Henry and Ralph decided to cut a little more wood for the restaurant. An hour or so later as they were splitting wood they looked up and saw the bully from the night before and his three friends coming towards them from behind the houses along the road. Ralph moved away from he wood pile and into an open space. Henry saw the move and moved away to give his friend room to move and he stood ready to join in if needed. The young man with the broken nose walked toward Ralph and said.

"You caught me unexpected last night, let's see what you can do now that I know what to expect."

Ralph had noted the positions and movements of the other three and as they all moved in he waited for the right time to move. As the bully pulled back to take a swing at Ralph, Ralph spun and doubled him over with a kick to the stomach and then he was in position to grab one of the other guys by an outstretched arm and throw him into the wood pile head first then catch a third man in the groin with his left foot, doubling him over. Henry had feinted and then caught the fourth man on the side off his face with a strong right fist which knocked him to the ground.

Just then the sheriff came running from the restaurant and joined them. The man that Ralph had thrown into the wood pile was the first to get back on his feet and he just stood there looking at the sheriff and holding his head where he had hit a block of wood which had been very hard. The man Hank had hit and knocked down and the one Ralph had kicked in the groin were the only ones still on the ground. The bully had got some of his breath back but was still gasping and holding his stomach as he stood up and was looking at Ralph and the sheriff.

"He doesn't fight fair." he managed to get out as he looked at the sheriff.

"Do you call four to two fair fighting?" the sheriff asked him.

The bully just looked at him, then at Ralph. The sheriff waited till they were all standing up and looking at him. Then he said.

"You boys do not know how lucky you really are. Ralph was pulling his punches and trying not to hurt any one of you. That type of fighting was taught to him long ago in the country of "Tanga", it was taught only to kill the opponent, not to just stop him. Ralph was modifying his fighting to only stun or slow down you guys. You were lucky. What have you got against him anyway?"

"He killed Junior" the bully said.

"No he didn't." The sheriff said. "I did. Junior had a double barreled shotgun and he took a shot at Ralph and missed then aimed at Henry and was about to shoot when I told him to stop and he didn't so I had to shoot him to stop him from killing Henry."

"We didn't know all that." the bully said as they looked at each other and started walking away.

The restaurant started filling up about eleven o'clock and a lot of help was needed in the kitchen and table cleaning. Ralph and Henry both helped in the cleaning off of the tables and sometimes the serving. All eyes were on them most of the time but they were polite and seemed not to mind.

Ralph went to the piano and played through the dinner hour. As it neared the important hour and the place became packed, he played softer and was ready to stop when the sheriff came to the podium. The small band had left their microphone and amplifier on the stage for the sheriff to use and Ralph had turned it on and tested it out.

At one o'clock the sheriff walked out on the small stage and stood by the Podium waiting for the talking to subside. As it quieted down he reached for the microphone and said,

"I want to thank you all for coming. Some of you will thank me and some of you will wish I had kept my mouth shut. There is a stranger in town, he is here now. Please stand up, Mr. Warring. And face the audience. He is going to tell you something that will change this town drastically in the next few months and possibly years. Mr. Warring, will you come up here please."

Mathew Warring stepped up on the platform and walked to the sheriff's side waiting to be introduced. The sheriff then said.

"Citizens of Baxter, this is Mr. Mathew Warring. Asked to come here by his son Henry to talk to you folks, he has something important to tell all you landowners." and went back to his table.

"Folks" Mr. Warring said. "I have set up sort of an office in one of the cabins beside the restaurant, feel free to come in and talk to me any time you wish. What I want to say is this, I am relatively sure there is a lot of oil under this area; we will have to drill several wells to be sure. There is surface seepage on Harry Braddock's property. There are probably other spots around these hills that are visible as well. If we find oil it will mean prosperity and work for the general area and a lot of wealth for landowners who have property over the bed of oil. Only the drilling will show us just how much oil there is. We will sign contracts with landowners who will let us drill on their property. Thank you all for coming."

The restaurant turned into a roaring mob of people. Everyone wanted to say something at the same time. The sheriff sat watching for any sign of trouble but it seemed they were just talking to whoever was next to them.

The girls were busy serving coffee and clearing off tables and the roar continued. They were not eating, just coffee and drinks of some kind. Soon the crowd started to move toward the door and the restaurant started to quiet down and some of the people who had not had a chance to eat, called to the girls for service.

Mr. Warring went to his makeshift office and was soon talking to individuals about drilling and signing contracts.

The two men the sheriff had called back were soon walking through the crowd breaking up small arguments as they broke out. Ralph and Henry were helping the girls clean up the tables and dishes and helping out in general.

The afternoon went by and it was near time for the dinner hour. Henry and Ralph had stopped working and were sitting at a table with cold lemonade and talking about the future with the prospect of an oil boom in the area. There was bound to be a construction boom and lots of work. Most of Harry Braddock's property was fairly level and would bring a good price per acre for lots for family construction and even business construction. A large portion would have to be cleared of trees for residence buildings to be built. A lot of planning was called for so a lot of work was needed. The county would need to construct new roads and residence and business zones would have to be separated.

Henry and Virginia were spending more and more time together and Ralph could see the signs. He knew all about falling in love and knew he had practically lost a pal, but he was happy for both of them. It looked like they were truly in love. He was left alone in the restaurant a lot more these days and Ralph was beginning to wonder when it would be time for him to leave and continue traveling. Karen was nice, but there was not the love feeling he needed to continue a relationship. He needed a car to travel on with so he would have to stay around long enough for money to come his way or for Henry to offer to sell him the station wagon reasonable. The way it looked to Ralph. Henry and Virginia would be married soon and would be taking the restaurant off her parent's hands so they could travel. Ralph knew that if the oil was there money enough for them to go anywhere they wished would soon follow. Harry's dream would soon be coming true.

Time went fast now. The little town formed committees for everything and new streets were planned, Trees began to fall and a lumber company was formed by Junior's father. Now that Junior was not around to make trouble by trying to control everything, his father and mother were coming out of their shells and enjoying life.

A surveyor was brought in to perform a lot of the laying out of the much larger village, and even plans for a future small city.

Nearly all of the landowners within ten miles of the little town had signed contracts for the drilling of a test well on their property and some of them were already receiving monthly advance royalty checks from the expected oil. The incoming money was already having it's effect on the town. The first drilling rig was already being set up on the east end of Harry Braddock's property and would be drilling soon.

A sort of tent city was set up for a lot of workers that were drifting in and of course the restaurant was doing all the business that it could handle. Harry was adding ten new rental cottages and adding on to the restaurant dining area. The band was asked to play more and more dinner hour and then later for dancing. The money box was collecting a lot more money than they ever had before so Ralph and Henry were getting a lot more money.

Ralph was saving to buy a car of some kind so he could be on his way. Times were changing and so were people. Ralph could see the writing on the wall and it was not good.

There were of course brawls occasionally, but the sheriff handled most of them as they started. The young men that had tried to fight with Ralph and Henry became apologetic and were now friends of theirs. They worked with them when the work involved a lot of cooperation and a lot of men were constructing something. Like a large storage barn or the new Grocery store that was put up where the little store had been.

A new post office had been built near the Webster house, which was owned by the postmaster Peter Webster. Pete had used one room extension on his home as the post office. The increased population called for a larger Post office. Pete donated the ground and remained Postmaster.

Two months after the first well was started on Harry Braddock's property, the nitro was lowered and then the "go-devil" was dropped and the explosion was heard and felt for miles. The following gush of black oil shot into the sky and hundreds had come to see it happen. There was hardly any wind that day but a lot of people ended up covered with the black smelly and slippery liquid. There was shouting, yelling and dancing into the night by a bunch of happy people. It was a day to be remembered.

Two months later, Ralph and Henry were sitting in the restaurant having coffee and Henry said "Ralph, I know you are thinking about leaving. Times are changing. I want you to know that you are my best friend and we have had some good times together. You are the first one I'm telling this to, Virginia and I are getting married, and soon. I want you to be my best man. With the money Virginia and I are making together we can get another car and I want you to have the station wagon. I'll sign it over to you and you can leave whenever you wish."

"Thanks, Old buddy" Ralph said. "I am getting itchy feet and winter is on its way. I don't really care for so many people around all the time. I do like the scenery, but this place is a mess with the new workers and all the buildings going up. When is the wedding?"

"The first week in September, the fifth I think. Virginia is thinking it out now, I'll let you know when she tells me." Henry said. "And you can go with us into the big town and we can transfer the car title and get another car on the same trip. Virginia has some shopping to do in preparation for the wedding. Her mother is probably going along too."

On the morning of the fifth of September, Ralph took all his things out of the little cottage they had used as living quarters and packed them in the back of the station wagon. He didn't have much so it did not take long. He wasn't one to say too many goodbyes. He figured to leave before the party ended and get in the station wagon and drive away. They would not miss him till someone looked for him and could not find him. Goodbyes were no fun at all, the memories were and he had a lot of them.

The wedding was beautiful and the Bride was gorgeous; two very happy people, deeply in love and ready for the future. Ralph did not wear a Tuxedo. He dressed in his best and was ready for whatever came up. He stayed around for the reception to start and enjoyed the dinner. When the dancing began, he danced with Karen a few times then sat down at a table for a while.

A while later, when Henry looked around for Ralph, he could not find him. He went outside to look and noticed that the station wagon was gone.

The station wagon was a few miles down the highway, its driver relaxed and looking ahead.

As Ralph drove away from the little village, now growing into a big village, he was thinking of the times there He had enjoyed the people and he loved the countryside. He hated to leave his good friend Henry, but Henry would have no time for his friend Ralph as a newlywed with a beautiful wife like Virginia. It was time for him to move on to whatever the future held for him.

He had been working for the past two months and had saved most of the money he made working. Because of his playing the piano he was never charged for his food and drink, so he had saved most of the money he got each night when the band played, which was nearly every night since the workers started coming into the town. They spent most of their evenings in the restaurant and they spent their money as fast as they received it.

He drove steady, stopping only to refuel or for food. Two days later he entered the foothills of the Rocky Mountains and was really enjoying the scenery as he drove. The road became narrower and was winding around with very sharp curves. According to a sign he had seen a few miles back, there was a small town twenty-five miles ahead. He planned on stopping there for the night and resting up. Maybe stopping for a day or two as it was beginning to cloud up and look like it might rain.

A few miles later it started to rain and he slowed somewhat and suddenly came to a sharp curve. His foot hit the brakes and he started sliding. The car would not follow the curve and at the speed he was going he could see that he was going to go over the cliff on the left side of the road. He opened the door on his side of the car and jumped clear of the vehicle as it went off the edge of the road and out into space. The drop was straight down and he was going out into space, then he started dropping straight down out away from the trees and brush that was on the side of the cliff. He heard the station wagon hit with a big crunch and continue crashing on down the side of the cliff. He felt some branches catch his clothes then hit a huge rock and darkness came.

Li Chan knew her host body was doomed and when the body hit the rock she felt the bones break and penetrate the life giving organs of the body, she waited for it to come to a stop near the bottom of a small canyon, she slipped out and rose above to look down. She could not at first see the body. It was lying on top of a huge boulder sticking out of the side of the canyon and was still beneath the canopy of trees. She then looked for the station wagon and finally found it beneath some huge trees near the bottom of the canyon. It was on its side and wedged between two of the trees; neither would be visible from the road above. There had been no cars on the road and he had not passed any other vehicle, so no one knew what had happened.

Li Chan had enjoyed willing and controlling Ralph. It had been a learning experience for her and she rather hated to leave, but again she was eager to look around again, maybe she could again get the feeling when she was near Chen Li. She must find her way back to Tanga and her people. The soul of Li Chan was soon moving slowly away from the scene of the crash. She could do nothing for Ralph and so she moved on.

CRIME

As the soul of Li Chan drifted in the earth's atmosphere she drifted lower where she was aware of the objects on the surface. They brought memories alive and she liked to think of the different situations she had been in. They amused her and she liked that. She had learned so much since she had left the body of her childhood. It was like an addiction, she wanted to learn more.

She was drifting over land in the lower area of the North American continent when she became conscious of the vibrations of an accident on surface. She drifted lower until she could see the surface clearly. There was a rising cloud of dust and smoke coming up from a winding road below her so she drifted lower until she could see the reason for it. It appeared that a car had been speeding on the road and had failed to complete the curve and had left the road and crashed into some large rocks at the bottom of a large hill. The force of the crash had smashed the car badly and the occupants had been thrown from the vehicle and were lying on the ground. The vehicle had caught fire and was burning.

The soul of Li Chan dropped lower and examined one of the bodies. It was the body of a young woman, and was badly mutilated. There were no signs of life in the woman so Li Chan drifted to the other body. She found life so she quickly entered the body and absorbed the memories. It was the body of a man of twenty-four years of age and American. She now was the soul of John Barrow. He had been thrown from the vehicle before it had hit the rocks and was unconscious from a blow to the head. She could find no other problems. Li Chan felt some little resistance and she took over control of the body. The young soul was not very confident and did not have much memory bank to call upon to help the body so it gave in and became part of the new Soul.

John Barrow was coming out of his unconscious state and was trying to sit up with the urging of Li Chan. He was soon completely conscious and stood up and quickly went to the woman and felt for life. Finding none, he hugged the body and burst into tears not so much for pure love, for he had just met her the night before, but because something had taken something away from him that he still wanted. His sadness was short lived for the police were coming.

A few minutes later he heard the sound of sirens in the distance and knew it was the police. He stayed where he was, a tall man tanned from much time in the western sun. Light brown hair covered most of his head and a almost blonde hair covered most of his face. He had not shaved for at least four days and his beard was thick. Dark brown eyes under thick eyebrows gazed out with a rather blank look at the world around him. His clothes were standard western plaid shirt and ragged blue jeans.

As Li Chan now knew he had robbed a bank earlier and had escaped with a large amount of money. He had stopped earlier at a country church and buried the money, so they would not find that. There was no other evidence now except the cashier and her identification of him as the robber, so he just stayed with his girlfriend crying until the police arrived.

There were two police vehicles and two officers in each car. They quickly left the vehicles and with guns drawn approached John and the woman. One officer quickly returned to the squad car and called for an ambulance, then returned to the scene of the accident.

One of the officers holstered his weapon and reached to grab John and handcuff him. Seconds later he found himself on the ground trying to catch his breath again, and John was standing up looking at them. Two of the remaining officers holstered their weapons and approached John telling him to hold still so they could put the handcuffs on him. John said,

"I am not armed, I'll go peacefully, just don't lay your hands on me, I don't like that and it is not necessary."

The fourth officer holstered his weapon and approached to help his fellow officers put the cuffs on John. As they reached for John Li Chan's memory went into action and an officer got the breath knocked out of him with a kick to his stomach as John turned and the other officer received a hard blow to the side of his head from John's other foot as he spun around. With two down, the third officer was more careful as he came in to box with John. As he came in John stepped out and brought his right foot up into his groin and he dropped to the ground holding his crotch. John said.

"I said I will go with you, with the cuffs on, but I will not be manhandled, otherwise you will have to shoot me."

The first officer was getting up now and he looked at John, and said

"Ok, come here and let me put the cuffs on."

John walked over to the officer and held out his hands and as the ambulance drove up he watched as they put the body of his girlfriend onto a stretcher and lifted it into the ambulance and left. He noticed how the ambulance crew had looked at the officers as they worked. No one said anything. One of the officers motioned John toward one of the police cars and opened the rear door and motioned John in and John climbed in and sat down, no one said anything.

One of the officers asked John

"Where is the money?"

John just looked over at the burning vehicle and said

"If it wasn't thrown out in the crash it is still burning, I guess."

Three of the officers then went to the road and followed the skid marks and small trees out to the rocks and burning car, looking everywhere for the bag of money. They found nothing.

John sat in the patrol car and watched as the car burnt. He never could figure how a car made out of metal could burn so completely and so hot. The policeman that had called the ambulance had also called for a fire truck and soon it arrived and was soon putting out the raging fire, but there was nothing more than burnt metal and a few wires. No sign of the bag of money. They spent another half hour looking for the money but none was found. They were soon on their way to the little town.

The new soul of John was having a small problem with the weaker and more carefree soul she had absorbed. It was thinking in a different category of things she had been used to thinking. It was somewhat shocking to the Li Chan part of the soul, which was dominant. Thoughts of killing, robbing and sex were playing a dominant role and she was not used to that in a violent way. The memories she had found in the man's soul had been more of violence, hate and thievery with very little love. There were some tender thoughts of the young woman that had been killed in the accident. Some were of a kind of love, but mostly sexual, not true love for the person.

There were memories of past killings and robberies, evidently a lot. Li Chan's memories were shocked as she recalled things she had absorbed when she took over the soul. She was to study those findings later when she could take her time in doing so. John had been a very busy man over the twenty some years he had been alive so far. He had practically no education at all, having been kicked out of nearly every school he had attended. He had a sister and a younger brother somewhere, but he had no idea where they were now or his parents either. He had ran away form home at the age of fourteen and had never returned or wanted to. If he wanted something he would steal it or fight for it.

The young lady who had died in the crash had been picked up the night before in a bar in a little burg he had stopped in a few miles back up the interstate. He had wanted to stop and eat and have a few drinks and a place to sleep. The bar had been nearly empty so he had been picked by the girl to provide her with a meal and a place to sleep. They were nearly two of a kind and got along well. He did not even know her last name or she his.

The next morning he had bought her a breakfast and then told her he would get some money out of the bank and they would take a little trip. He pulled up in front of the Bank and stopped. He told her to stay in the car, he would be right back. He returned in a couple of minutes, got in the car and drove away on one of the back roads leading into the mountains. Later came the accident that killed the girl and now he was on his way to jail, under arrest for bank robbery. He had not intended to be caught so quickly. He had not known that the Police station was directly behind the Bank and they were connected. The Police knew what had happened within seconds of the door closing behind him as he left with the money. It was a wonder that they had not caught up to him at the country church a few miles out of town when he had stopped to hide the money. The dirt was soft and he had heard sirens so he had worked fast.

It was a very small village and the Jail was two rooms on the side of a larger building which housed a garage and an office for the four officers to work out of.

Two of the officers left to go on patrol and the other two led John to a chair in front of a huge desk that sat in the center of one of the two rooms and told him to have a seat so they could interrogate him and file charges. The Captain of police sat in the chair behind the desk and the First officer stood behind the prisoner.

"What is your full name"? The Captain asked as he looked at the prisoner.

"John Barrow" John answered.

"Where do you live?" The Captain asked.

"I have no residence, I live wherever I am at the time" John answered.

The captain continued gathering information from the prisoner and filling out the necessary forms until it finally dawned on him that he had heard the name John Barrow before. He suddenly stopped and looking at the prisoner, said,

"Were you the John Barrow that was arrested and held for murdering two men over in a city called Westerville about ten years ago? They did not have enough evidence to hold you and they let you go. Then later they sentenced another man for the murders."

"Yeah that was me. I was innocent. I got out of there fast" John answered.

"Well," The captain said. "I need your signature on this form, just sign on the bottom line where the X is".

John pulled the paper to his side of the desk and signed the bottom line as the Captain looked at the first officer and said, "You sign below his signature as witness."

The first Officer moved from behind John forward to the desk to sign the document.

As he did so, it brought the first officer's gun nearly in front of John, who knew an opportunity when he saw it.

It took only seconds for him to get possession of the weapon and fire two quick shots, one for each of the two officers in front of him.

The first officer died instantly. John's second shot missed a vital spot, but it immobilized the Captain and he slumped over the desk. He was still conscious and was looking up at John.

John stood up, then bent over to the first Officer and searched his pockets for the keys to one of the patrol cars.

With the keys in his hand he looked down at the captain and said,

"Oh, by the way, that killing over in Westerville, you got the wrong guy. I killed those two men and took the money. Come to think of it, the money is still buried under the sign in front of the little church. I never did go back for it. Well I gotta go, thanks for the loan of a car, see yuh."

John Barrow got in the patrol car and drover slowly out of the little village and went into the mountains alone and with the stolen gun. He needed another vehicle, this one was hot. He was not worried about being caught. He had traveled before and always found someone with money enough to keep him going. He could not remember just how many people he had shot when he needed money. He tried to find people who were alone or were traveling alone and were sitting alone in a car resting or eating. He shot them where they were and left them there after he had found all the money and things that he wanted. He knew it would be a while before anyone would discover them and call the police.

The Soul of Li Chan was having a hard time getting used to the living habits of John Barrow, her willing and controlling was not doing exactly as she wanted. What was the soul of John Barrow did not consist of much knowledge of the normal human being. It consisted mostly of self satisfaction and no concern for any other member of the human race. There was no trace of compassion for another human, no thoughts at all of his relatives including his mother and father. He was doing the things he knew and wanted to do. Normally he would have shot the Captain again to be sure he had killed him, but Li Chan's thoughts were trying to make him show some compassion for the Captain and he had not shot again. She was also trying to tell him to admit to the killing of the couple he had killed years ago so the innocent man might go free. She was getting through to his true soul and having a little effect, but it was a slow process. Some habits are easy to change, but bad habits are usually very hard to change, but she was trying.

A few hours later he noticed the gas gauge was reading low he spied a little cottage with a fairly new vehicle parked beside it and there were no other houses in sight so he pulled in and parked the police car off the road and walked to the door and knocked. An elderly woman came to the door and opened it.

John Barrow pushed his way into the room and held the gun ready. No one else was in sight so he said.

"Get me some money and the keys to the car outside and be quick about it if you want to live."

Li Chan was trying to make him think of the fact that he did not have to kill these people because there were no telephone lines into the building and there were no near neighbors, so they could not get any word out for several hours at the least. He had seen no other vehicles on the road and probably none would be coming by.

The elderly woman put her hand to her mouth, looked at the gun pointed at her and turned toward the doorway to another room. John Barrow followed. She went to a dresser, opened the top drawer and reached in as John watched and pulled out a woman's purse. She opened it and pulled out a small billfold and handed it to him. Then she picked up a set of keys off of the top of the dresser and handed them to him also.

As John Barrow drove away in the old lady's car he was wondering why he had not shot her to make sure she could not recognize him in a lineup. His conscience was acting up. Nothing had bothered him before and he was disturbed that he was even thinking about it now. The conscience that Li Chan had brought to his body was overpowering and absorbing the conscience that was his only source of right, wrong and indifference. He was confused and did not understand what was going on in his mind.

He had always done as he wanted, with no thought of what the effects of his actions were, or what they did to the other people around him. He had never been exposed to love and had seen nothing but antagonism since he became aware of things around him as a baby. He knew nothing and learned by what he saw and replied in kind.

This knew knowledge had suddenly appeared and he had not been prepared for it. It was all knew to him and he wondered where it came from. He liked some of it and was curious about the rest. When he had seen the old lady, an odd feeling came to him. His first thought was that she looked like a very nice old person. He had never thought that way about any one else and the feeling was new, but he liked it and wondered why.

Other things were coming to his mind now that he had never thought about before. The beauty of nature came to him and he wondered why he had never thought about it before. He began to enjoy looking at the trees now, noticing the differences in them and the beautiful tall pines. He knew a lot of things now and he also had the memories of where he had been and how he had learned the things he now knew. That information was coming into his thoughts slowly and he was amazed at how much he could think up and know now.

This new knowledge did not come to him all at once. It came to him when his eyes would see something and his memory would try to figure out what it was, then Li Chan's conscious would bring it to him and he would know about it. It would scare him a little but he was getting used to it coming to him and was unconsciously beginning to understand a little of what had happened to him at the time of the accident. He was aware now that this new stuff had started at the time of the accident and was directly related. He was aware now that nearly everything he had done before the accident was against the laws of the people around him and that he was in deep trouble, all caused by the way he had been living and getting the things he wanted. He was not feeling much guilt yet but he knew he had done wrong and would probably have to pay for it sooner or later.

Now his thoughts were of what to do now. His new conscious told him that he would have to get out of the western part of the country. That was where he had committed most of the crimes and killings and he knew he was a very wanted man, so he must get clear of the western part of the states so he could figure what to do to live the way his new conscious was telling him that he should live.

First he had to get rid of the old lady's car, but it would be a day at least before the cops would find out about the car, the old lady had no phone and so she would have to wait till some one came by and she could tell them.

As he came down out of the foothills and the ground leveled off he came to some railroad tracks and it occurred to him that he might hop a slow freight and ride far away from this area provided it was going east. He suddenly remembered that he had just passed a small gully back the way he had came, and it had been filled with small trees and there might be a space he could hide the car so it could not be seen from the road, He could easily walk the short distance from the patch of trees to the tracks the train would be on.

He suddenly realized how he was thinking and how fast the thoughts were coming to him and he was amazed and a little scared at the things and the way he was thinking. It was a new thing for him and as he turned the car around and started back to the little gully he was feeling good about himself in a way he had never felt before.

The gully was empty and dry when he looked for a way to drive the car into the trees. He left the car and walked a little ways off the road and finally found an area where he could leave the car and it would not be seen from the road. There was also a hard enough surface from the road that there would be little tracks for anyone looking to see where a car had been driven.

He drove the car off the road and across the hard surface to the hidden area he had found and parked it deep into the brushy area, left the keys in the ignition and walked back out of the brush and looked back to see if the vehicle was visible. He could see nothing of the car and as he left the brushy area he picked up a rather heavy branch that had broken off and used it to brush away any marks of the tires he had made on the way into the brushy area, and off of the road. After checking the area again for signs of footprints or tire marks he walked on hard surfaces eastward parallel to the train rails for a while till he came to an area close to the tracks where he could hide until a slow freight came by and he could hop on and get into one of the boxcars so no train detective could see or find him, he found a little shaded area, lay down and waited.

It was not until the next day that he finally heard the rumble of an oncoming train. He was sitting under a low bush and waited for it to come into sight. He was anxious to be out of where he was an be on his way to a big city where he could get something to eat and a change of clothes. As the train came into sight he recognized it as a passenger train and that it was coming far too fast for him to get aboard. Cursing to himself he sat back down in the shade and waited.

It wasn't until late evening that he felt rather than heard another train approaching. He could tell by the rumble and sound that it was a slow freight and that this might be his chance to get out of here and be headed East. As he thought, it was a very slow freight and when it came within sight he hid himself in the brush as the engine went past for fear the engineer would see him and know what he was going to do. There were a lot of "Hobos" on the trains these days.

It was a long train, perhaps a hundred or more cars, so he waited till the engineer was out of sight and the big box cars began to go by before he ran along side and grabbed the steel rail beside the door and swung himself up and into one of them. He walked to the front of the car, stretched out on the floor and soon was sleeping.

Hours later he felt the boxcar lurch and woke up to darkness all around him and the train seemed to be slowing down. As his eyes became accustomed to the darkness he stood up and found his way to the huge door that he had came through when he boarded the train. Sticking his head out where he could see ahead he was surprised to see the lights of a rather large city. There were street lights along a road and the sky was lit up from the lights on the ground.

He was very hungry and he backed into the car a little ways and waited till he thought the train was going slow enough for him to jump out of and not be hurt when he hit the ground ready to run. He did not want to go very far into the city either. He wanted to stay in the suburbs where people would be inside their houses and where he could stay out of sight in the dark.

As the train slowed, he saw a grassy area ahead and as it came by he jumped out. It was a little too soon and he could not keep on his feet as they hit the ground and he went tumbling and ended up flat on his stomach. The train rumbled on past as he lay there catching his breath. He felt fine, he didn't feel any pain or hurt and he quickly got up and walked away from the tracks before the caboose came by. He knew that there was a signalman in the caboose at the rear end of the freight trains. He hid quickly in the brush beside the grassy area as the train slipped away down the tracks. As the Caboose disappeared into the darkness he stood up and tried to figure out what kind of area he had landed in.

He listened, then wondered why he had stopped to listen. His new conscience was telling him to listen and see if he could hear a dog barking. It told him that if there was a dog in the area it would be the first to see or hear him as he went looking for food or clothes. He must be careful and not be discovered unless he wanted to be discovered. There was a time for everything and he did not want trouble. He still had the money that the old woman had given him when she gave him her car keys.

He walked along the train tracks till he came to a road crossing, and discovered that it was a busy street and also a lived on street with lots of houses and there were sidewalks. He stopped and looked both ways along the street and saw a small restaurant about a block away that did not look too busy. He looked down at his clothes, brushed his pants off with his hands, tucked his shirt into his pants and figured he did not look so bad, then started up the street to the restaurant. He knew that he looked rough, with his beard and unshaven condition, but there was nothing he could do about that until he could find a store and get a razor and clean up and shave.

There was only one man in the restaurant at a table eating when he entered and sat down at the nearest booth. The waitress brought him a glass of water and handed him a menu, then left. He grabbed for the glass of water, maybe a little too fast, and drank it. He hoped that no one had been watching, he sat the glass back down a little slower, and looked at the menu. The girl had noticed and came and picked up the glass an brought him another and sat it down smiling and asked "Would you like to order now?"

"The special looks good." he told her, then added. "Some coffee also, please."

He wondered at the way he was talking. It seemed that he was being different, but he liked being this way. His new conscience was rather making him feel like he was important somehow, and he liked the feeling. His conscience gave him flashing pictures of other times in restaurants when he had not been so nice and now he did not like what he was seeing in those flashes.

He drank half of the new glass of water and waited for the food. When the food came and the waitress had put it before him, he thanked her and immediately started to eat. He was really hungry.

From the advertisements posted on the walls of the little restaurant he found out that he was in the little town of Santee. He had never heard of it so probably the people had never heard of him either, except through the news or newspapers. Maybe there had been no pictures and no one would recognize him. He ate rather fast at first then slowed down and really enjoyed the rest of the meal.

While he sat and enjoyed the second cup of coffee he became aware of his whiskers and he felt the need for a bath and a shave. When he went to the cashier and paid his dinner tab he spoke to the waitress who worked the cash register;

"Can you tell me if there is a drug store near here that I can buy a razor, some soap and a towel? I lost mine this morning and I would like a shave and wash up if I can find a rest room somewhere."

"Why yes, there is a small drug store about three blocks down the street, just past the first red light." She told him, smiling.

"Thanks." John Barrows said as he turned and walked out the door.

As he turned and started down the street that the girl had told him to go down he heard someone call,

"Hey, Mister".

He turned and saw the girl from the restaurant looking at him and motioning for him to come back. He walked back and as he came closer she said;

"Mister, I get off duty in a few minutes and I will be going that way, I can drop you off at the store if you want. Just wait here a moment and I will be with you."

"Ok, thanks." John said, and he meant it and he wondered at how nice he felt saying it.

There was an old porch swing type of bench on the sidewalk in front of the store and John sat down on it and relaxed. That had been a nice meal and he felt pretty good. As he sat there thinking about his situation, a car pulled into the small parking lot beside the restaurant and turned off it's lights. It looked to John like there was only two people in the car. They seemed to be talking and were in no hurry too get out. He was no rookie when it came to casing a place you were about to rob so he became alert and kept an eye on the car and the two people inside it. He had no watch and he had not noticed a clock in the restaurant, but if she was getting off duty, the restaurant may be closing and that would be a good time to grab the days income before the manager could take it to the bank drop. As a matter of fact he seemed to remember doing something like that a few years ago himself.

He saw some of the lights in the restaurant going out and watched the two guys in the car get out and start towards the restaurant so he got up and entered the restaurant and stood just inside the door. He looked at the girl and whispered"

"Stay behind the counter and stay down low, trouble coming, I'm with you."

The door opened and two men walked in, one going toward the cash register and one looking at John. John moved slowly toward the man looking at him but keeping an eye on the man at the cash register also. Who now spoke up and asked the girl;

"Is it too late to get some food, we're pretty hungry?"

The girl looked up and answered;

"We're in the process of closing, most everything is pretty much put away, sorry."

"Well then," the man by the register said, "Just give us the money out of the register and we'll be on our way"

As he finished talking his right hand came up with a small handgun. John was expecting something like that and as he saw the gun his right foot came around and struck the other man in the midriff, knocking the wind out of him and putting him on the floor. As John continued his spin the man with the gun turned in time to receive the left foot on the side of the head knocking him against the counter and in position for John to grab the gun hand and twist the gun out of the hand and drop it to the floor. Dropping a little lower John then threw his body under the gunman and heaved, throwing the man toward the door.

Picking up the gun, he held it casually the short barrel aimed directly at the man who had dropped it.

Both men were now looking at John and could tell that he meant every word he said when he started to speak;

"I have your license plate number and if you give this woman any trouble from now on I will personally find you and I will kill you both." He said as he opened the cylinder on the little gun and dropped out all six of the bullets. And tossed it to the man he had taken it from. The man he had kicked in the stomach was trying to get up and John kept an eye on him and said;

"Keep those hands where I can see them, and you and your partner get the hell out of here and keep going".

The man he had tossed the gun to was holding his head where John had kicked him and was looking at John with hatred but he said nothing as he turned and walked out the door. The other man followed. John watched as the car left the parking lot and went down the highway.

The girl grabbed for the phone and said,

"I'm calling the Police."

"Let's not." John said, then added "They didn't get anything but what I did and they are now out of here and I don't think they will ever be back. If you call the Police we will have to go down to the station, fill out a lot of paper work and answer a lot of questions and it will be a lot of trouble the police will probably have to let them go anyway. I would just as soon let them go."

The girl looked at him a while, then said;

"I suppose you are right, by the way my name is Barbara Shaffer, my father owns this little restaurant. He is usually here, but he felt a little sick this afternoon and went home early and asked me to stay and close for him, and I want to thank you for what you just did. Let's not tell him what happened. He will just worry more." She hesitated a moment and John spoke up and said:

"My name is John Sanders and I just jumped off the slow freight that just went through town. I am headed east to my family and stopped here to get something to eat and a change of clothes and a suitcase to carry them in. Mine were stolen by another train hitchhiker and I did not feel like trying to catch him. I like the rails, it is a fun way to travel and see some of the country".

"Well then, Mr. Sanders, Let us get you to the store and get you some replacements for what you lost. You don't mind if I stop by the bank drop on the way do you?" Barbara asked.

"Of course not." John replied "I am ready when you are."

"Ok, let's go." Barbara said as she started for the door.

John watched as Barbara turned out the lights and closed and locked the doors to the Restaurant, and followed as she went to the remaining car in the parking lot. He was thinking fast about what had happened in the restaurant and what he had told Barbara. He had come up with a fairly good reason for not wanting the police into the situation. He hoped that she would believe him and go along with the situation the way he wanted to handle it. He did not want any police checking on him now. He would be in real trouble if that happened.

They talked as they headed to the bank. Their personalities were very much alike and by the time they reached the drug store they were behaving like good friends. She insisted on going into the store and helping him shop and he did not object.

When they were back in the car and John asked her if she knew where there was a public rest room where he could shave and clean up, Barbara quickly said:

"You're coming home with me. Mom and dad will not mind, you saved me a bundle."

John was highly satisfied with her answer. The less publicity he got the better he liked it. He was a little confused at the way he was thinking, but the thoughts that were going through his head and mind pleased him. The memories of the past were still there and he found himself giving them little attention. He was so pleased with the new memories and the way they were keeping him out of trouble that he thought of little else. He had acquired an education overnight practically and he knew so much of the world that he found other things to think about.

John thought a lot about the last thing she said, but did not say anything. There had been a bundle of cash as she had said. Now why hadn't he grabbed that bundle and ran, like he would have done in the old days which were not so old really. Just a week or so ago he had been robbing banks and killing people.

"Boy I've really changed, what has happened"? He thought. Then he remembered the funny feeling he had had after the crash. That must have been when he had acquired the memories he had now. That was the only thing different that had happened. He felt happy and funny at the same time. He loved the way he was feeling and was not going to question it too much, he felt too good about it.

Barbara had helped him pick out a sport outfit and some shirts and other necessities and now they returned to the car and they headed toward her place, doing small talk on the way.

When Barbara pulled into the driveway and stopped in front of a garage, she said.

"It looks like Mom and Dad are gone, there car is gone, you will have time to clean up and change, you look a mess".

"I feel a mess, I will be glad to get out of these rags, shave and shower." John told her.

Barbara led him directly to the bathroom and left him to his own business, showing him how to turn the hot and cold water on.

It took John a little over an hour to make the conversion. He had never even thought about his appearance or whether he needed a shave or not and he had not known just how to trim a beard or mustache, but now he just seemed to know what to do and how to do it, which surprised him and again gave him thought about how such a thing could happen. There was so much new stuff in his memories that he could hardly remember any of the old stuff he had thought about so much and had got him into so much trouble.

He was happy and he knew that it was because of the new memories. When he was finished everything and walked in front of the large mirror he did not at first believe it was his reflection that he was looking at. He backed up and then walked out again in front of the glass, not really believing what he had seen. The face he saw was nearly new to him. He had been dirty or covered with hair when he had looked into a mirror before. Now he was neat looking and had a clean rather handsome face and with a clean white shirt and light tan trousers and new brown shoes, he made a striking figure, although he did need a haircut. He thought perhaps Barbara knew where he could find a barbershop.

He cleaned up the mess he had made and picking up his dirty clothes walked out of the bathroom and into the kitchen were Barbara was cleaning up some left over dishes. He asked her,

"Do I look any better now?"

She turned and looked at him, and a really surprised look appeared as she said;

"Wow; what a transformation, if you looked in the mirror in the bathroom, you know you look much better. There is no part of the old John. You look like a high class gentleman now and are very handsome, all you need now is a little hair trim and you can get that tomorrow just down the street."

John walked out into the kitchen and said;

"I really am a little hungry, and whatever you are cooking smells really good."

"My parents will be home in a little while, I don't know where they are, but they are usually in the house by now. They'll be here anytime and we'll eat, you can relax in the living room and listen to the radio." Barbara told him and she motioned toward the large room just off of the kitchen

John walked into the room she had indicated and soon saw the radio and headed toward it. Barbara turned back to her preparing of the evening meal. Soon the sound of music came to her and she hummed along with the tune she knew very well, it was one of her favorites. She thought it sounded a little different, but she could not place the difference. It seemed even prettier somehow. The next song was also one she knew and so she kept humming and occasionally singing alone with the music.

The Soul of Li Chan was quite pleased with the transformation she had made in the mind and thinking processes of John Sanders. His mind was thinking good things most of the time and she had little trouble keeping him thinking along those lines.

His soul now had the loves and likes of a few other beings and their thoughts had been guided by the strong Soul of Princess Li Chan into the mind of John Sanders. He truly loved the way he now looked. He could hardly believe what he had seen when he had looked in the mirror after he had finished dressing. He still had the memories of the man he had been, but he was now ashamed of his past and was trying to put it out of his mind altogether.

When he had left the kitchen and walked into the living room, the first thing his eyes noticed was a large piece of dark furniture in the far corner of the room. He was not sure at first what it was, but he remembered another piece of furniture he had seen with a double folding lid. And it had been a piano. Memories came to him of playing music on one of them, so he walked over to it and slowly looked at the beautiful keyboard as he lifted the lid and folded it back into its up position.

Pulling out the beautiful bench he sat down and ran his fingers over the keys, then as the memories came to him, he drifted into a beautiful melody that he loved. His mind, locked now into his new found love of music, brought the old favorites from his new memories and he played them now as he had never played them before.

It was into this scene that Barbara's mother and father walked in to as they quietly entered their house. They heard the music and looked toward the piano. They saw a man sitting there softly playing beautiful music and totally involved in what he was doing.

They then looked toward the kitchen where their daughter was singing along with the music and getting ready to serve dinner. Neither their daughter nor the young man at the piano had heard them enter the house. They stood there and listened for a few minutes then slowly walked toward the kitchen. Barbara sensed, rather than saw them, then glanced around and said;

"Hi, you guys are just in time dinner is ready to be served."

"Barbara, who's the guy playing the piano, he's really good, where did you meet him?" her mother asked.

"That' just the radio, and I want you to meet the guy sitting in there somewhere, I met him today at the restaurant."

"No Barbara. That is not the radio, there is some man sitting at the piano playing beautiful music, is he the guy you met at the restaurant today?" Her mother asked her. Barbara stopped what she was doing, stood up, then rushed to the door and looked in. John was still sitting at the piano and the soft music was still coming from it as John, still deeply engrossed in what he was doing, played on.

"I did not know he could play the piano." she said, keeping her voice low and she sounded surprised, then continued "I wonder just who that guy is. I just met him tonight at the restaurant. He came in for a meal and we got acquainted when he stopped two guys from holding me up and taking the day's receipts."

"You almost got held up" Her father asked, surprise in his voice. "Let's hear more about that."

When Barbara started toward the piano, her mother grabbed her arm and said.

"Let him play awhile, I haven't heard that piano sound that good in a long time"

Barbara turned to the kitchen, turned off all the stoves and they all went into the living room and found places to sit as John continued to play the soft music.

They listened for another half hour, and Barbara thought the food should not get cold so she went to the piano and tapped John on the shoulder and told him that it was time to eat. He turned, saw the parents and said,

"Oh, I am so sorry, I was engrossed in what I was doing, I forgot everything else, I haven't played a piano for quite a while and it felt so good, Barbara, you should have stopped me"

"It' your own fault, your playing was so good I thought it was the radio and I was singing along with you, I did not know you played piano" Barbara told him, then continued, "Come on lets eat, I will introduce you to my parents and we'll talk at dinner".

The introductions were made over dinner and Barbara told her parents about the two men trying to rob her, and John's place in the action. He did not say much and looked embarrassed. He was trying to think what he was going to say if they began to question him about his past. He had a lot of memories now in his head and he wondered where they had come from. There were a lot of people's names and a lot of places he knew he had never been, and he wondered why and when these memories had came into his head. Then he remembered, the day of the crash, his head had hit a rock and he had blacked out. When he had come to and the police had come, his body had gone into action in a way he had never done before and he had tossed the police around like tenpins. That must have been when the knowledge had come to him. He had never known all this stuff before that accident. It was a little scary, but he liked it. In his life before the accident he had been running all the time and now he was a changed man and knew a lot of nice things and he liked it.

Li Chan's Soul was still having a little trouble as the soul of John Sanders. The old soul was still trying to push him into trouble, and a life of crime. During the attempted robbery she had tried to get him to take the money and Barbara's car and run. Fortunately Li Chan's willing was a bit stronger and she had kept control. She was given a large amount of help from the fact that John had felt attracted to Barbara, and did not want to hurt her in any way. That feeling was new to him, but he liked feeling like that.

As the meal ended they all got up and walked into the living room to talk. As they sat down in the chairs and divan, Mr. Shaffer looked at John and asked,

"How did you happen to end up in this little burg, anyway?

"Oh," John said. "I was living with my parents and working the range for my Uncle to spend the time until I decided what I was going to do next. I had just quit my regular Job, and do something different. I had saved a little money and decided to go east and see some of the eastern seaboard, We all had joked about the hoboes riding the rails so I decided to give it a try so here I am. I got hungry and dropped off when I saw the lights of this little town. I found your little restaurant just before closing."

"Barbara took me shopping to get some new clothes after she closed the restaurant, then she brought me here to clean up and put them on. I am sorry to have been such a bother and I want to thank you all for the kindness, I need to get a haircut and be on my way." John finished.

Barbara's father spoke up. "We have a spare bedroom and you may as well stay the night and you can do that tomorrow, there is a barber shop just down the street and he opens at about 8:30 am. Now, how about giving us some more of that piano music, that was beautiful."

John just turned and went to the piano. He was thinking how glad he was that they wanted more music, it would give him a chance to think about his situation. He would play for an hour or so then say how tired he was and go to bed. He needed more time to think.

His luck was still holding as they showed him his sleeping quarters just off the downstairs bathroom with a single bed and small dresser. There was another door into a hallway which led to the living room. Just what he needed, he thought.

Three hours later as he held the rear door knob turned to open position as he quietly closed it and slipped into the darkness hoping that no one had heard him preparing to leave. He had been very quiet and knew that he had all his belongings. He headed toward the railroad tracks and kept in the darkness so he would not be seen. Now he hoped all the local dogs were sleeping too.

As he neared the tracks, he tried to remember where there had been a thicket of trees or low bushes that he could find and use as a hideout till the evening train came by the next afternoon.

Maybe there would be an earlier slow moving one he could catch, he wanted out of here.

Several times he thought about staying and having a goods breakfast in the morning and then catching the train, but the questions stopped him. He had never been around a bunch of people and talked so much and it was making him uneasy just thinking about it He could think pretty fast when he needed to but he knew that there would be a lot of questions and he could not fool them very long, so he wanted out of here quickly.

He went back to the tracks the same way he had came to the restaurant and soon approached the rails and walked along the till he came to a bunch of small trees with a lot of low bushes on the ground around them. He had bought a rather heavy jacket when he and Barbara were shopping, because he knew that the nights could get rather cold sometimes and he would be sleeping outside when he could not find a shed or some protection from the elements. The store had given him a shopping bag to carry his purchases in and he had kept it and it now held all his belongings. He still kept the police special under his belt beneath a sweater he had bought. I must get some cartridges for that too, he only had three cartridges left and he never knew when he might need more. With the heavy jacket on he crawled into the bushes and found a bunch of tall grass, curled up and went to sleep.

John went to sleep thinking that he would have to wait till the next afternoon or evening for the next slow freight. A few hours later he was awakened by a weird sort of noise and the shaking of the ground he was sleeping on. It took him a few minutes to figure out that it was a slow freight train coming slowly from the west. Minutes later he saw the gleam of the beam of the big headlight on the front of the huge engine as it approached.

He stayed in his hiding place till the engine passed then moved closer to the tracks and began looking for open boxcar doors. The train was moving rather slowly and he wanted to get into one of the cars in the middle of the train if possible. He watched fifteen or twenty cars go by, then seeing one with the door half closed he threw the shopping bag in and caught the hand rail and swung himself into the half open door. Picking up the shopping bag he walked to the forward end of the car, curled up in the corner and with his head on the shopping bag of clothes went to sleep to the clickety—click of the wheels.

The train had evidently just filled it's boilers for it was late the next day before it slowed down. John was getting hungry and tired of the clicking of the wheels and as the train slowed he began to look for a place to jump off without being seen. He preferred jumping off while the train was rounding a curve, no one on the front or rear of the train could see him in the middle of the curve, and if there was cover of some kind he could hide quickly. As it happened there was a slight curve while the train was still out in the rural area due to the water tank being a mile or two away from the busy roads and intersections which the train could not block while taking on the water.

It was not dark yet but as the section of the train he was in started into the curve and at the same time he spotted a section of trees, he grabbed the bag of clothes and jumped. The train had not slowed enough for a good landing so he let himself roll and gripped the bag. He stood up and checked himself. He was not hurt and the gun and bag were still with him so he headed toward the woods for cover and a place he could look around and figure out which way to go for food.

The train seemed to take forever to fill the boilers, but it finally started to move Slowly at first then it gradually increased speed and was soon gone and John got a good look at his surroundings. He had jumped off on the north side of the train which looked like rural country, and had not paid much attention to the south side of the tracks. Now he could see nearly all the surrounding country and he could see a large cluster of houses off to the south. He could see cars moving along a road a half a mile or so away. He stayed in the shelter of the trees until dark and then picking up his shopping bag he headed toward the road and the cluster of buildings.

As he entered the small village he noticed a sign near the center of the buildings which read, "Baker's Bar and Grill". He headed that way. All his clothes were nearly new and he was still rather neat looking so he acted natural and walked in and picked a table in the corner and sat down. When he was seated, he pulled out his leather wallet and checked his cash to see how much was left of the money the old lady had given him. There was only a few dollars, and he began to think about where he was to get some more. He counted it to see how much he could order and still be able to pay for it. The waitress came over and put a menu on the table. After looking at the prices and the food description he discovered he could eat a good meal and still have a few bucks for the road.

He was very hungry and was glad to see how good the food looked when the waitress put the large plate down in front of him. He finished the food in short order and was sitting there enjoying the second cup of hot coffee when he noticed the old Piano sitting near the Bar section of the building. There was only one person sitting at the bar so he took his coffee and sat on the bench in front of the piano. Sitting his cup of coffee on top of the piano he let his fingers move across the keyboard lightly while looking at the Bartender. The Bartender looked and listened then gave a slight nod. John then put more pressure on the keys and increased the volume so that the soft music could be heard throughout the room.

There were more people in the restaurant half of the room than there were drinkers at the bar. And most of them were listening to the sound of the music and glancing occasionally toward the piano and smiling. The buzz of people talking filled the air. The waitress came and took the cup and saucer, smiling at John as she did so. John kept on playing. A half hour later he stopped and returned to his table and picked up his check and went to the cash register to pay for his meal.

As he handed the check to the cashier, a man stepped up behind her and took the check, looking at John he said;

"If you're not in a hurry and will stay around and play the piano for an hour or two I'll take care of this for you."

"Well Thank you", John replied. "I'll be glad to, I haven't played for a while, but I'll do my best".

John went back to the piano and sat down and started to play. A few minutes later the waitress came over and sat a large glass on the piano, turned and walked back to the food counter. John played on and soon the glass had a dollar in it. John played on.

Soon a glass of beer appeared and someone asked for a favorite tune and the evening started.

It was near two A. M. when John finally finished the fourth beer and stopped playing and the owner finally shooed the last customer out the door and turned too John and asked,

"You got a place to sack out?"

"Not really," John replied "But I'll find one."

"If you don't mind a small bunk, there is one in the back room and you know where the "Jon" is". The owner said, then, "See you in the morning"

John took the money from the glass and stuffed it into his pocket and went into the back room. He had no intention of staying the night, just till it got light enough he could find his way back to the little group of trees by the train tracts. He did not want to get involved with people any more than he had to. He wanted back on the trains and headed east.

His mind seemed to tell him when daylight seeped in and in an instant he was up and found his way to a rear door which he easily slipped open and out into the early morning. It was a little chilly and he was wearing his jacket so he was comfortable as he found his way back the way he had came to this place. He hoped no one had seen him leave. It was nearly full daylight as he slipped into the small thicket and curled up on the grass and went to sleep.

It was nearly noon when he heard the rumble of a slow moving train and moved to the edge of the brush and watched as a long line of box and freight cars came into sight and slowed down. He knew that when the engine stopped to take on water, the center of the train would e somewhere close to where he was and that he would have a chance and plenty of time to locate the car he wanted to jump into. So he waited.

Soon the cars came to a halt and he looked for an open door on one of the box cars. He saw one just where the curve started so looked first for any sign of a railroad detective, which he would have to evade as he swung up into the car. He stayed under cover till he got as close as he could to where the car was and then waited.

Soon the train began to move and John wanted to get on before it was moving too fast, so he ran to the open door, kept pace with it as it moved, threw his shopping bag in on the floor of the car, then he grabbed the iron bar beside the door opening and swung his body up and into the open doorway. He immediately moved back away from the opening for he knew that the car would be moving through the suburb of the city and he could be seen by someone and they might call the police, probably not, but there was a chance. Few people would pay attention to a railroad bum sitting in a box car.

The Soul of Li Chan was quite content with things as the days were passing. John seemed to be really enjoying himself and there had not been any hard decisions to be made. He now had some money and he had enjoyed the earning of it. Now he could just enjoy the ride east and see what comes next.

It was rather dark in the boxcar due to the half closed door, but his eyes were becoming used to the darkness as he got up with his shopping bag and started toward the front of the car.

"Well, what have we here?" a loud voice said out of the dark area toward the rear of the car.

John turned and saw a big whiskered man coming toward him from the rear of the car. He was looking at John with a silly grin on his face.

"Let me see what's in the shopping bag." he said as he reached for the bag.

John said nothing as he moved slowly toward the open door, carrying the bag with him.

"Give me that bag." The big man said as he lunged for the bag.

John tossed the bag behind him, grabbed the extended arm, turned and heaved the big man over his back and out through the open door. The train had left the outskirts of the city as John had noted and the big man hit the ground and rolled. There was no way the big man could get back on the train as it was now traveling much too fast for him to jump back on even if he was able too.

John picked up the bag, then made a tour of the car to see if the big man was traveling with a companion. There was no one else in the car, so he went to the front of the car, put down the bag in a corner. With the bag for a pillow he lay down and went to sleep with the clickety-click of the wheels.

A brief thought came to him before he fell into sleep, "Why hadn't he just shot the big man?

The Soul of Li Chan knew why. She was still in a controlling and willing position and John seemed to be following her direction, but she knew she was not yet in full control. During the past few days she knew that John had been giving much thought to where he had learned to play a piano and had wondered about this new fighting ability. He knew he was fast with his fists, but just how to use them had not been with him until the car accident. The question was, "What had taken place during the crash and fire?" Where had he known a Robert and a Jessica? A few other names had come to him, but not as strong as those two. He still had the revolver, but he was more reluctant to use it now than he had been before that accident. Why?"

The really nice thing that he knew now was the ability to make music on the piano. He loved to feel his fingers going over the keys and listening to what came out. He had always liked to listen to music, some songs more than others, so he naturally played is favorites, but he seemed to know so many more and wondered where the memories came from. Dreams came to him now of traveling to far places, different countries and many different people of different races.

The big man was John's first encounter with what the country called a "Hobo". For years there were hobos on the trains criss-crossing the country. They begged for food wherever they were at the time. Some offered to work for food; others just begged for it or looked in the trash cans in the towns behind the grocery stores. There were "Hobo camps" along nearly all of the railroads. The camps were usually in a woodsy, sheltered area near a city or town of some kind.

As the train moved east, John jumped off at nearly every place it stopped and ran to the nearest building that looked like a store and bought whatever they had to eat or drink, then, being careful to look for railroad detectives, jumped back on and continued his ride east. He was traveling fast and steady until somewhere in the mid west he was pretty hungry and the village was a mile or so away from the train and he did not make it back in time to catch the train before it gained too much speed for him to jump back on.

The countryside was changing and John liked the greenery and the growing amount of woods and valleys. They were different from the western areas, though still flat in some areas as they entered the farm belt.

As he sat leaning back against the side of the boxcar, looking out the opposite door, he noticed that they were slowing down and entering a city of some kind. The train slowed to a slow steady speed, slow enough for him to jump if he wanted to, but he decided to wait and see just where it was going to stop.

They were entering what looked like a big railroad intersection, with tracks all around the train and there were other strings of freight cars on both sides of the one he was on. He had heard about this place in the center of the country and it was a large city near the lakes in the center of the country. Boy, he thought, I've came a long way. There are probably a lot of railroad detectives here too; I had better be on the lookout.

When the train came to a full stop, he jumped to the ground and started walking toward the nearest buildings, watching for any sign of another person. He came to a bunch of large buildings that looked like warehouses, entered one and stood still as he looked around. There were small rooms built on the floor of the big building, which he saw was in bad disrepair and was full of mostly trash, He walked slowly out through an Isle down the center of the building, watching and listening. Out of habit he kept his right hand inside his shirt and had a good grip on the butt of the revolver held behind his belt. Near the other side of the building he suddenly stopped and listened. He thought he had heard something, sounded like voices.

Off to his left toward the back corner of the building he saw another small room and there was light coming out of some of the cracks in the walls. He stopped and stood for a while listening and watching, then slowly walked toward where the door seemed to be, it looked slightly open and light was coming through the opening. Staying about fifteen or twenty feet away from the opening he moved to where he could see into the center of the little room.

There were several men in the room; they seemed to be sitting on the floor in a circle. He could not see them all, some feet with old shoes on and some men in dirty wrinkled clothes.

They were all trying to talk at the same time it seemed for he could hardly make out any of the words. He could see why, on the floor in front of them in the center of the room was, of all things, a huge pile of paper money. He could see different denominations from where he was.

One of the men sitting out of sight said,

"Where the 'ell did she get all that money?"

The man who seemed to be in charge was sitting where John could see him and John figured he was the man to keep an eye on was looking at the stack of money and as John watched, reached into the pile of bills and pulled out a piece of white paper.

"It says 'ere that this bag she was carrying is the property of the South Market St Holy Church. She must have been on her way to a bank drop and we lucked out when old Pete there grabbed her and brought her here to play with." He said, looking across at the man that had spoken.

It was then that John noticed a pair of slim legs between two of the men. They were tied together and were not moving. He figured that her hands were also tied and she was probably gagged as well. John could see four men and there may be more. He suddenly thought of a possible guard and where he might be, probably at the main entrance to this place.

"Rafe," Old Pete spoke up. "Lets divvy up the money now and get to the girl; I didn't bring her here to talk about."

"We can split the money later Pete, I kinda like your idea, we'll have some fun first, get rid of the wench then split the dough." Rafe said and reached behind him and picked up the cloth bag. John watched as Rafe shoved the pile of bills into the bag and picked it up as he stood up.

John stepped into the opening in the doorway, his revolver in his hand and said,

"I'll take that". He said looking at Rafe over the gun barrel.

"We'll see." Rafe said as he reached into a pocket.

John pulled the trigger of is revolver and shot directly into Rafe's chest. The big man was jolted backward and to the floor. John was watching the other men and all of them, there were four of them, were reaching for something in their clothing, so he fired as fast as he could, once at each one, at this range he could not miss. Two came up with a gun in hand and the other two each had a wicked knife. All were on the floor, some moving and some still. He watched, he knew he only had one shell left in his revolver so he reached in his pocket and found five good loads and waited for what he thought was the right time and reloaded, all the time keeping his eyes on the men on the floor.

When he had determined that they were all either dead or dying he went to the girl and pulled her out where he could check her and see if she was still alive or seriously hurt. She was gagged and her hands were tied behind her back. When she could talk, she started talking so fast he tried to quiet her. She was talking and when he heard the word "Guard", he remembered and reached for his revolver. As he grabbed it and turned he felt a sharp pain in his side and heard the shot. As he fell he saw the guard and raising his gun, he pulled the trigger. The guard disappeared as John hit the floor.

John opened his eyes, still conscious and looked around on the floor in front of his face was one of the knives that had been drawn against him. The girl was lying there in front of him also. He had to get her free someway. He picked up the knife and reached around to her wrists and tried to slip the blade between them. Finally it felt to him that the blade was in the right place so he started a sawing motion as his strength was leaving him.

She had quieted down and when she saw what he was trying to do, she tried to help him. When she felt the cloth part and her arms come free, she untied her feet and stood up. All was quiet, the men were all still, even John had gone into a coma. She ran for help.

The girl ran to a phone booth about two city blocks away. When the operator answered she screamed into the microphone,

"Help! Send the police and an ambulance to the old Sommers warehouse on Epson Ave. fast. Someone has been shot. Hurry please". She slammed the mic back on the hanger and headed back to the warehouse.

When she entered the little room the men were all in the same position they were in when she left. The only sound was a low moaning she discovered coming from John. She rolled him over on his back and made him as comfortable as she could. His eyes slowly opened and he tried to say something. It came out as a whisper and she had to bend down to hear what he was saying.

"Are you Ok, are they all dead?" He managed to ask.

"Yes, I think so, they aren't moving, you know you saved my life, they were going to kill me, I heard them talking." She said through her tears.

"Good," John whispered and his eyes closed.

"Oh Lord, don't let him die." She said as she cradled his head in her arms.

The last thing John felt were the warm wet lips of the girl as she kissed him on the forehead and held him close.

The Soul of Li Chan now found that she could no longer control or will anything so she slowly left the body of John Barrow and hovered above. She was remembering the time she had spent in that body. Her experiences had been vastly different than any of the other bodies she had entered. It had been a real shock finding a soul that possessed such evil ways of thinking. It took a lot of controlling and willing, using the memories she had received from the other bodies to begin to move them to the recesses of his memory cells where he might not think of them.

She watched as the Police arrived and discovered that all the men, including John were dead. Some of them were well known and all were wanted by the authorities except John They did not recognize him as yet. She watched and listened as the girl showed them the money and told them the facts of the case. She also explained that she knew none of them, even John. He had not told anyone his name and he had no Identification on him. They might find his shopping bag outside the room, but his clothes did not indicate that he was one of them. With three guns on the floor they would not know which was the one he used. The girl probably had not noticed.

Li Chan found no reason to linger any longer so she let herself drift off into the upper levels where she could ponder her next move. Again the thoughts went back to her teenage years and her life as a Tanganese Princess and of the fatal evening she and her two hand maidens had fought it out with a band of would be kidnappers in the little park where she was to be met by her lover, a young Army officer. The battle had gone well till one of the bandits had slid a wicked short sword into her side from behind. She had died there and she had left her physical being and had traveled ever since, experiencing life in other human beings by entering their near death bodies and prolonging their lives as their souls.

As the Original Soul, Li Chan had kept herself in control of the other Souls she encountered and so now she gave some thought of going back to the country of her origin and trying to find some trace of her first lover Chen Li. Since the visit to the little room with her things she had been amazed at the memories that she was having. She loved her country and now more than ever she wanted to go back and spend some time there. After all they were her people and they worshipped her, she must go back, she thought.

She had noticed that when she was thinking of a particular time or place she would usually find that it would appear and she would be there without her making any effort to get there.

Now as she was remembering the time in the little garden waiting with her handmaidens for Chen Li to arrive, she found herself above the little bench they had been sitting on as they waited. For Chen Li. She was remembering that evening and wondering what had become of her two faithful handmaidens, and the way they had left the palace so that her father would not know she had went out. She had found out that he knew all the time and at times had her followed. This night she had left earlier than usual and he had not dispatched his men in time to prevent what had happened. A thing he had regretted the rest of his reign.

Li Chan's Soul drifted to the different locations as she thought about them. She entered the little room that had been her bedroom and discovered that it was nearly the same as the one in the museum. She discovered that the ones in the museum were the original and the ones in her real room were fakes. The only thing missing was the little Ninja short sword with the jeweled handle.

She had not kept time of years and now she was amazed at the change in the castle and the surrounding area. She had to pick out the things that had not changed and then look for the other things that were related to them in order to keep oriented, the new buildings, schools and houses, and so many people. The cars and modes of travel were a surprise. She had seen them and had memories of them from the experiences she had encountered as the souls of the different bodies she had entered and lived in, but to find them in her own country was unexpected. They had not been in her memories of Tanga and now it surprised her. She knew now that she should have expected it but it still shook her up. She had seen the cars and some of the changes when she had been in Tanga with the body of Jessica, but she was in a different environment and had not had the time to notice those things. She drifted through the halls of the old castle she had lived in and saw the huge pictures of her father The people, she observed had been loved by his people and was still remembered fondly by them. There were some large pictures of her as a young princess. She had been quite beautiful and she remembered now, how she had been pampered and catered to by the people of the castle and even she had traveled outside of the castle.

Li Chan had been a quiet Princess and had not been demanding or overbearing, just friendly and courteous to her people. Her father, the Emperor, had taken her with him a lot as he rode around the country and she really enjoyed those times. It had been a very good time to be alive. The country was in peacetime and she had never known times of war.

She now saw signs of what must have been a bad time of fighting and warring, for there were remains of buildings having been destroyed and she saw that there were many more roadways and even some canals had been built. It all added up to a lot of change that she was not prepared for, it would take some getting used to.

The Soul of Li Chan, with all her memories, drifted slowly around the now, big city and saw the many new buildings and even factories that had sprung up to make the city the capital that it was. There were even some new buildings that she was glad to see were colleges, Universities and other buildings used for the Education of the people of the country. Around these buildings there was an almost continual flow of young people either walking or riding in some kind of conveyance, a lot were on bicycles of their own.

There did not seem to be much system or order to the way the traffic was controlled and she marveled at the lack of accidents in the hustle and bustle of the mess that was going on below on the surface as she hovered and felt the excitement of it all.

Everything was moving as it should until a few weeks later in late afternoon she suddenly sensed something unusual. Locating it she saw that there had been an accident. One of the little automobiles had evidently been going too fast and had turned sharply and collided with a young lady on a bicycle and she had been injured.

She was now lying on the pavement and people were gathering around her to see if they could help her in any way.

She appeared to be unconscious to Li Chan, so she proceeded to approach the body and slip inside to see if it was possible to keep her alive. The other Soul was rather young and inexperienced and the Soul of Li Chan quickly absorbed the knowledge and memories of it and took over the willing and controlling of the young body.

Her new senses told her that there was nothing but a slight bruise on the side of her head where she had hit the pavement when she had been knocked from her bicycle. She appeared to be even now gaining her consciousness so Li Chan took over and she soon was sitting up and talking.

Li Chan was not quite in full control yet so she was babbling about just heading home from her classes and had seen the little car but did not expect the sharp sudden turn it had made. Li Chan let the young Soul ramble on about classes and school while she got all the information from the young girl's memory banks.

The girls name was Akina and she was a little over eighteen years of age and was soon to graduate from a very prestigious and well known University. She as not a very bright student and was just going to clear the required points to graduate at the rate she was going. The final exam was in a few weeks and she had not prepared too well. Li Chan soon knew all there was to know about Akina and slowly took over control and absorbed the soul of the girl as the Souls became one with Li Chan as the main controlling force.

A short time later, with Li Chan's knowledge and control, Akina got back on her bicycle and went on her way to her room at the dormitory a couple of blocks away. Megume, Akina's roommate had reached the small apartment ahead of her and was a little concerned about the bruise on Alina's head and helped her to check it out and apply some ointment.

The two girls were somewhat alike, both near five foot ten, dark black hair and slightly oriental looking eyes and skin texture. Both were very beautiful as beauty goes and were built nearly the same with Akina being fuller breasted and more rounded across the hips. The skin texture of Megume was a little darker than Akina's, but both were quite beautiful.

The two girls had been in constant conversation since Akina walked in the door and soon Akina noticed that Megume was looking at her in an odd sort of way.

"Why are you looking at me that way"? Akina asked.

"What way?" Megume answered.

"As if something is different." Akina told her.

"Akina" Megume answered "I have known you since our youth and I know something is different about you, you must have hit your head pretty hard. How do you feel now?"

"Megume, you are my best friend and you are right. I have changed. I feel the same except for the bump on my head, but there is something else. I seem to have a lot more knowledge in my head and different things come to my mind that I do not remember ever learning, but I am so sure that I know them and that they are true. Different languages come to mind and I can understand them also and the only foreign one that I studied in the university and earlier in school was English. We almost all learned to speak a lot of that as it is becoming almost universal, but please do not say anything to anyone else?" Akina asked her.

Akina's Soul, now controlled by Li Chan, had been going to let the young Soul of the young Akina keep on talking about all the new things that she now found in her memory banks but changed her mind and thought she had better not let all the surprises out at one time so she took over and stopped the conversation. There was no reason now to reveal the true intelligence now of the new Akina. There would be plenty of time later if the occasion called for it.

"Right now I just want to stretch out and get a little rest before we go out to eat, OK?" Akina asked Megume, as she stretched out on her cot.

About two hours later they both got up and took turns in the small bathroom and soon were on their way to the local snack bar for food. The streets were crowded with people and bicycles, but they were used to the mess and took it all in stride.

There was very little talking as there was really too much noise so they waited till they were in the little restaurant before they tried to talk.

Megume spoke first.

"How are you feeling now Akina?" She asked.

"Fine". Akina said. "That little bit of rest done the trick. "I feel great and am ready to eat now, but let's find a better restaurant next time."

When the waitress had taken their order and they were waiting for it to come, Akina brought up the subject of the upcoming final exam.

"I am a little scared about that." she said. "I am not sure I am prepared. I haven't done too good with all my subjects."

"You will do ok." Megume told her "Your grades are not all that bad, you can probably make it if you study a little. I'll help you all I can."

"We've got a little over a week yet to prepare and if we hit the books a little in the evening, by the time the day comes we'll be ready." Megume said.

The Soul that had been through so many other physical beings and was controlled by Li Chan now searched the new memory section of her memories and when she found the memory of what the test might be she knew that she would have no problem with it now as Akina.

She thought that she better not tell Megume just how much she knew. She would let her find just how much her new room mate's brain held a little at a time. A little later, after they had left the snack Bar as they were nearing their apartment, a group of boys began following them. They had done it before and the girls had not responded so they were getting braver. Talking louder and becoming more vulgar with their language. One of the larger boys made a crude remark about the bruise on Akina's head. Akina stopped, turned around and moved a little toward him as she said.

"It sounds a little like you haven't been knocked on your ass yet today, smart ass."

"And just what are you going to do about that?" the tall youth asked.

Akina had placed herself at just the right distance away from the boy and now she spun to her left and brought her right foot around and placed a hard kick to the young man's mid-section, driving him backwards and knocking all the wind out of him as he was slammed back into the rest of the group of young men and went to the ground gasping for breath.

Akina stood there then with her hands at her side waiting and looking at the young men. They had all stopped and most were looking at Akina. A couple had went to help the one Akina had kicked.

"You had all better learn how to treat and talk to your equals before you open your mouths" She said, then she turned to Megume and continued, "Come on

"Meg", we've got some studying to do." and the two girls continued on to their apartment.

The young men just stared after them,

Megume just glanced at Akina a few times but said nothing until they were inside the apartment. Then she spoke up.

"I knew something in you had changed Akina, "She said, "But, boy, that was so fast, if I had blinked I would not have seen it. Where in the world did you ever learn to fight like that? That guy never saw it coming. You will probably have to fight some of them again because most of those guys have had some of that kind of training and think they are pretty good. So you had better be ready all the time."

"I know quite a lot of that kind of self defense, Meg, but that kind is not what I am worried about. There is an ancient technique that I know very well. I don't like to use it because it is meant to kill and I do not want to kill anyone. I am afraid that I might accidentally throw a killing blow sometime instead of just a judo or Kung fu blow." Akina told her, "But please do not tell anyone." she added.

"There is a lot more that you are not telling me, isn't there?" Megume said, then added.

"Ok, I won't give away any of your secrets, but I hope they are all legal and for all good reason."

Megume thought for a few minutes then looked at Akina and asked.

"One thing, Akina, Just when did you acquire all this knowledge? I have known you for a long time and you did not know that stuff then. What happened?"

"When that car hit me and I was knocked off of it for a while I was unconscious for several minutes. When I regained consciousness, I had all these memories and all this knowledge and I do not know where it came from. I am still a little confused and mixed up from all the things that I know and have knowledge about, people's names that I have met or know real well and things that have happened. I have even experienced childbirth. It's wild story. And one day I will probably tell you a lot more so that you will believe me. Believe me it is all a little overwhelming and really unbelievable, even to me and I lived it.

Megume looked at her for a little while, then said,

"After seeing the way you handled 'Tora', and the speed you used, I can really believe you. It will be interesting to see what happens tomorrow when we go into the university. No one has ever stood up to him before. I'll bet he doesn't want to believe it happened himself. The guys with him did not know what to do. They were so surprised they just stood there and looked."

Megume opened one of the text books she had brought home to study and Akina did the same and they looked through them. Akina said "All of this stuff looks so easy. I must have gained a lot of knowledge at the accident. It all looks so easy; can I help you with some of the things you need to brush up on 'Meg'?

"I wish you would." Meg answered, and the two girls spent the next two hours together studying before going to their respective cots for the night.

The two girls were up early and sat at the little table in the little kitchen and each had a bowl of oat cereal to eat before they left for the university there was a little girlie chit chat on the way but neither knew exactly what to say. They were both waiting to see how the day would go. Most of the kids must not have heard of the incident for they nearly all were acting the same way they always did. The ones that seemed to have heard about it just stared and did not say anything. They entered and each went to their classroom.

By the end of the day more and more of the students were staring at Akina and Megume with odd expressions on their faces when they were passing in the halls.

When 'Tora' and some of his friends would pass them, they just looked down until they were passed.

When the day's classes were over the two girls met on the front steps of the huge building and they walked back to the little apartment.

Meg, broke the silence,

"I got some of the weirdest looks today Akina". She said. "Nobody really said anything and they weren't nasty looks, just curious". She added.

"I got the same thing, but they just kept a distance away from me when they passed me in the halls and in the classrooms" Akina said. "The instructors even noticed it."

"We'll see what happens when we go out to eat'. Meg said. "We'll go to the same place tonight. If they try to get back at you it will happen tonight."

Akina spoke up. "I hope they learn from it and forget it, I don't want to have to be on guard all the time when we go any place at all." Then added "Let's get to that homework before we go out for dinner."

They sat down at the table with the books and opened them.

A couple of hours later they closed the books and put on their light jackets and started down the street toward the little diner. Both were on the alert but they were talking about little things as they walked. Soon a small group of young men appeared behind them. "Tora' was of course one of them, and he was in the lead. They were about two city blocks from the little restaurant and walking side by side as the small group got closer. Akina whispered loud enough for Meg to hear. "Meg, give me fighting room when it starts." Meg said, "You got it".

They were walking beside a long warehouse when 'Tora's voice said.

"Akina, you with the bruise on your head, do you think you can do that again, I am looking at you now and it will not be a surprise?'

Akina stopped, motioned to Meg and then put her back against the warehouse wall as Meg moved on ahead of her. The young men came on and stopped in front of her, but kept their distance.

Akina just stood in a ready position, smiling slightly. There was no sign of fear or even anger on her face, but the way she stood, they knew she was ready.

When Tora saw her and looked in her eyes, he saw too the confidence, the lack of fear and the readiness. He began to feel that he was not quite ready for that kind of an encounter. He remembered the speed of the blow he had received from this girl. He could almost feel the hardness of that blow, and it had been in a soft part of his body. What would it have felt like if it had been on the side of his head? He spoke up.

"We'll save you for another time, com on guys, let's get on to the restaurant and eat.'

The two girls followed them at a distance. Meg said as she looked at Akina with an odd expression.

"That guy did not want any part of you back there, he's scared to tackle you, he remembers that kick". Her amazement was still showing on her face.

As they entered the restaurant they saw that the men were in the back of the room so they sat next to the cash register on the stools and ordered their food and drink. As it was getting a little cool in the evening they ordered hot tea with their meal.

For a while there were people coming up to the register to pay their bills and it was somewhat annoying to Akina who sat next to the cash register. It soon quieted down and they began to enjoy the meal.

Suddenly a gun with a hand holding it came into sight between Akina's eyes and the cash register and a voice said to the young man that had been working the cash register,

"Nice and easy now, just open that register and hand me all the paper money and don't try any funny stuff"

At the same time a voice behind them said to the diners at the tables.

"Everybody just stay as you are and keep quiet and no one will be hurt"

Akina had been looking in the mirror behind the counter and she had seen the man behind the guy with the gun. he did not appear to have a gun.

The cashier opened the drawer and started to pick up the paper money. As he tried to hand some of the bills to the robber, the robber reached out to get it and at the same time the cashier reached for a handgun he kept on the shelf under the cash register.

Akina saw what was happening and as the robber fired at the cashier she threw a cup of hot tea into the face of the robber with her right hand as she grabbed the gun with her left hand and pulled him around to face her as she brought her right hand up to his neck with all her strength in a bone crushing punch. At the same time she slid off the stool and bracing herself she brought her left foot up between the legs of the other robber as he turned to see what was going on. As he bent over with the pain of it Akina delivered a powerful blow to the side of his neck and then again on the back of his neck. Both men now lay on the floor. Akina had the gun and she turned and told one of the waitresses to call the police. As it happened one of them had already pushed an alarm button, and they were probably on their way.

The cashier had fallen off his stool and now lay on the floor seemingly unconscious. The two would-be robbers were lying crumpled together on the floor in front of the cash register. The diners who had been at the nearest tables had jumped up and now were backing away from the area.

Akina put the gun on the counter beside the cash register and stood where she could watch both of the men on the floor. When the Police came rushing in both Akina and Megume backed away and stood at the edge of the crowd.

"What happened here?" asked one of the officers.

The Hostess, who had been standing a few feet away from the cash register on the opposite side of where Akina and Meg had been sitting, stepped forward and said to the officer.;

"Our cashier has been shot, I've called an ambulance, he is on the floor behind the counter. These two men", She indicated the two men on the floor, "Tried to hold up the cashier and he reached for the gun on the shelf under the cash register, and the man lying there" she indicated the one who had fallen closest to the counter. "Had a gun pointed at him and he just shot".

Then she continued, "When he shot, that girl over there grabbed his gun hand and jerked him around so she could use her other hand to give him a blow to the neck or head. He went down and she then twisted off of the stool and kicked the other robber in the private parts which put him in position for some blows to the head and neck, which put him down also. She put the gun down beside the cash register."

The officer asked, "Who are you?"

"I am the Hostess and I was standing right over there and saw the whole thing." she said

The ambulance pulled up and the interns came in and put the cashier on a stretcher and took him out. They were soon on their way to the Hospital. Another ambulance pulled up and the interns entered and were checking the two men on the floor.

"This one is dead." One intern said as he checked the man next to the counter. Then he went to the other. When he rolled that man over he discovered he had a gun in his right hand which was still in his coat pocket. The officer took the gun. As he did he looked at Akina and asked;

"Did you see him reach for this?"

"After I put this one down", She pointed to the dead man. "I turned to this one and as he turned toward me I saw him reaching in his pocket for something, so I put him down too"

"How did you manage to kill that one?" The officer asked.

"He had just shot the cashier and I knew he would not hesitate to shoot again so I used a killing blow instead of something less. I don't like to do that, but I felt I had to protect myself and possibly someone else." Akina told him.

Unknown to either Akina or Megume, The group of young men that had followed them to the restaurant had left their table and were in the group of people that had encircled the area of the cashier and were hearing every word.

The still alive robber was taken away and finally the dead man was also taken out The officer in charge came over to Akina and said;

"Will you come down to the station; we will need some more information from you and what happened here. We would appreciate it, it won't take long." Then he turned to the hostess and continued. "We would like you to come and repeat what you told me for the records"

The Hostess nodded and the police left and the diners wandered back to the tables. Akina and Meg sat back down at the counter to finish their meal. Meg was still looking at her lifelong friend with an amazed expression as she sat down. Finally she said,

"You really meant what you said when you said there was a lot more to tell and that most of it would be unbelievable. I have just seen some of it and it is unbelievable. If I had not just witnessed it I never would have believed it."

The group of young men was now at the tables and did not know what to say. Finally one of them, a short stocky boy of about eighteen spoke

"Two full grown men down in less than a minute, and one of them dead how could she do that?" Then added "And one of them had a gun out."

"She said she did not like to use the killing blows, but in this case she did to protect herself. Tora said, and added. "That means that she knows there are more blows that can kill and she knows them well."

A boy named 'Haro' spoke. "I have seen a lot of fighters and I do not think I have ever seen anyone faster than that, I could not follow the blows."

Nearly everyone in the restaurant kept glancing at the two girls and talking until they got up, paid their bill and left the restaurant. The police station was not far so they walked and enjoyed the cool night air.

When they entered the station they were met by the same officer that had talked to them at the restaurant and led to a conference room and seated at a large table with the Hostess and two other people, one looked like an undercover cop. and the other was an elderly gentleman with an air of authority.

The table was soon filled and some other people brought in chairs and sat along the wall close to the table. The first officer, whose name was Makoto, spoke;

"Akane", The Hostess, "Will you tell us exactly what you witnessed at the restaurant this evening, Please?"

"Of course." Akane said and repeated what she had told the officer at the restaurant.

Officer Makoto asked her:

"When did you first see the young Lady Akina start her actions?"

"She did not start any movement till after the first shot was fired and the cashier started falling off the stool." Akane said.

Officer Makoto looked at Akina and asked;

"Is that when you first joined the action?'

"Yes, I wish I could have joined earlier but I thought maybe no one would be hurt. When the cashier reached for the gun under the counter I made ready to try to stop any killing, but the robber shot first. By the way how is the young cashier?" Akina answered.

"He will recover, but it will take a while." Makoto answered, then added' How did you know your blow would kill or disable that man when you hit him?

She looked at him then at the other people around the table before answering, they waited and she finally started.

"This will be very hard to believe. Some of you will maybe remember. There is or was an ancient art of fighting that was only used when the battle was nearly lost. It was the art of instantly killing an enemy with one blow. It was used very little and only taught to a select group of people."

As she paused to figure what she could say next, the old man at the end of the table said one word.

"Machedo"

Akina turned and looked at him and nodded.

The people at the table and in the chairs were putting two and two together and not coming up with answers. You could have heard a pin drop as the people tried to understand what the words all meant.

Akina started talking again;

"I will not try to explain how I knew the art of Machedo, it is much too complicated and unbelievable, but I knew I had to stop the use of that gun. Officer Masajun, I think will back me up on that."

"I knew of the art of Machedo, but I was never taught it. There was one man, but he died years ago that knew it and as far as I knew never used it, but there really was such a thing."

Masajun said. Then added "The technique was said to increase the speed as it blended all motions together".

Akane, the hostess spoke up. "I can believe that. I have never seen anything happen so fast before, it was over before I could say anything."

Officer Makoto spoke now.;

"I think that is all we need from you three" he said to the two girls and the hostess, then added the only question left for you, Akina is, ""Where and when did a nineteen year old college student that has lived here all her nineteen years ever learn how to fight like that, two men down in less than a minute and one dead and she doesn't carry a scratch. Don't try to answer that. I can see that it is quite beyond comprehension. If you would, I would like to talk to you for a while some day out of curiosity. I can see that there are more things about you that would be interesting. Would any of you people like to ask her any questions before we let her go?"

No one spoke up.

Akina and Meg both got up and Makoto showed them to the door where he thanked them for coming. To their surprise he asked one of his men to drive them to their apartment. They waited till they were safely in the apartment before talking.

Megume was quiet for a while, all the time, looking at Akina with an odd look on her face. Then she said,

"It has been only a week since your accident and look at all that has happened. You look nearly the same as you did before the accident but the change in your actions and attitude is completely out of your other character that it is unbelievable. I do not know which I prefer, the quiet one or the one full of action and knowledge. It has been exciting to say the least, but I have no idea what will happen next. That guy Tora was in the restaurant and heard what the hostess said to the officers. He probably saw you floor those two guys and how little time it took you, unbelievable. If he has any sense at all he knows he had better leave you strictly alone, he should know he is not even near being in the same class as you when it comes to that kind of fighting. We'll have to wait and see."

For the next week the two girls went to classes and studied at night in preparation for the upcoming exams. Meg was an easy student and a quick learner and Akina explained every thing that she needed help with. The other students had a few questions and the girls answered what they could. They stayed mostly on the subjects of the University and the coming exams.

On Friday, after classes, they went to the huge Auditorium to sit and talk about the exams. As it happened they went down front and were sitting in the front row. As they were talking Akina's eyes caught sight of the Piano and the sight brought up memories. AKina said to Meg;

"I think I can play one of them."

Meg looked at her and said;

"If you think you can, you probably can, after what has happened, I don't doubt it a bit. Go over and sit down on the bench and look at it close. I'll sit here and wait to hear the music."

Akina got up and walked over, pulled out the bench and sat down. She looked at the keyboard for a while then put her fingers on the keys and started playing, first slowly and softly, then slowly increased the tempo till it sounded right.

As the memories came to her she brought up all of the ones on Piano and the music filled the auditorium. They were all old songs from Italy and America, but they were soft and beautiful. Unknown to the two girls, people were starting to come into the huge hall and gather behind Megume.

The part of Akina's Soul that was Li Chan was remembering a little girl named Jessica in a little grape vineyard in southern Italy. Jessica had become a famous well known pianist over all of Italy and then in America. Her young soul had been taken over by Li Chan after a violent rape and beating. Li Chan's soul had really enjoyed her time as part of the Soul of Jessica. She had learned much and had enjoyed the piano playing. She loved good music. She was really enjoying it now in this great university Hall here in Tanga.

Akina was now playing softly, but the Tanganese [people were ahead of most of the world in the development of electronics and the system in the auditorium was one of the best so that the music from the piano was picked up and could be heard the same throughout the great hall.

Meg heard a movement behind her and turned with surprise to see the people assembled there. She was not really surprised, because the music was very beautiful and it could be heard even out in the hallway.

One man, an elderly gentleman clearly not Tanganese came down and sat beside Meg. No one was talking. They all sat quietly and listened.

Akina, at the moment was not Akina. Li Chan's part of her soul was remembering her times on stage in front of huge audiences in Italy and America as Jessica Levanti, the internationally known Pianist. Akina was lost now in the music and the memories, she played on unaware of her surroundings.

Over an hour later she ended a very popular internationally known song and her fingers stopped and she sat there a few seconds before she turned around to say something to Meg.

Suddenly a thunderous applause rose from the people in the great hall. Loud clapping, whistles and shouts brought a broad smile to Akina as she slid off of the bench and bowed to the admiring audience that were showing their appreciation of her playing.

Akina had just been thinking of crowds just like that as she quit playing so it was nearly expected and she was of course surprised but was quick to accept it. She bowed a couple times more then walked over to Meg somewhat embarrassed and sat down beside her. The old gentleman on the other side of Meg spoke up and said:

"That was very beautiful music, and we do not hear Italian songs very often, especially any of the national favorites, I heard music like that many years ago, played by an American on tour here one summer. I believe her name was," and he stopped to think, and Akina spoke up and said,

"Jessica Levanti."

"That's it" The old man almost screamed in Italian and continued. "How did you ever learn to play exactly like her?

Akina answered in perfect Italian. She said. "I had several of her recordings for a while and I practiced a lot. Then I sold them all. They are very beautiful."

That she had answered him in his own language had apparently been missed in the excitement but he walked away scratching his head.

Megume had not spoken, but she had an odd look on her face as they started toward their apartment. Finally she opened her mouth but nothing came out, then she tried again;

"Akina, you're driving me crazy, will you try to explain this all to me when we get back in the apartment so I can at least feel like I am still sane and not seeing and hearing things that are not and can not be true?"

Akina put her arm around Megume and said:

"Meg, you are my best and now my only friend and I promise you I will give you a true explanation as soon as we get to the apartment. It will be hard for you to understand what I will have to say, but you are an intelligent girl and with a little imagination it will all make sense to you and I hope you will keep what I will have to say a tight secret between the two of us,"

They came to the apartment and entered. Putting their books away they went to the sleeping area and got comfortable, on the cots as young people do.

Meg said, "I can do that, no one would believe me anyway and it would make more weird situations. Did you notice that that old gentleman, his name is Professor Delgado, he is our Italian language instructor, did not notice that you answered him in perfect Italian instead of Tanganese. I know perfectly well you never took an Italian language course because I've known you all my life. I am anxious to hear how that happened. He will be too when it dawns on him that it happened that way." She paused for a few seconds and then continued. "That music, when your fingers started moving across those keys, it looked like you were caressing them and the softest music I have ever heard came out of that box. I could not believe it. To my knowledge you have never been near a piano, let alone learn to play that kind of music on one. I am half afraid to hear what you have to say, There is no way that you can give me a reasonable answer to what happened. There is no known method of transferring information from brain to brain that anyone that I know is able to use. It is not possible yet, probable maybe, in the future.

Akina said;

"When I give you an explanation and you hear what I have to say I am sure you will have a satisfactory and almost believable explanation with a little stretch of the imagination you know that I am not the same as I was a few weeks ago. You know that I, meaning the person I am now entered Akina's body at the time of the accident and took over and am now in control of the body of the Akina you grew up with and knew" She paused for a moment.

"But before I start telling what I have to say I want to show you something and tell you about it. How far is the Historical Museum from here and is it still open this time of day?" Akina finished.

Megume answered her;

"The museum is about four blocks and I think the museum stays open till Nine O'clock. We can get a cab and be there in a few minutes."

They both grabbed their light jackets and headed for the door. Akina said,

"We can eat a little later after we leave the museum."

Meg hailed a cab and a few minutes later they were dropped off at the steps of the museum. As they were walking up the steps of the museum, the part of Akina that was Li Chan was remembering the other time, many years ago that she walked up these same steps with her good friend Jessica and they found the little room that Li Chan remembered so very well.

As they walked back the huge hallway to where the little room was, Akina thought I hope everything is still the same. To herself, she wondered if the little old man was still behind the curtain. At that time he seemed to be ageless and said; "Li Chan, we know you will return and we are looking forward to your return."

They came to the little room which was the little chapel she was remembering. She had no shawl so she put a scarf she had over her head and as Meg did the same, They walked in together, heads bowed and approached the little statue at the end of the row of ornate polished marble tiles. Akina knelt on one of the little blue pillows that were on the raised step that was there, Meg knelt beside her. Inreverence. Akina was muttering an ancient prayer as Meg listened. Akina was watching the silken curtain behind the Idol, but there did not seem to be anyone behind it.

With their heads bowed, they slowly backed out of the little chapel. When they were outside of the chapel door Akina turned and entered the little room next to it. Meg's eyes opened in amazement as she saw the ornate and beautiful items that were neatly arranged around the little room. On the wall directly above the center of the beautiful glass display case was the huge picture of the young Tanganese Princess,

Li Chan at the young age of eighteen. That had not been there when Li Chan had returned the first time as Jessica. Akina stopped and just stared at the picture for several minutes, then said to Megume;

"Megume," She said softly, "These are the truest words I've ever spoken. That is a true picture of me, taken by the best photographer in all of Tanga when I was eighteen. My father, The Emperor was very proud of me." These things in this room are the things that were in my bedroom when I was killed. Even the beautiful little jeweled dagger that I used in the fight the night I died. After I left my physical body and was watching from above, I saw my hand maiden Su Lin reach down and pick up the little Ninja short sword my father had secretly had made for me with a secret compartment and Jewels in the handgrip. I loved that little knife, and there it is.", Akina pointed at the little weapon in the glass case.

Akina then told Meg about the other items and clothing that were in the other cases and even the little ornate single bed that sat on one side of the little room.

Nearly an hour later the two girls walked slowly out of the little room and out to the street. Where they hailed a cab and were soon on their way to the little restaurant for something to eat. They were a little early for the same crowd that had witnessed the fight the night before and they were hoping it was a new crowd and they could avoid a lot of questions.

They were dropped off at the door and walked into the restaurant and went to an out of the way table. Where they could talk and not disturb anyone, they hoped. Akina looked at Meg and asked her,

"Do you think you could think about what you have seen and not talk about any of it till we get back to the apartment where it is private?"

"Of course," Meg said, "I've seen enough in the last two days to keep me busy thinking for two months."

Meg asked:

"Are you going to pay that officer a visit like he asked?"

"Yes, I'll have to come up with some thing to tell him about my use of Machedo."

Akina told her, and she continued.

"Maybe there are some books in the Library I can check out."

About that time the Hostess for the restaurant came to their table and brought a waitress with her. She said;

"Why, hello you two. We're glad you came back. We want to thank you, Akina, for what you did for us yesterday. You probably saved the cashier's life and you did save us some money so tonight you can have anything in the house and it will be on us, so eat up and Thank you again."

They enjoyed the free meal and then walked back to the apartment. Megume was a lot less talkative on the way back she was apparently in deep thought. Several times she looked over at Akina and looked like she was going to say something, but nothing came out. Once she said,

"Boy, you sure were a beautiful girl at eighteen, no wonder your father was so proud of you."

Later, in the small apartment, relaxed on their cots Megume asked,

"When were you here the first time when you talked to the old man and he told you that they were waiting on you to return?"

"About six months after the big war when we lost everything." Akina told her, "A long time ago."

"Now you seem to have a problem." Meg said. "You do not know if your people still want you back or not. It is a different world today than it was even at that time, let alone at the time you were killed and you left. Tanga. Did you come back for a particular reason this time or just traveling, so to speak?"

"Meg," Akina said, "There are or were a couple of reason's, One I wanted to see my own home country and second I was still hoping to run across my original Lover Chen Li. Whom I loved dearly. We had a very close relationship. We could tell when we were near each other. A couple of times in our travels, our paths crossed and we both knew it I'm sure, but we could not stop. I am hoping that will happen this time and we will be able to stop and see if it is so. If he is doing the same thing I am it might. And if our current ages are relatively close we could marry and be together. Of course he would have to be in a boy or man's body."

"When the physical body I happen to be in when it dies, I can leave it and I take all the memories with me. That is how I know so much and how I learned Piano and Italian.

The old man that I saw and talked to in the little chapel we visited, said that a man was doing the same thing I was doing and that he had came back for a visit." Akina said then continued.

"If that is Chen Li, then we may meet if he is still traveling like I am, the times of living and dying will have to be right for us to get together in life. We will have to take it as it comes and hope for the best. If we can meet in real life and the age and sex differences are right it would be great, but that is not likely. Are you beginning to understand what is going on with me now?"

Megume looked at her friend for a while then said;

"If I am getting this right, it looks like both you and your lover did not like leaving each other and when you died, your Souls decided not to stay with their bodies like good souls should, and left the bodies to go in search of the soul of the one they loved, wherever it might be. Is that about right?"

Akina replied:

"I never thought about it like that, but that is about right. And going in and out of people near death and living their lives with them has taught us both probably, a lot about life and people and has made the time fly."

They both decided that if Akina was to find her lover they would have to travel the country and see if she could sense any presence that she might think was Chen Li. Before then they would have too take the Exams and graduate before they could travel. As they talked they determined that they were both well enough prepared to take the Exam.

The next day was Thursday and both Thursday and Friday were the days set aside for the final exams. The two girls were kept occupied with the exams and the other students talking to them about the exams so that the two days went by rapidly.

On Friday Akina was finished with the last test early and Meg was still in the classroom so Akina went to the huge Auditorium and sat down at the piano and started playing. As the music became noticeable, the seats began to fill as she played. She was really enjoying the music and so she just sat there and played nearly all the songs she knew.

Megume came in and sat down at the last hour of the school day and listened too. Akina turned once to see if she was there and then a few minutes later she stopped playing and went to talk to her.

"Have you got anything planned for the summer months?" Akina asked Meg as she sat down beside her.

"No, I haven't thought about it." Meg replied.

I've been thinking about Chen Li," Akina said. "And we know where all the military bases are so we would have no trouble visiting them and seeing if I could feel Chen Li's presence if he was there in whatever form."

"That sounds like a good idea, where are we going to get the money for all this travel?" Meg asked.

Akina sat and thought for a while then said:

"I haven't asked my parents for much since I have acquired this new soul. They are somewhat puzzled by the change in me but they think it is just me getting to be an adult and learning new things. They haven't heard me play the piano yet. That will be a surprise when it happens. I think I can talk them into financing a trip around the bases."

"Good', Meg said. "I am looking forward to it and meeting this long lost boy friend. Your story is so out of this world that I'll believe anything you say and not be surprised. Boy, you sure were a beautiful girl at eighteen, no wonder your father was so proud of you. How long have you been living away from your parents now?"

"We've had this apartment now, what, about six or eight months and we lived in the other place at least a year. That's a year and a half at least and I've only been back a few times. They live a very busy life and have plenty of money. They won't be surprised at anything I do. As long as I am not giving them problems, they're a happy couple. We can go to them and tell them what we want to do but not why we want to do it and they will probably give us the money and tell us to enjoy ourselves." Akina told her.

The next day was Saturday and the two girls decided to visit Akina's parents and find out if what they were thinking would work out. Neither girl had access to an automobile so they were going to talk Akina's father into buying her one. They were both two years older now than they were when they had entered the University. Neither of the girls had a job but both had personal checking accounts and their parents saw that they both kept a little money for keeping the apartment and little things that they needed for the university requirements to see their daughter show up for a visit. They welcomed Megume nearly as much, Megume had been a close friend of Akina since childhood, they had met in grade school and had been as sisters ever since.

When they all sat down to talk, Megume said;

"You two should be very proud of your daughter, she has learned to play the piano and she did not want me to tell you till she became quite good. She does not think she is good enough, but I think she is. The College music instructor has asked her to play at the Farewell address on Wednesday this week and she has consented. You two will be welcomed if you would like to attend."

Akina's mother spoke up and said to Akina;

"When did this sudden interest in music start, you never showed an interest before"

"About two years ago a classmate of mine invited me over to hear some American records and there were some by a young woman named, "Jessica Levanti." Akina answered. "They were so soft and beautiful I wanted to learn how to play that way."

Akina started talking again;

"Dad, Megume and I have been taking taxis on longer than bicycle trips and it takes a lot of our money. We have saved a little money and we were wondering if you would help us buy a good little used vehicle. We want to do a little traveling this summer break and we don't want to use the bicycles. Will you think about it? We will be out of classes next Friday."

"We would kind of like to take a few days and tour our country and see some of the sights and some military bases and a lot of other parks etc. and not have to be in a hurry like on a tour bus." Megume said. Akina's father looked at his daughter and she nodded. Her father then said;

"Akina, you haven't been keeping track of your father for the last couple of years have you? You haven't noticed that I have been elected Governor of this small

State and am aiming at being the president of this country of Tanga sometime in the future. I will be tickled to come to the Farewell address on Wednesday and hear you play. They may even ask me to give a little speech, which I will be glad to give. I will also get you an acceptable automobile for you and your friend to use in your escapades. Will you check with the principal and ask what time he would like me to appear and if I should prepare a short speech?"

"Oh Dad," Akina said. "I am so happy for you, I know that you have wanted to enter politics but I was so busy I didn't know that you had made the first step." Then she looked at her mother and said. "Mom, are you happy about that change?"

"Oh yes, "Her mother said. "It is something he has always wanted and as long as he is happy it is OK by me."

Small talk went on from there until the girls left and returned to their apartment.

On Monday, Akina and Megume went to the university and met with the Coordinator for the day of the Fairwell address and talked to him about Akina's father. He told them that he would be glad to have The Govenor speak for up to a half hour.

Akina called her father to give him the news that evening so her father would have time to write his speech.

Wednesday arrived and both the girls were looking forward to the days happenings. The principal had given Akina a list of music and the sequence they were to be played. He was still a little surprised that Akina was the daughter of the Governor. It had really never occurred to him before. He was still mystified by the talk about Akina in just the last few weeks and he wondered if the girl's father had heard the talk about her as a silent fighter and the deadly aspect. The girl certainly did not look the part.

Akina's father spoke up and said;

"I kinda like piano music and if you think they will let us in I would like to go and hear her play."

"Your daughter has changed a lot since she started living with me near the University, you will certainly be surprised." Megume told them.

Akina started talking again; until the girls left and returned to their apartment.

Since the first incident with Tora, Akina had developed a habit of doing aerobics whenever she could to build up her strength and muscles, and had spent some time in the gym. The original Akina had been an athletic trainer.

Starting time for the formal part of the Address was listed as one o'clock PM, so the girls did not get there till a little after twelve o'clock noon. There seats were reserved so they had no trouble finding a place to sit. When they arrived the huge auditorium was nearly filled to capacity. Akina's father was seated off the stage in a chair in a group of six chairs put there for the speakers to use. As Akina passed that area he caught her eyes and waved as she went on to the seat reserved for her near the piano.

As it neared one o'clock, the principal walked out on the stage and approached the microphone, tested the audio level and said as the noise quieted;

"Welcome to this Farewell Address. Some of you may not have heard that the Governor of this state has been asked to give you graduating students some pep talk before you face the world. Some of your teachers and Professors will also have something to say to you. I wish to say to all of you. I am very proud of the way you have all behaved and conducted yourselves over your stay as students of this University. Now to start the proceedings, the lovely daughter of our Governor will honor us with her music, which some of you may have heard before in this auditorium. 'Akina', you're up".

Akina walked to the piano, sat down on the bench and the sound of the school song filled the huge hall as she played louder than she ever had before then slowly softened the music till it was beautiful to hear. She played some of the verses twice before she finished and the hall was filled with applause as the crowd showed their appreciation.

When the noise stopped, the principal thanked the audience and introduced the first speaker.

Akina was to provide music when the stage was not being used so she played when the speakers were changing or when there was a lull in the action on the stage. When the first speaker appeared on the stage, Akina's mother was ushered to a seat beside her. Where she remained for the entire performance they talked when they could but there was not much time. Akina was going back and forth from her seat to the piano bench.

Akina's father was the last of the speakers, and as he led up to the conclusion, the Principal of the Universty went up on the stage and thanked the Governor and the audience for coming, then signaled Akina to start the music as the crowd began to leave.

Her father came down off the stage and went to sit with his wife and daughter. Akina was still playing so they just sat and listened to the music along with a lot of the audience.

Akina played for over half an hour until the Principal signaled her she could quit anytime. When she left the piano bench, her father got up and put his arms around her and gave her a nice hug, which was rather new to the soul of Li Chan. It brought a warm feeling to the body of Akina, and both the new soul and the memories in the old one felt the pleasure. Her father then led her, with her mother and Megume following toward the exit. Her father was speaking;

"That was the most beautiful music Akina, it must have taken you a long time to learn to play like that. I am so proud of you. I will buy a piano now and keep it in the house so you can play when you visit us."

The parking lot had been full but kind. They stopped in front of the Lincoln and were talking. Both the girls were looking at the little sports car and Akina said;

"Dad that is the kind of car we would like to take on our trips this summer, but that one would probably cost too much, about that size would be about right though."

That was what her father and mother were waiting for. They both reached, her mother into her handbag and her father into his pocket to get something. Her mother brought out a large envelope and her father a set of car keys, and they handed them to Akina. Her mother said;

"I pretended I was you and got your registration and tags and your father has the keys. You are all set to go. You will have to get your own driving permit, but that should not be a problem. Just be careful enjoy it."

Akina threw her arms around her father's neck and said;

"Oh father, thank you, thank you, I couldn't be happier." As tears came as she hugged both of her parents.

Megume would have to drive until Akina secured her permit.

There was a small parking lot next to their apartment and they parked the little sport car there and locked it. They were quiet till they entered the apartment, then they burst out in happy talk, both trying to talk at the same time. Finally Megume said;

"I did not see your father give you any money, do you think he will?"

"He usually deposits it in my checking account when he thinks about it; I'll go to the bank and check tomorrow. We'll go to the University first and check out. Then we can start planning our trip." Akina said.

The next day as they were leaving the building and going toward the little sport car they saw three boys looking at it, one was sitting on the hood. As they got closer Akina said;

"Hi guys, how do you like them wheels?"

"Neat, you the owner?" one of them asked.

"Yeah" Akina answered. "Just got it yesterday."

"We figure you'll give us a ride downtown." One of them said.

"Not today" Akina said. "I've got to go to the motor vehicle office and get my permit and it is near closing time. Sorry about that, maybe some other time."

Megume had opened the driver's side door and was starting to get in. One of the guys grabbed her, pulled her back and started to get in the back seat. The back doors were both locked. Akina ran around the back of the car and the other two guys started to grab her and pull her away from trying to stop the first one from getting in the car.

The one closest to her felt a blow to the stomach and the second one got a blow to the side of his head as she spun. Both were on the ground as she walked to the car and told the one that had entered the car to open the back door and come out quietly. He looked at the two on the ground, then put two and two together and recognized now who the two girls were. There had been a lot of talk about the restaurant attempted holdup and now he had met the two girls and especially the one that had killed the man that had shot the cashier. The man in the car quickly opened the back door and got out quietly and went to see if he could help his buddies.

Akina just looked at them, then seeing Megume in the car went around and got in the front seat beside her and they drove away and went to their apartment.

ENTER CHEN LI

Now in the Capitol City of Kaloku, events were shaping up that would make a world of difference in the lives of Akina and Megume. In a busy intersection two blocks from the capitol building a bank robber, fleeing from the local bank, rushed the intersection, ignoring lights, and tried to find his way through the traffic and ran directly into the side of a government vehicle. Hitting it a glancing blow on the driver's side of the vehicle, sending it in front of another car which hit it again on the left side and crushed the driver inward.

As the police directed traffic around the damaged vehicle. The ambulance personnel removed the body from the passenger side first as it was easier to remove, then the drivers body which had already been pronounced dead. They were soon on their way to the hospital.

The Soul of the driver had left the body of the driver when it could not do any thing to keep it alive any longer. The sixty year old body had been his to control and will for at least thirty years and he had enjoyed the time spent. He had really liked the man he had been chauffeuring around and now he followed the Ambulance to the hospital to see if he could be of any help to him. When he was finally taken into a ward and placed on a cot, the Soul dropped down and seeing the movements of the fingers and seeing that the man was still breathing, entered the body and took over the Soul that was faintly trying to keep the body alive.

Chen Li had found his sixth body to live in and control. He had traveled far and wide in his quest to find the Soul of his lost love 'Li Chan'. He had come close a few times when he felt her presence but could not locate the person before he or she had left the area. He would keep trying. He had just missed her when he visited the Museum. The old man had not seen her at that time.

The body he had entered was that of a thirty year old man that had recently entered the service of the Tanganese Government as a Foreign Diplomat and was unmarried and loved Politics and the public Domain.

Chen Li absorbed all the information and memories and was quite impressed with the extent of knowledge the man possessed. This body would carry him a lot of places and new countries and he would be on the lookout for his Li Chan.

The man, Yutaka, was a native of Tanga and liked to travel. Honest, and a hard worker, he was well liked by all who met or knew him. As such he was frugal and his new job would pay him an amount he could easily live on and even save a little.

His body had not been hurt seriously in the accident. A bruise on the head had kept him unconscious for a while but he was soon conscious and talking.

He was back on the job in the statehouse the next morning with nothing but a slight headache. He was a little sad because of the death of his driver. He had known him for about five years and had become quite fond of him. He will have to get used to a new driver, but that is the way life is.

Akina and Megume were anxious to be on their way.

They went directly to the division of motor vehicles where Akina filled out the necessary papers and had her picture taken. After a short wait they left and went to their apartment where they got out a map of the country and located some of the military bases to plan their trip around the country.

Finally Megume asked Akina:

"Akina, have you checked to see if we have enough money to make the trip? I checked my account and I still have some, but I want to buy some clothes before we go."

"We'll stop at the bank tomorrow and check, but I am sure Daddy put in some money. He always does." Akina said. "Then we'll go shopping. We don't need to leave till Monday so that will leave us a couple of days for shopping and whatever else we need to do." The girls did not want to travel in dresses so they bought several pants sets and a variety of blouses and tops to go with them when they finally saw a small village where they could get something to eat and possibly a place to stop for the night. There was no one outside when they pulled over and stopped in front of a little sandwich shop which advertised sandwiches and drinks. They entered and sat at a table in the empty end of the room. There were four young men sitting across the room at another table but they ignored them and looked for a menu of some kind. There was an older man behind the counter and they assumed that he was the cook and also waiter. He picked up some papers off of the counter and brought them to the girls and handed them each a sheet.

The girls looked them over then each ordered a sandwich and drink and then gave back the menus. The man then returned to the spot behind the counter and fixed two cups of coffee and brought them out to the girl's table.

"Those guys are talking about us and I bet we have trouble with them". Megume said.

"I hope not." Akina replied.

A few minutes later one of the young men approached their table and said;

"We would like you two to join us; we have put two tables together and made it long enough for all of us to be comfortable."

"We like it here and we are here only for a sandwich and coffee, nothing else, thank you anyway." Akina answered.

"That is not being friendly and this is a friendly town and we expect to be treated that way."

The young man said.

"We are only passing through and are in a hurry, now please leave us alone and mind your own business." Akina said as she stood up and faced the young man

"I'll take your coffee, you follow me". He said as he reached for her coffee cup.

As the young man reached for her coffee cup, Akina grabbed his hair and as she brought her knee up she pulled his head down. Nose and knee came together hard and the young man flipped over backward and then hit the floor, his nose spurting blood.

Akina stood by her chair and watched as he put his hand to his face and felt the blood. One of his friends came rushing over and started to help him up. No one spoke. The men just looked at Akina and then went back to their table.

Akina sat back down and sipped her coffee as their sandwiches were brought to their table. They finished their meal and as they got up too leave, the young men also got up to leave.

"Meg" Akina said as she watched the men. "Take care of the check, I'll wait". And she stayed close to Meg as they walked out to the car.

They let the men go out first then followed at a distance. The men were watching the girls and seemed to be waiting for something, but they did not like the ready position that Akina kept. There was no fear or care, she was just there and ready. The girls got in the car and drove away, glad to be gone.

It was getting late so they decided to stop at the next decent hotel or rooming house for the night. Two hours later, they pulled into a parking lot of a large hotel and checked into a double bed room for the night. Later, in the room as they relaxed Megume said:

"Akina, we will be going pretty close to the capital, so you think we could stop for an hour or two and look it over? I have only been there once and I would like to see more of it."

"I don't see why not, we are not in any big hurry and I haven't seen it at all yet." Akina replied.

"Ok" Meg said. "See you in the morning." as she crawled into the blankets.

They were up early the next morning and after a good breakfast in the Hotel restaurant they were soon headed up the road toward the capitol city of Kaloku. The ride was peaceful and three hours later they were inside the city limits of the Capitol and looking for a place to buy a sandwich and a cool drink. They were nearing the center of the city when they noticed the Dome of the capitol building so they headed for it to see it closer. On the west side of the Dome they found a little sandwich shop so they pulled in and parked.

They were sitting at an outside table enjoying a sandwich when Akina suddenly exclaimed;

"Chen Li, he is near!"

The girls both started looking around. Megume did not know what to look for and Akina wasn't sure. A couple of minutes later Akina said;

"He's gone, did you see anything?"

"Nothing that was different but a long Limousine. With all this traffic it is hard to see anything for long." Meg remarked.

"Which way was it going?" Akina asked

"That way." Meg answered, and she pointed toward the Dome building.

"If it was going that way, it was probably going to the dome for some reason. Let's go there for a tour and see what it gets us?" Akina said. Now she was excited and anxious. She felt that her long ago lover's Soul was somewhere in the area and that the Soul of Chen Li was here in the Capitol. She had felt the attraction, a little weaker perhaps, but still there.

She was feeling like a little lost child who knew that something was near but could not see it and in the confusion did not know were to look to find it. If it was the Soul of Chen Li and it had been in the Limousine that would mean that he might, in some way be connected to the Government. They must go through the Dome building and then she would know.

There was a big circle around the Dome building so Akina pulled out of the sandwich shop parking lot and entered the circle traffic and started looking for the Dome parking lot. When she saw the sign' Dome Parking' she pulled in and they walked toward the Dome Entrance.

They were asked to sign their names at a desk inside the front doors and were given a pamphlet of information. They walked on into the center of the building where they saw a building layout that showed where each office and Department was located. The name of each office holder was listed as well. There were only two floors to the building and the layout was simple. The building was shaped like a wheel and the hallways were like the spokes of a wheel. There were other people milling about and the girls walked slowly out one of the hallways then turned and walked around the rim hallway to the next spoke hallway then followed it back to the center. It was an easy way to check the whole building.

They had covered nearly half of the first floor when Akina stopped and started to smile.

"He is close now." She said. "I wonder if he is in a male or female body."

The presence was becoming stronger and stronger until a man suddenly appeared. He was walking slowly and had a strange look on his face. To Megume he looked to be about twenty-five or thirty years of age, very handsome and a great looking body build. He was looking at the two girls with a strange smile, expectant, yet reserved. His eyes finally centered on Akina and he walked slowly toward her. When he was directly in front of her he stopped, looked into her eyes and Akina said;

"I am Li Chan."

They came together like two magnets and held each other in a tight embrace, both were shedding tears of joy. Years of waiting, searching and dreaming had finally come to a close. Now they were together. There was no talking. This was not the place. As one, they turned and walked toward the entrance they had used coming in. Megume followed slowly, out to the car. Akina and the man got in the back seat and Megume got behind the wheel. The man spoke;

"My name is Yutaka, we will go to my apartment for now. I will give you directions. It is not far."

Ten minutes later Megume pulled into an apartment driveway and the three of them went into a second floor apartment and relaxed so they could talk. The apartment was a five room Condominium so there was room for a little privacy if they needed it. First they had to introduce each other, and then they all started to talk at once. Megume knew enough about their travels so she was very interested as well.

They talked all afternoon. His travels were nearly the same as Li Chan's. Megume sat through it all, shaking her head in wonderment at the tales she heard.

They finally decided to go out for dinner, and then of course stay the night. Li Chan and Chen Li never left each others arms. Megume watched in amazement as the two moved around and did the different things required for daily routines. Their movements were so coordinated and precise that one watching knew that they were both thinking the same thing and in most cases did not even have to talk. Their happiness was apparent on their faces and in their attitudes. Megume knew enough of their history that she could fill in the parts she had not been told so she understood the whole story and was happy for them both.

They had eaten late so it was rather late when they returned to the apartment. They found comfortable positions in the chairs with Akina and Yutaka curled on the couch and Megume in a lounge chair to watch Television and talk a little. Finally Akina said to Meg;

"Meg, we're going to bed, we'll see you in the morning then decide what to do tomorrow. The trip of course is off now and everything has changed. Ok?"

Yutaka and Akina walked into the bedroom together and sat on the edge of the bed holding each other for a few minutes then stood up and helped each other remove all their clothing. Yutaka then stood for a few minutes caressing and kissing Akina until she let herself fall backwards onto the soft sheets on the bed.

Then began the most pleasant night of their lives, as they gave each other the ultimate and most pleasant gift possible in this world, they had waited a very long time.

An explanation of the actions and happenings of the next few days would take pages and pages if it was all to be told. Needless to say they were both very surprised when they found out whose body they each had ended up being in as a soul. Akina, as the daughter of a State Governor that was headed toward running for the Office of President at the next election and Yutaka, who was to become a very well known Foreign Ambassador.

Li Chan and Chen Li had been in nearly similar situations when Li Chan had been killed. Now they were back in the employ, so to speak of their country and both in positions where they would be serving their country and helping their countrymen. They were not too far apart in age to become husband and wife. They were already planning for the wedding, but of course for the sake of protocol they would have to wait an appropriate length of time before the ceremony. As Ambassador for Tanga Yutaka had already met Akina's father as State Governor so it was a rather happy situation and everyone was delighted.

Needless to say the names, Li Chan and Chen Li were used a lot and the two of them spent hours and hours together and had more that enough things to tell each other about the long years they had been separated, There was not a happier couple in the world and they were looking forward to children and a very happy life together.